W9-CYD-206

*"A little revulsion
is good for the soul."*
Stephen King

Keeping this in mind, award-winning editor
and author Charles L. Grant has put together
eighteen tales of nastiness and horror. Rang-
ing from extraordinary demons and creatures
to deceptive dolls, cats, and swimming pools,
these stories are realizations of your ultimate
fears by masters of the macabre.

Witches and Spells
CHELSEA QUINN YARBRO

Werewolves
BARRY N. MALZBERG

The Living Dead
DENNIS ETCHISON

Alien Animals
ALAN DEAN FOSTER

A Child Demon
MELISA MICHAELS

Ghouls
J. MICHAEL REAVES

The Thing in the Pool
WILLIAM F. NOLAN

The Toy That Can't Be Thrown Away
STEPHEN KING

HORRORS

HORRORS

EDITED BY
CHARLES L. GRANT

BERKLEY BOOKS, NEW YORK

HORRORS

A Berkley Book / published by arrangement with
the author

PRINTING HISTORY
PEI edition / October 1981
Berkley edition / August 1984
Second printing / July 1986

A BERKLEY BOOK ® TM 757,375
Berkley Books are published by The Berkley Publishing Group,
200 Madison Avenue, New York, NY 10016.
The name "BERKLEY" and the stylized "B" with design
are trademarks belonging to Berkley Publishing Corporation.

PRINTED IN THE UNITED STATES OF AMERICA

CONTENTS

INTRODUCTION

Stephen King, whose skills overwhelm the usual best-seller list fare, once said that a little revulsion is good for the soul. In the best works it comes like a thunderclap in the midst of a snowstorm, and it is so much a part of the story that removing it would give you something considerably less than what you paid for. And it would be missed. But this revulsion, this sudden shock to the nervous system by a scene or incident graphic in its violence or matters gruesome, appears all too often either out of place or out of character. It goes without saying that a fair amount of skill is required to handle such things properly and that the absence of this skill gives the reader only bloody details without the necessary accompanying emotional shock.

The best horror stories, whether they deal in the supernatural or not, use shock minimally. Too much of it, and there's no shock at all; too little, and it stands out unsupported and weak. In this sense it causes the reader to react to it as he would to sexual excess: He turns the page, or he skims until the story gets moving again.

There is, too, the matter of a definition of that which is horrid (literally) to the reader—there is none. Each reader reacts differently to various types of horror. One person reacts violently to snakes, and another loves them; the same with spiders, blood, thunder and lightning, dark graphic violence, and so forth. The supernatural bothers some people not at all, while it turns others to racing through the house to switch on the lights.

Yet writers persist in attempting to reach all readers, not by piling on as many diverse types of horror as they can (though there are those who do that, usually quite badly) but by assuming certain kinds of situations: Either they are so normal that *anything* will, for the moment, produce a moment of horror, or they are in themselves horrible enough to induce a reaction directly the story begins. In either case it's the skill of the writer that quite candidly manipulates the reader's mind, coupled with the ability of the reader's mind to compound and intensify the experience.

It doesn't always work, however.

But in this volume there are sufficient tales of nastiness and horror, of bludgeons as well as scalpels, that somewhere along the line you're bound to be shuddering once in a while. The reprinted stories have been chosen for their effects as well as their aftertaste; the original material has been written especially for this book's guidelines. There are no funny stories here, no science fiction, and no poetry. There is, on the other hand, a lot of fun—on the writers' part in creating the horrors, and on the readers' part in knowing that as soon as the story is over the horror is too.

Of course it is.

None of this can actually happen in "real" life, and so it's safe to allow yourself to be momentarily startled or scared.

Of course.

You and I both know that because it says so right here on this page.

Of course.

And if I happen to be wrong . . .

CHARLES L. GRANT
Budd Lake, New Jersey 1980

Dennis Etchison wields words like a scalpel, cutting and slicing through pretense with a quiet style that in no way diminishes the onslaught of horror. Rather, the style heightens the shock, and far better than most blood-and-gore-in-glorious-color films that currently are making the rounds. Proof positive, I think, that the image produced on the printed page is immeasurably more powerful than any celluloid version.

THE DEAD LINE

by Dennis Etchison

This morning I put ground glass in my wife's eyes. She didn't mind. She didn't make a sound. She never does.

I took an empty bottle from the table. I wrapped it in a towel and swung it, smashing it gently against the side of her bed. When the glass shattered it made a faint, very faint sound like wind chimes in a thick fog. No one noticed, of course, least of all Karen. Then I placed it under my shoe and stepped down hard, rocking my weight back and forth until I felt fine sand underfoot. I knelt and picked up a few sharp grains on the end of my finger, rose and dropped them onto her corneas. First one, then the other. She doesn't blink, you know. It was easy.

Then I had to leave. I saw the technicians coming. But already it was too late; the damage had been done. I don't know if they found the mess under the bed. I suppose someone will. The janitors or the orderlies, perhaps. But it won't matter to them, I'm sure.

I slipped outside the glass observation wall as the technicians descended the lines, adjusting respirators, reading printouts and making notations on their pocket recorders. I remember that I thought then of clean, college-trained farmers combing rows of crops, checking the condition of the coming harvest, turning down a cover here, patting a loose mound there, touching the beds with a horticulturist's fussiness, ready to prune wherever necessary for the demands of the marketplace. They may not have seen me at all. And what if they had? What was I but a concerned husband come to pay his respects to a loved one? I might have been lectured about the risk of bringing unwanted germs into the area, though they must know how unlikely that is with the high-intensity UV lights and sonic purifiers and other sanitary precautions. I did make a point of passing near the Children's Communicable Diseases Ward on my way there, however; one always hopes.

Then, standing alone behind the windows, isolated and empty as an expectant father waiting for his flesh and blood to be delivered at last into his hands, I had the sudden, unshakable feeling that I was being watched.

By whom?

The technicians were still intent on their readouts.

Another visitor? It was unlikely; hardly anyone else bothers to observe. A guilty few still do stop by during the lonely hours; seeking silent expiation from a friend, relative, or lover, or merely to satisfy some morbid curiosity; the most recently acquired neomorts usually receive dutiful visitations at the beginning, but invariably the newly grieved are so overwhelmed by the impersonalness of the procedure that they soon learn to stay away to preserve their own sanity.

I kept careful track of the progress of the white coats on the other side of the windows, ready to move on at the first sign of undue concern over my wife's bed.

And it was then that I saw her face shining behind my own in the pane. She was alert and standing for the first time since the stroke, nearly eighteen months ago. I gripped the handrail until my nails were white, staring in disbelief at Karen's transparent reflection.

I turned. And shrank back against the wall. The cold sweat must have been on my face, because she reached out shakily and pressed my hand.

"Can I get you anything?"

Her hair was beautiful again, not the stringy, matted mass I had come to know. Her makeup was freshly applied, her lips dark at the edges and parted just so, opening on a warm, pink interior, her teeth no longer discolored but once more a luminous bone-white. And her eyes. They were perfect.

I lunged for her.

She sidestepped gracefully and supported my arm. I looked closely at her face as I allowed her to hold me a moment longer. There was nothing wrong with that, was there?

"Are you all right?" she said.

She was so much like Karen I had to stop the backs of my fingers from stroking the soft, wispy down at her temple, as they had done so many, many times. She had always liked that. And so, I remembered, had I; it was so long ago I had almost forgotten.

"Sorry," I managed. I adjusted my clothing, smoothing my hair down from the laminar airflow around the beds. "I'm not feeling well."

"I understand."

Did she?

"My name is Emily Richterhausen," she said.

I straightened and introduced myself. If she had seen me inside the restricted area, she said nothing. But she couldn't have been there that long. I would have noticed her.

"A relative?" she asked.

"My wife."

"Has . . . has she been here long?"

"Yes. I'm sorry. If you'll excuse me—"

"Are you sure you're all right?" She moved in front of me. "I could get you a cup of coffee, you know, from the machines. We could both have one. Or some water."

It was obvious that she wanted to talk. She needed it. Perhaps I did, too. I realized that I needed to explain myself, to pass off my presence before she could guess my plan.

"Do you come here often, Emily?" It was a foolish question. I knew I hadn't seen her before.

"It's my husband," she said.

"I see."

"Oh, he's not one of . . . them. Not yet. He's in Intensive Care." The lovely face began to change. "A coma. It's been weeks. They say he may regain consciousness. One of the doctors said that. How long can it go on, do you know?"

I walked with her to a bench in the waiting area.

"An accident?" I asked.

"A heart attack. He was driving to work. The car crossed the divider. It was awful." She fumbled for a handkerchief. I gave her mine. "They say it was a miracle he survived at all. You should have seen the car. No, you shouldn't have. No one should have. A miracle."

"Well," I told her, trying to sound comforting, "as I understand it, there is no 'usual' in comatose cases. It can go on indefinitely, as long as brain death hasn't occurred. Until then there's always hope. I saw a news item the other day about a young man who woke up after four years. He asked if he had missed his homework assignment. You've probably heard—"

"Brain death," she repeated, mouthing the words uneasily. I saw her shudder.

"That's the latest Supreme Court ruling. Even then," I went on quickly, "there's still hope. You remember that girl in New Jersey? She's still alive. She may pull out of it at any time," I lied. "And there are others like her. A great many, in fact. Why—"

"There *is* hope, isn't there?"

"I'm sure of it," I said, as kindly as possible.

"But then," she said, "supposing. . . . What is it that actually happens, afterward? How does it work? Oh, I know about the Maintenance and Cultivation Act. The doctor explained everything at the beginning, just in case." She glanced back toward the Neomort Ward and took a deep, uncertain breath. She didn't really want to know, not now. "It looks so nice and clean, doesn't it? They can still be of great service to society. The kidneys, the eyes, even the heart. It's a wonderful thing. Isn't it?"

"It's remarkable," I agreed. "Your husband, had he signed the papers?"

"No. He kept putting it off. William never liked to dwell on such matters. He didn't believe in courting disaster. Now, I only wish I had forced him to talk about it, while there was still time."

"I'm sure it won't come to that," I said immediately. I couldn't bear the sight of her crying. "You'll see. The odds are very much on your side."

We sat side by side in silence as an orderly wheeled a stainless steel cleaning cart off the elevator and headed past us to the observation area. I could not help but notice the special scent of her skin. Spring flowers. It was so unlike the hospital, the antisepticized cloud that hangs over everything until it has settled into the very pores of the skin. I studied her discreetly: the tiny, exquisite whorls of her ear, the blood pulsing rapidly and naturally beneath her healthy skin. Somewhere an electronic air ionizer was whirring, and a muffled bell began to chime in a distant hallway.

"Forgive me," she said. "I shouldn't have gone on like that. But tell me about your wife." She faced me. "Isn't it strange?" We were inches apart. "It's so reassuring to talk to someone else who understands. I don't think the doctors really know how it is for us, for those who wait."

"They can't," I said.

"I'm a good listener, really I am. William always said that."

"My—my wife signed the Universal Donor Release two years ago," I began reluctantly. "The last time she renewed her driver's license." Good until her next birthday, I thought. As simple as that. Too simple. Karen, how could you have known? How could I? I should have. I should have found out. I should have stopped your hand. "She's here now. She's been here since last year. Her electroencephalogram was certified almost immediately."

"It must be a comfort to you," she said, "to know that she didn't suffer."

"Yes."

"You know, this is the first time I've been on this particular floor. What is it they call it?" She was rattling on, perhaps to distract herself.

"The Bioemporium."

"Yes, that's it. I guess I wanted to see what it would be like, just in case. For my William." She tried bravely to smile. "Do you visit her often?"

"As often as possible."

"I'm sure that must mean a great deal."

To whom? I thought, but let it pass.

"Don't worry," I said. "Your husband will recover. He'll be fine. You'll see."

Our legs were touching. It had been so long since I had felt contact with sentient flesh. I thought of asking her for that cup of coffee now, or something more, in the cafeteria. Or a drink.

"I try to believe that," she said. "It's the only thing that keeps me going. None of this seems real, does it?"

She forced the delicate corners of her mouth up into a full smile.

"I really should be going now. I could get something for him, couldn't I? You know, in the gift shop downstairs? I'm told they have a very lovely store right here in the building. And then I'll be able to give it to him during visiting hours. When he wakes up."

"That's a good idea," I said.

She said decisively, "I don't think I'll be coming to this floor again."

"Good luck," I told her. "But first, if you'd like, Emily, I thought—"

"What was . . . what is your wife's name? If you don't mind my asking?"

"Karen," I said. Karen. What was I thinking? Can you forgive me? You can do that, can't you, sweetheart?

"That's such a pretty name," she said.

"Thank you."

She stood. I did not try to delay her. There are some things that must be set to rest first, before one can go on. You helped remind me of that, didn't you, Karen? I nearly forgot. But you wouldn't let me.

"I suppose we won't be running into each other again," she said. Her eyes were almost cheerful.

"No."

"Would you . . . could you do me one small favor?"

I looked at her.

"What do you think I should get him? He has so many nice things. But you're a man. What would you like to have, if you were in the hospital? God forbid," she added, smiling warmly.

I sat there. I couldn't speak. I should have told her the truth then. But I couldn't. It would have seemed cruel, and that is not part of my nature.

What do you get, I wondered, for a man who has nothing?

I awaken.

The phone is silent.

I go to the medicine cabinet, swallow another fistful of L-tryptophane tablets, and settle back restlessly, hoping for a long and mercifully dreamless nap.

Soon, all too soon and not soon enough, I fall into a deep and troubled sleep.

I find myself trapped in an airtight box.

I pound on the lid, kicking until my toes are broken and my elbows are torn and bleeding. I reach into my pocket for my lighter, an antique Zippo, thumb the flint. In the sudden flare I am able to read an engraved plate set into the satin. Twenty-Five Year Guarantee, it says in fancy script. I scream. My throat tears. The lighter catches the white folds and tongues of flame lick my face, spreading rapidly down my squirming body. I inhale fire.

The lid swings open.

Two attendants in white are bending over me, squirting out the flames with a water hose. One of them chuckles.

Wonder how that happened? he says.

Spontaneous combustion? says his partner.

That would make our job a hell of a lot easier, says the other. He coils the hose and I see through burned-away eyelids that it is attached to a sink at the head of a stainless-steel table. The table has grooves running along the sides and a drainage hole at one end.

I scream again, but no sound comes out.

They turn away.

I struggle up out of the coffin. There is no pain. How can that be? I claw at my clothing, baring my seared flesh.

See? I cry. I'm alive!

They do not hear.

I rip at my chest with smoldering hands, the peeled skin rolling up under my fingernails. See the blood in my veins? I shout. I'm not one of them!

Do we have to do this one over? asks the attendant. It's only a cremation. Who'll know?

I see the eviscerated remains of others glistening in the sink, in the jars and plastic bags. I grab a scalpel. I slash at my arm. I cut through the smoking cloth of my shirt, laying open fresh incisions like white lips, slicing deeper into muscle and bone.

See? Do I not bleed?

They won't listen.

I stagger from the embalming chamber, gouging my sides as I bump other caskets which topple, spilling their pale contents onto the mortuary floor.

My body is steaming as I stumble out into the cold, gray dawn.

Where can I go? What is left for me? There must be a place. There must be—

A bell chimes, and I awaken.

Frantically, I locate the telephone.

A woman. Her voice is relieved but shaking as she calls my name.

"Thank God you're home," she says. "I know it's late. But I didn't know who else to call. I'm terribly sorry to bother you. Do you remember me?"

No luck this time. When? I wonder. How much longer?

"You can hear me," I say to her.

"What?" She makes an effort to mask her hysteria, but I hear her cover the mouthpiece and sob. "We must have a bad connection. I'll hang up."

"No. Please." I sit forward, rubbing invisible cobwebs from my face. "Of course I remember you. Hello, Mrs. Richter-hausen." What time is it? I wonder. "I'm glad you called. How did you know the number?"

"I asked Directory Information. I couldn't forget your name. You were so kind. I have to talk to someone first, before I go back to the hospital."

It's time for her, then. She must face it now; it cannot be put off, not any more.

"How is your husband?"

"It's my husband," she says, not listening. Her voice breaks up momentarily under electrical interference. The signal re-forms, but we are still separated by a grid, as if in an electronic confessional. "At twelve-thirty tonight his, what is it, now?" She bites her lips but cannot control her voice. "His EEG. It . . . stopped. That's what they say. A straight line. There's nothing there. They say it's nonreversible. How can that be?" she asks desperately.

I wait.

"They want you to sign, don't they, Emily?"

"Yes." Her voice is tortured as she says, "It's a good thing, isn't it? You said so yourself, this afternoon. You know about these things. Your wife. . . ."

"We're not talking about my wife now, are we?"

"But they say it's right. The doctor said that."

"What is, Emily?"

"The life-support," she says pathetically. "The Main-tenance." She still does not know what she is saying. "My husband can be of great value to medical science. Not all the usable organs can be taken at once. They may not be matched up with recipients for some time. That's why the Maintenance is so important. It's safer, more efficient than storage. Isn't that so?"

"Don't think of it as 'life-support,' Emily. Don't fool your-self. There is no longer any life to be supported."

"But he's not dead!"

"No."

"Then his body must be kept alive. . . ."

"Not alive, either," I say. "Your husband is now—and will continue to be—neither alive nor dead. Do you understand that?"

It is too much. She breaks down. "H-how can I decide? I can't tell them to pull the plug. How could I do that to him?"

"Isn't there a decision involved in *not* pulling the plug?"

"But it's for the good of mankind, that's what they say. For people years from now, even for people not yet born. Isn't that true? Help me," she says imploringly. "You're a good man. I need to be sure that he won't suffer. Do you think he would want it this way? It was what your wife wanted, wasn't it? At least this way you're able to visit, to go on seeing her. That's important to you, isn't it?"

"He won't feel a thing, if that's what you're asking. He doesn't now, and he never will. Not ever again."

"Then it's all right?"

I wait.

"She's at peace, isn't she, despite everything? It all seems so ghastly, somehow. I don't know what to do. Help me, please. . . ."

"Emily," I say with great difficulty. But it must be done. "Do you understand what will happen to your husband if you authorize the Maintenance?"

She does not answer.

"Only this. Listen: this is how it begins. First he will be connected to an IBM cell separator, to keep track of leucocytes, platelets, red cells, antigens that can't be stored. He will be used around the clock to manufacture an endless red tide for transfusions—"

"But transfusions save lives!"

"Not just transfusions, Emily. His veins will be a battleground for viruses, for pneumonia, hepatitis, leukemia, live cancers. And then his body will be drained off, like a stuck pig's, and a new supply of experimental toxins pumped in, so that he can go on producing antitoxins for them. Listen to me. He will begin to decay inside, Emily. He will be riddled with disease, tumors, parasites. He will stink with fever. His heart will deform, his brain fester with tubercules, his body cavities run with infection. His hair will fall, his skin yellow, his teeth splinter and rot. In the name of science, Emily, in the name of their beloved research."

I pause.

"That is, if he's one of the lucky ones."

"But the transplants. . . ."

"Yes, that's right! You are so right, Emily. If not the blood, then the transplants. They will take him organ by organ, cell by cell. And it will take years. As long as the machines can keep the lungs and heart moving. And finally, after they've taken his eyes, his kidneys and the rest, it will be time for his nerve tissue, his lymph nodes, his testes. They will drill out his bone marrow, and when there is no more of that left, it will be time to remove his stomach and intestines, as soon as they learn how to transplant those parts, too. And they will. Believe me, they will."

"No, please. . . ."

"And when he's been thoroughly, efficiently gutted—or when his body has eaten itself from the inside out—when there is nothing left but a respirated sac bathed from within by its own excrement, do you know what they will do then? *Do you?* Then they will begin to strip the skin from his limbs, from his skull, a few millimeters at a time, for grafting and regrafting, until—"

"Stop!"

"Take him, Emily! Take your William out of there now, tonight, before the technicians can get their bloody hands on him! Sign nothing! Take him home. Take him away and bury him forever. Do that much for him. And for yourself. Let him rest. Give him that one last, most precious gift. Grant him his final peace. You can do that much, can't you? *Can't you?*"

From far away, across miles of the city, I hear the phone drop and then click dully into place. But only after I have heard another sound, one that I pray I will never hear again.

Godspeed, Emily, I think, weeping. *Godspeed.*

I resume my vigil.

There is a machine outside my door. It eats people, chews them up and spits out only what it can't use. It wants to get me, I know it does, but I'm not going to let it.

The call I have been waiting for will never come.

I'm sure of it now. The doctor, or his nurse or secretary or dialing machine, will never announce that they are done at last, that the procedure is no longer cost-effective, that her remains will be released for burial or cremation. Not yesterday, not today, not ever.

I have cut her arteries with stolen scalpels. I have dug with an ice pick deep into her brain, hoping to sever her motor centers. I have probed for her ganglia and nerve cords. I have pierced her eardrums. I have inserted needles, trying to puncture her heart and lungs. I have hidden caustics in the folds of her throat. I have ruined her eyes. But it's no use. It will never be enough.

They will never be done with her.

When I go to the hospital today she will not be there. She will already have been given to the interns for their spinal taps and arteriograms, for surgical practice on a cadaver that is neither alive nor dead. She will belong to the meat cutters, to the first-year med students with their dull knives and stained cross sections . . .

But I know what I will do.

I will search the floors and labs and secret doors of the wing, and when I find her I will steal her silently away; I will give her safe passage. I can do that much, can't I? I will take her to a place where even they can't reach, beyond the boundaries that separate the living from the dead. I will carry her over the threshold and into that realm, wherever it may be.

And there I will stay with her, to be there with her, to take refuge with her among the dead. I will tear at my body and my corruption until we are one in soft asylum. And there I will remain, living with death for whatever may be left of eternity.

Wish me Godspeed.

David Morrell is the best-selling author of The Totem, *one of the best horror novels of the past decade. He is not a prolific writer, nor does he deal with horrors of the supernatural kind; rather, he manages to combine the grisly with the emotional in a way that no other writer to my knowledge is able to do. "Black Evening" is a superb example of that awesome, and gruesome, combination.*

BLACK EVENING

by David Morrell

So we all went out there. I can see that you're apprehensive as we all were, and so I'll tell you at the outset that you're right. The house was in the poorest section. It had been among the best homes in the 1920s, I'd been told, but its shutters long ago had fallen, its porch was listing, paint was chipped and peeling, gray at dusk, though I could guess that it once had been brilliant white. Three stories: gables, chimneys, dormer windows, balconies. Nobody could afford to build so large a home now, and no doubt it had required someone rich to build it then: a mansion in its dotage. Sad, I thought, imagining the pride of those who first had owned it and their sickness should they see it now. But they would all be dead now, and so it didn't matter. All that mattered was the stench.

I say that we all went out; I mean my deputy, the doctor, and myself. We stood beside the cruiser, staring at the dark and silent house. We saw the neighbors on the porches of the other ill-kept houses, silhouetted by the dying sunset. Then we held our breaths and started toward the gate. It fell off in my hand, a broken picket gate that once must have been white. We moved up toward the front steps, and the sidewalk was weed-cracked, the yard overgrown. We felt the cool air, almost misty, as the sun descended totally; and in the dark, our flashlights on, we stepped up on the cracked and creaking steps that led up to the porch. We had to work around some broken boards on the porch, and then we stared down at last week's newspapers, which had been left but never picked up, and we squinted through the stained-glass window, dusty and opaque, the darkness in there absolute. At last I twisted at the grip that rang the bell. The tone was flat, without enthusiasm, and no echo or reverberation followed.

No light came on. No weak footsteps shuffled near to let us in. I twisted at the bell again. We waited.

"And what now?" the deputy was saying.

"Give them time. They're old," I answered. "Or they're maybe not at home."

"Just one," the doctor told me.

"What?"

"There's only one. Her name is Agnes, and she's in her seventies at least."

"She's maybe sleeping."

"You don't think so. Otherwise. . . ."

I twisted at the bell again. I hadn't lived in town for very long, I'd brought my family to what I'd hoped was some place better, and as new chief I was hardly eager to antagonize the townsfolk by disturbing some old woman.

All the same, the stench was horrible. It made my stomach rise, my nostrils widen with disgust. The neighbors' phone calls had been so persistent that I couldn't very well ignore them.

"All right, let's go in."

I tried the knob. The door was locked. I leaned against the door, and it came open with a sound as if the doorjamb had been cardboard. No sharp crack—instead a rip, a tear, so soft, so effortless. The wood was rotten at my feet.

"Is anybody here?" I called.

No answer and no echo.

We looked at one another, and we stepped inside. The hall was dusty and the odor more intense.

We flashed our lights. The living room, or what I guess had once been called the parlor, was beyond an oval entrance to our right. The room was filled with papers from the floor to far above my head. There was a corridor we could walk through, but the papers towered on each side.

"This could be it," I told the doctor. "Papers, wet and musty. If they mouldered. . . ."

"You don't think so."

We went through another oval doorway.

"Anybody home?" I called.

I saw the grand piano, cobwebbed in my flashlight's glare. More papers towered all around it.

"Hoarding. Some old folks . . ." the deputy was saying. He was young and hoping, but he coughed now, gagging from the stench.

"I guess we do it room by room," I told them.

We went up to the attic, starting downward, trying for some order, some sane balance. Papers, 1925 and 1936, each room devoted to a decade, 1942 and 1958. We found a bedroom on the second floor, and it at least was normal, if by that is meant no clutter and no useless objects. But the bedroom, all the same, was from the 1920s I guessed. I have no eye for furniture. The canopy above the bed, the stained-glass fixtures, and the heavy hopsack covers on the chairs—these clearly were from another time.

The bed had not been slept in. We had tried the lights. They didn't work.

"She didn't pay her bill, I guess," the deputy was saying.

And the dust, the cobwebs, that pervasive cloying stench. We went with flashlights to the first floor; the cellar is the place that you suspect you ought to check first, but you always wait till last.

We stood inside the pantry on the first floor in the back. The stench was even worse there, and I held control and pulled the door. The stench was like a veil that struck us, wafting up. We went down slowly, board by creaking board.

You know that I'm a trained observer. I've been taught to stop emotion, just to take in what I see. But that is difficult, especially when you are staring by the aid of flashlights and you only see one object at a time, the horror mounting until you think you can't bear it.

First, the woman's headless body on the floor, the stench like old potatoes that have turned to liquid in their jackets, seeping out as something had seeped out from her. The urge to vomit was uncontrollable.

Then, for no reason you can understand, you scan up with your flashlight, and you see her head jammed in the noose, the white hair dangling, the flesh now viscous on her cheeks, the open eyes dissolving toward you.

But that isn't it yet, not the final detail; once more, without a reason you can understand, as if you knew that it would be there, you are aiming with your flashlight toward a corner, toward a tiny table meant for dolls and set for tea, where tied

upon a toy chair, slumping, is another body, small and lonely
—a young girl. You know this from the long hair and the
bow and dress; you wouldn't know it from the face, which has
been forage for the insects. And that isn't it yet, not the final
detail, for the clothes she wears are not from our time, rather
from the old days: straw hat, button shoes, and yellowed
crinoline, a moth-holed satin party dress, as if she wore a
costume or had been compelled to act a part she didn't like,
the bow around her neck so tight that her blackened tongue is
bulging out.

"My Christ," the deputy has moaned behind me, and the
bile that spews up in my mouth is bitter, scalding.

"All right, help me understand this," I am saying.

We are in my office downtown, lights aglare. Although the
night outside is cold with the gust of autumn, I have opened
all the windows, turned the fan on—anything to clear the
stench.

"She killed the child, then hanged herself, that much is
obvious," I say. "But why? I'm new here. I don't understand
this. What would make her do it?"

I can hear the rattle of the fan. The doctor clears his throat.
I am waiting.

"Agnes lived there since the house was new," the doctor
says. "She and her husband built it."

"But I thought that. . . ."

"They had money then," the doctor goes on without pause.
His voice is weak. "He was a banker. They were prosperous."

"The husband?"

"Andrew was his name. In 1922, the world was theirs.
They had a child, a daughter who was three. She died that
fall. Diphtheria. I know this from my father, who was always
fascinated by the case. He couldn't save the daughter, and he
watched the parents ruined by their loss. The husband left one
day. The wife remained, a recluse. It's so easy now, in retrospect, to understand. You see, from time to time there have
been children missing, usually in autumn, just as now. That
girl we found, for instance. All the people who've been looking for her. You'll soon have to notify her parents. I don't
envy you. My guess is that as Agnes aged, became more
lonely and reclusive; she went crazy, sought to find a substitute for what she'd lost. She kidnaped children, but, of course,
she couldn't let them live to tell what she had done. She killed
them but believed that they were still alive, her own child."

"Like a doll, the way that children make believe?" I ask.

"If that analogy is helpful to you. This is a sickness that is so bizarre, it threatens sanity to think about it. As I said, it's easy now in retrospect to know that Agnes kidnaped all those children. Who'd have thought it at the time, though? And I wonder where she put the rotting corpses of those children. Surely when they reached an awful state of decomposition, she could not sustain her make-believe. This final time she must have for a moment understood what she'd become and hanged herself."

"It works," the deputy says, sickened, face ashen. "It makes sense."

"And that's the trouble," the doctor says. "A lunatic is always logical if we but understand the system."

There were many things to do. I'd put off calling in an ambulance. I'd wanted first to understand before the scene became disturbed, a clue destroyed; after all, in a small town such as this one, it would take a while to get things organized.

But I knew that I had to act, make those phone calls, tell the parents. I was reaching for the phone, but it was ringing in anticipation.

"Yes?" I said, and then I listened and realized how wrong we'd been.

"I understand. I know what's happened."

I set the phone down, and I peered at them.

"It wasn't her. It wasn't Agnes," I was saying.

"What?" the doctor answered. The deputy was staring.

"It was Andrew," I now told them. I was rushing toward the door.

"He left in 1922," the doctor was repeating.

"No, he *never* left."

They ran out with me toward the cruiser.

"He's still in there," I was saying.

"But we searched the place," the deputy insisted.

"He was in there. We were just too dumb to see him."

We were in the cruiser. I was squealing from the station's parking lot.

"But I don't understand," the doctor said.

I didn't have the will or time to argue. I was skidding around corners, racing up the side streets. At that once-great, now-dilapidated section of the town, I surged out, running past the ruined gate and up the weed-choked sidewalk, past the porch holes, through the stained-glass door.

"I know you're in here, Andrew!" I was shouting. "Come out now! Don't make me look for you!"

The house was silent and grotesque as I flashed my light and charged in toward the parlor.

"Damn it, Andrew! If you've harmed her, I will punish you the way you punished all those children!"

I was yanking at the stacks of paper.

"Chief, you'd better get control," the deputy was saying.

I was pulling, yanking, and the one side of the room was no good. I was swinging toward the other.

"Help me!" I yelled to the deputy and the doctor.

We found him in the music room, or rather in a room within a room, a room whose walls were stacks of paper. He was in there, almost eighty, brittle and yet strangely spry. He glared up at me, smelling old like ancient papers, squirming now to hide his secret. But I grabbed his shirt and yanked him to one side, and there she was, another young girl, dressed in 1920s clothing, gagged and bound and staring, wide-eyed, fearful. For you see, it had been Andrew all along who had grabbed the children. He had never left. He'd only lost his mind; and Agnes, to protect and preserve him, had hidden him. But each time he killed a child, her loyalty had weakened, until finally disgusted, faced with awful choices, she had hanged herself, unable to betray him.

And I'd guessed that he was there because that phone call had informed me of another missing child, a child who now from fright was white-haired, always would be: if Agnes hadn't done it, then who else but Andrew? Yes, that child, an adult now, is white-haired, I can prove it, for that small child was my daughter, and she sometimes seems to know me when I visit her on weekends.

R. Bretnor's skills as a storyteller, editor, and anthologist are unquestioned, his contributions to writing are generally described in superlatives, and his ability to touch his characters with that added and delicate dimension of realism is unequaled. It is no surprise, then, that when he turns to an evocation of horror (a case all too infrequent), the result is much like the buildup of a thunderstorm: tension, electricity, and finally, explosion.

PARTY NIGHT

by R. Bretnor

Anger never made Carse Hannock drive dangerously, not even now. Except occasionally on turns, when he held speed too fiercely, the fury in him showed only in his cold mastery of his car. It was a new car, wider than most, named for a famous race its make had never entered, and he drove it at a steady seventy. Seventy!—when most of the characters he knew would've been pushing ninety and a hundred, trying to work their mad out. Seventy!—after what Anne had said to him—Jesus Christ, *seventy!*

The moonlight through the windshield showed him his own hands, long, hard and competent, dictating to the wheel. Ahead stretched Highway 101, leading up over Gaviota Pass, leaving behind it Santa Barbara, and the taunting sea, and his fouled-up evening, and Anne herself. He had gone to college with her in L.A. his senior year, after he'd found his way out West. He'd dated her for several weeks—and he'd have made out, too, if Dickson hadn't come along. Herb Dickson, whom everyone called Dickie Boy. Dickie Boy! Big, slow, and sort of solemn Dickie Boy, who—my God!—played the *bagpipes*. Things had looked bright for Dickie Boy right then. UX Aggregates had picked him up six months before they hired Carse. Anne had married him within two weeks. Nobody'd seen he was a loser—nobody but Carse. He could tell them every time.

Carse had worked things right. Jim Teach, his chief, was nothing but a slob. But he had had a secretary, the sort of incredibly efficient woman who, only too often, devotes her life to keeping slobs in business. She was ten years Carse's senior, a little worn by waiting, but with a hell of a good figure. He'd made a play for her, not obviously, not spending too much money, and he had slept with her enough to keep her hungry. He never thought of her by name. She was a face, a body, an instrument. In two years, he'd caught up with Dickie Boy. Another two, and he'd been jumped ahead—not much, but just enough. Now his card read, "Carse Hannock, Assistant Executive Sales Engineer, Los Angeles Branch," and Dickie Boy, after being sidetracked first to Santa Barbara, was being shunted out.

That was what made it so damned queer. Anne must've known. She must have known that once UX dropped a man, his chances, except in small time, were exactly nil. You would have thought she'd have been doing a long double take at the crumb she had latched onto, looking around for someone on the rise, for fun if not for keeps. Yet all through dinner she had seemed relaxed, had bragged about how big a jump it was for Herb to go with Kaiser, had invited Carse to come and stay with them the way he always had. Just as if the story—complete with Dickie Boy's new salary—hadn't come to him straight, or almost straight, out of the Board Room.

Then later, back at her apartment, he had made his pitch. He had only hinted at what was sure to become of Dickie Boy; he had told her how really serious he had been, and how he'd always hoped to marry her himself, and how, while he knew it was too late for that, still chances like tonight didn't often come along, and they were too precious just to chuck away, and—

She interrupted him, pushing him off. "Carse," she said, looking at him out of her dark, dark gray eyes, "are you trying to tell me that I'm supposed to let you sleep here, with *me*?" She didn't let him answer. "Is that what you've been working up to all this time? All of that sideways talk about Herb's job, that's how you operate? Carse, I'm Herb's wife. And you're supposed to be his friend."

"I'm *your* friend, Anne. That's what I've always been." He reached for her.

She stiffened. She drew back. His instinct, infallible where women were concerned, told him she wanted him, that she was asking for it—his strength against her scruples. He seized her by the shoulders: he pressed her back; he said whatever it was he should have said. She did not struggle. She went limp—

And suddenly, as he brought himself down over her, her lax left hand lifted the ashtray under it, and dashed butts, ashes, everything, into his eyes, his mouth, his face.

He dropped her. She straightened and stared at him, as cold as ice. Blindly, for a moment only, he raged at her.

Evenly she said, "Carse, do you want to take it from me? Do you want to try?"

Then she waited there, while he went into the bathroom and rinsed his eyes out, and his mouth, and washed himself. When he returned, she had not moved.

"I could tell you several reasons," she said finally, "why I won't sleep with you. You wouldn't understand them. They don't matter, really. But here's the reason under all of them, and you won't understand it either." She laughed abruptly, a deep and angry laugh from the remote and personal center of her being. "I will not sleep with you, Carse Hannock, because I am real—and you are not."

He hadn't taken all that in, not at the time. He had tried a few smooth-overs, making out it was all a joke, reminding her again of how close they'd been at school. She ignored all of it, watching him silently while he found his coat, put it on, brushed off his lapels, went to the closet for his hat. He didn't argue—she was too cold, too certain of herself, for that. As he left, she said nothing to him. It was only after the door had closed behind him that he heard her wounding laughter, whipping him down the hall.

Carse Hannock thought of her breasts and thighs, the way she walked, the way her eyes had once looked into his. He thought of Dickie Boy. He started hammering at the wheel with his right hand—then realized its sheer futility. As he entered the Gaviota Pass approach, a sudden cross wind caught him, flipping him almost into the other lane, and he realized with a shock that he was up to eighty, eighty-five. He braked. Only suckers pushed too fast. Deliberately, as he drove through the hills, he made himself relax, lean his left elbow on the door casually, think of what he might make out of the balance of the night.

It was a Friday night, with October almost over, cold and

clear, a good night for driving, and not yet ten o'clock. Once in a while, you ran across a chick like Anne, frigid and all tied up inside with justifying it. Well, she was the first he hadn't spotted right away. She'd fooled him. And so what? Anytime before two A.M. he could make the grade at some bar along the road. Usually all it took to get things rolling was a nice slice of profile. He was not conceited—that was the way things were.

Carse Hannock's anger sank beneath the surface; his relaxation became more real. He turned the radio on; thought of Jim Teach's secretary; thought of how Dickie Boy would hit the skids when UX booted him; remembered how, back when he was just sixteen, his mom had caught him laying, or maybe just being laid by, the fat McCoy chippy who lived next door, and how, absurdly, she'd screamed out, "*Cur*tis Hannock, what*ever* are you *do*ing to that child?" What he'd been doing had been as obvious as a flagpole. Even though he'd had his tail beaten afterwards, his old man hadn't done it very hard— and later he had laughed like hell and made some crack like Ma had never showed *him* any sign of knowing what went on, and this just proved it.

Carse chuckled. Not a heavy drinker, he realized that what he needed was a drink or two to take the edge off things. He pulled in at Buellton, though the place didn't look like the hunting would be worth a damn, found a bar noisy with fights on its TV and farmhands with their girls. He belted down a couple on the rocks, ignored the coy attempts at conversation of a beefy off-duty eatery waitress, looked the situation over for maybe a half hour, decided that it stank, had another for the road, and shouldered his way out, not at all disappointed.

Los Alamos, fifteen miles on, looked more promising. He chose a bar where there seemed to be lots of action, and almost right away found himself making it with a pair of Latin girls, sisters in stretchpants, who said they were from Albuquerque but sounded more like Juarez or Tijuana. They had round, compact little bodies, and big black eyes, and too much makeup. They told him they were waiting for their boy friends, and winked and giggled at each other, and let him buy them drinks. When he asked when they expected the boy friends to show up, one of them said, "Mebbe tonight. Who knows?" and then they both went into another fit of giggling. They kidded him; he kidded them. Clarita and, of all things, Marlene. Their talk was uninhibited, provocative.

They told him, "Gee, you got beeg shoulders!" and hinted that he must be quite a man in many ways, and felt his muscles, giggled, pouted, said that they'd bet he had a wife and five, seex keeds. Back and forth, more and more friendly after every round. By midnight, convinced he had it cinched and with his hand under the table on Clarita's firm, round thigh, he was promising himself that the two of them together would really be a deal.

Then, at a quarter after, the boy friends came. Clarita swiftly disengaged herself. Marlene, giggling, explained that their friends, on duty at the base, had often to work late. The hot blood rushed to Carse's face as he realized that he'd been taken for a short, sweet ride. He leaned a little forward, each muscle tense, waiting for what would happen next. He understood abruptly what his mind had unconsciously recorded that there was a sameness to most of the men around him in the bar, that too many of them seemed to know each other, that most of them were military. If trouble started, he'd not exactly be on friendly ground.

The boy friends crossed the room, stopping occasionally to say hello, to slap a back. They were both older men than Carse; one of them tall, leathery, taffy-haired; the other dark, with the face and frame of a Camp Pendleton drill sergeant, wearing his sports coat as if it had three rows of ribbons on it. They didn't seem surprised to see him. When the girls introduced him as "Meester Hancock. Gee, he's a nice guy—he's bought us dreenks," they didn't look as if they believed the nice guy part, but they weren't hostile. Carse didn't get the tall one's name. The other was called Valenzuela; he was a master sergeant.

Carefully, Carse disciplined his breathing. He shook their hands. The pleasure had been his, he said, lucky break in the long run to S.F. To save face, he insisted on buying one more round, for all of them. They ordered. While the drinks were coming, the girls went off together to the john.

"Sweet kids," Valenzuela said. "Known 'em since I lived back in Albuquerq'." He looked Carse over. "Clarita, she's got a real keen sense of humor, hasn't she?"

"Real keen," Carse said.

"Been in the service?" the tall one asked, after a bit.

Carse shrugged. "The usual."

Glances were exchanged; there was a silence in which the two seemed quite at ease. Presently the drinks arrived. Carse paid the tab, tipped the waitress.

The tall soldier lifted his glass. *"Salud y pesetas!"* he said, speaking like a Texan who'd learned Spanish early.

"Y amor," added Valenzuela, *"y tiempo para gustarlos."*

They grinned at each other. "Especially *tiempo*," the Texan added. *"Poco tiempo, poco amor."*

"Cheers," Carse said.

"Speakin' of time, friend," Valenzuela remarked, "you figure to make Frisco by morning, you better get on your horse."

"I'll find a motel up around San Luis," Carse replied.

"This time Friday night, with the troops shackin' up and the weekenders? Don't be funny."

Carse started to snap back that his class of motel didn't fill up that quickly—and thought better of it.

"Yeah, it's real late," said the Texan, looking first at his watch, then back at the restrooms.

Carse had a rule; you didn't try anything if you couldn't win. "Maybe you're right," he admitted. "Weekends, they fill up pretty fast." He killed his drink in three gulps, spacing them decently with made conversation. Then he stood up to go. "Give my love to the ladies," he said.

"I'll do that," answered Valenzuela.

As Carse left the room, somebody gave a shrill wolf-whistle and there was a loud burst of laughter.

When he got into his car he was raging.

This time, he drove faster, hurling the car into the bright shaft of its headlights, into the turns. He savaged the brakes; let the tires scream bloody murder. He wasn't seeing red really —not quite. His control was still perfect, precise. After a few miles, when the chilling air had had a chance to cool him off, he realized suddenly that his rage was not at Valenzuela or the Texan, Clarita or Marlene. They didn't mean a thing; they weren't his kind of people. But Anne—Anne was. *Their* isolation, their imperviousness were of importance only as they accentuated hers. It had been she—she—who had made a triumphant night so suddenly go sour. Again his mind confronted her, cold and invulnerable behind the wall of her stupidity.

Carse's knuckles were white against the wheel. The radio blared, and he didn't hear it. The car, softly sprung, lurched and plunged in its efforts to obey him.

He stopped once, at a packed roadhouse, had one drink. Nothing had changed. There were two or three probable pick-ups, but they were pigs, real pigs.

He stopped at Santa Maria, at a bar-restaurant with lots of class, and nothing happened except that some swish character made a play for him.

He gassed up, bought himself a bottle at a package store, and hit the road again. He wasn't driving well now, and didn't give a damn. Under his anger and frustration, he began to feel the fatigue they had engendered. After four or five miles, he thought, "Oh, the hell with it! I need a good night's sleep." He'd find some place, take a hot shower, down enough bourbon to put him out, forget the mess.

He started looking for a motel. Nipomo, Arroyo Grande, Pismo Beach all went by. The Texan had been right; there were no vacancies. Sometimes neon signs taunted him, sometimes darkness. He knew that most likely at Pismo, where there were auto courts dating back to World War I, he could've found some kind of pad, but that was not what he was looking for. Now, as he turned inland towards San Luis Obispo, stretches of fog began to slow him down, and he became aware of the fact that he was drunk, not quite enough to foul up his reactions—they always were okay—but just enough to fuzz his thinking up a little bit.

He spent twenty minutes cruising San Luis; everywhere "No Vacancy" stared him in the face. It began to get to him, and again driving fast, he tore off for Atascadero. The fog thickened as he went up over Questa Pass. He took it as a challenge, riding the white line, trusting his road-sense, his disciplined and keenly tuned reflexes.

So, when it happened, he was braced for it. Abruptly, where there had been only the white line, he saw the big end of a wrecked trailer rig across the highway, yards of smashed crates and cartons, a State Highway Patrolman trying to light a flare—

He never could have stopped. It was too fast for consciousness.

There was a lightless flash of utter emptiness, a maelstrom of infinity, without duration, without beginning, without end, with neither sight nor sound nor self-awareness—

When he came to, he couldn't quite remember it—but it was there, something unseen, something behind his back. He was far down the road—how far, he didn't know and didn't care. He had blanked out, he told himself. His subconscious must have taken over, swerving the heavy car out on the gravel shoulder, wrestling it against its own mass and momentum with a skill no ordinary driver could have matched.

He shrugged off the uneasiness. Suddenly he felt sober. Suddenly, he no longer faced a hard, blank wall. His bitterness and fury were still with him, but this time he had won, and now they seemed less terrible enemies. Even his car responded to his victory. It no longer fought him. It no longer fought the road. Silently, it shared his power. Again, he and his car were one.

And the fog was gone. The full moon rode the sky, and he drove in its bright, fearful clarity.

At Atascadero, once again, no accommodations were available. One after another, the signs told him so. Finally, however, he found a nice, expensive, new motel, one with a heated pool and everything, where the sign said "Vacancy." He coasted in, stopped by the office door, got out, and rang the bell. At least he pushed the button, hard, time after time. And nothing happened. There was no sound, and no one answered him. He thought of shouting, of kicking the damned door— and then, recalling that Atascadero had a hospital for the criminally insane, decided not to. Somebody might be trigger-happy, or something might already have gone wrong and he'd be into it. Suppose some nitwit cop decided he was high? Publicity like that he didn't need.

He hesitated, wondering just what to do—and as he stood there a girl in well-filled slacks opened a door three units down the line and, keys in hand, stepped out to her car.

"Hi!" he called out.

She started to look back over her shoulder, shook her head a little, ignored him.

"Hi!" he repeated. "How do you shake these people out? Hell, I've been ringing fifteen minutes."

She opened the car trunk, took out a flight bag, locked the trunk again. Still ignoring him, she went back to her door. It closed behind her.

"Okay, so mama said don't talk to strange young men," he muttered after her. "You silly bitch!"

He gave it up. Almost without thinking, he turned back down 101, aiming for Pismo, where he knew he could at least sack in. He thought of Anne, went over all of it again. He tried to plan what he would do tomorrow, when he reached S.F., but found he couldn't concentrate. The car seemed practically to drive itself, demanding almost none of his attention; the ride was over with the swift timelessness of thought.

He left the highway. He could hear the soft, gigantic sighing of the sea. It was nearly three o'clock. The town slept. And all the best motels, of course, were full. He didn't care; he was too tired for that. He tried the side streets—found nothing, even there. At last, almost despairing, he saw a crudely painted sign, pointing toward a narrow lane. It said, "Love's Cottages."

Just what I need, he thought, and turned into the lane. It was a dead-end alley, and Love's Cottages lay athwart the end. There were ten or a dozen of them, built out on weed-grown sand. Each was square; each had a phony mission-style false front of vile pink stucco, faded and flaking; each was connected to its neighbor by an arch carrying the false promise of a carport. Another painted sign said "Vacancy"; it looked as though it never had been taken down. The place was even worse than he'd expected.

This time, when he pushed the button, he heard a ringing, thin and far away. He rang three times, then realized a light was on inside. Footsteps shuffled; the door opened on a chain.

"I see you've got a vacancy," Carse said. He took his billfold out; you didn't pay by credit card, not here.

The door swung wide. He saw a wisp of an old woman with thin lips and eyes like dull black beads, wearing a man's old overcoat over her flannel nightgown.

"You can have Number 3, dearie," she whispered to him hoarsely. "That's this one next to mine." He saw her peering at the car. "That'll be $8, single."

He knew that it was twice what she got usually and that she knew he had no choice. He paid her without protest, signed a cold, moist registration card, received his key.

He said goodnight to her, and she, sounding as though she suffered from some desperate illness of the throat, called after him, "You'll sleep real good, Mister. We always sleep real good down here."

Carse unlocked his door, snapped on the light. It was like the outside, only more so. The cracked ceiling fixture showed everything in all its dinginess, the bed as well worn as a wrestling mat, the obsolete TV, a nineteen-twentyish cheap print that looked like maybe it was made to illustrate *Three Weeks*, a tacked-up calendar of dogs. He switched on the bedside table light, and turned the other off. Things didn't look much better.

There was a gas heater. He tried to light it, but it wouldn't work. He brought his bag and bottle in, sat down on the bed, and poured a slug into his own plastic cup. While he drank it, he looked through the bedside table drawer. It held a Gideon Bible, the Book of Mormon, half a dozen used-up girlie magazines, a horror comic book, an empty condom can. He poured himself another drink, and started to undress, thinking of the shower, hoping to God there'd be hot water. He went into the bathroom; at least there *was* a shower. A rubber hose attached it to the faucet of the cracked, stained tub.

Naked, he stood beside the bed, drinking, letting his tiredness persuade him that messing with the shower would be a waste of time.

There was a knocking at the door.

"Oh, for Christ's *sake*!" Carse muttered. "Now what?"

The knocking came again, and he heard the manager's ruined voice asking him if he was yet asleep. Suddenly, the idea hit him that maybe she had come to fix the heater. He called out, "Just a minute," put his bathrobe on and went to the door, drink in hand.

She stood there with another woman, a woman somewhere in her middle years, fat, pendulous, smeared with lipstick, powder, rouge, and clad in a flowered wrapper as old as she, with just a tragic hint about her that once, somewhere, she had been young, and, unbelievably, perhaps attractive.

"This here's Mimmy," said the manager. "She's a friend of mine."

"I spell it like it sounds," Mimmy put in, "not Frenchy-like." Coyly she smirked. "My ma named me Mimosa. That's what it's short for. We got a party goin', and Bobsie said how you was so good-lookin'. We figured maybe you'd sort of like to come."

Carse ignored her. He was about ready to blow his stack. At the manager he snarled, "Look, Lady Love, I'm on my way to bed. Don't pester me again."

They snickered; they nudged each other. "Lady *Love*," crowed Mimmy. "Oh, my fat tail—*Lady Love*. She ain't Mrs. Love, hon. She's Mrs. Prewitt."

"Love sold out here twenty years back," giggled the manager. "I left the name because it sounded good. *You* know."

Carse wasted no more words. He grasped the door to bang it shut.

And at that point he saw the girl.

She was behind them, half in shadow. His own light showed her oval face. A fainter light from another cabin outlined her figure. Carse understood her at a glance. Her eyes were huge, her lashes long. Her mouth was full and brooding; her glance at once a promise, a caress, an aphrodisiac, and a surrender. He felt the passion in her—and he felt, too, her utter vulnerability. Here were no walls. Here was no cold imperviousness. Here was a person who could be hurt and hurt again, and finally broken. Here was his late reward, the cure for what ailed him. All his exhaustion left him. He knew he had to have her, and he knew as well that he would have to proceed very, very carefully.

He stared at her, his eyes taking in the fact that there were several other people there, but not quite understanding it. Shyly, she smiled at him.

"That's Laura—" Mimmy's voice reached him, suggestive, insinuating. "You'll *like* her."

Carse threw the door open. "Come on in," he ordered. "We'll have the party here."

They entered, calling back to others, and there were more of them than he had guessed, twelve, thirteen, fourteen. He wasn't sure; it didn't matter anyway. Some, Mrs. Bobsie Prewitt introduced; some shook his hand and introduced themselves. They crowded in, bringing their own bottles. Some brought in chairs. Some sat around his bed, some on it. Some leaned against the wall. Laura, passing with lowered lids, seated herself on the dressing table bench. She had a pint of brandy; from time to time she drank from it.

Carse had wondered what kind of people patronized that sort of dump. Now he learned. There were some who looked as if they'd bought their clothes out of Salvation Army salvage shops. There were one or two who seemed to have been trapped, like him, by lateness and no-vacancies. There were those in between. He met a sailor, hairy and big bellied, in rumpled whites with three stripes and hash-marks showing fifteen years of service; he kept wandering round and coming back to Carse to tell him about ports he'd helled around in, and his VD, and how a baker in the Navy couldn't make a quarter what he could outside. He met an old man with a wrinkled skin loose enough to hold two of him; he wore a crazy Herbert Hoover suit and whined interminably about how rough life was for a travelling man in notions, findings, and suchlike. Lately the railroad fares had forced him to start driving; cackling evilly, he recalled the pushovers he'd met in Pullman cars.

There were the others. A blocky, short-haired, brutal woman and her flaccid girlfriend. A small, dark man who sat all by himself, drank cheap sweet wine, kept looking at the pictures in his billfold, and wept. A tall, handsome, obviously expensive couple, whose hatred for each other burned in their eyes. And several more with no distinct identity. Most of them were grotesque. None of them meant anything to Carse. They were around, and they were in the way, and for a little while they'd have to be endured. Somehow, they kept getting between him and Laura, cornering him to tell their troubles, or stale dirty jokes, or stinking little bits of gossip or braggadocio. He let it all go in one ear and out the other. Laura was wearing a sleeveless green dress, cut very low. Under it, her body promised infinite warmth, infinite pliancy. He stared, ravishing her with his eyes. Occasionally, she glanced towards him, always indirectly, and very faintly smiled.

Slowly the endless minutes wore away. Mechanically, Carse drank his tasteless liquor, watching her, his hunger for her eating into him. Mimmy was making a nuisance of herself, being drunkenly affectionate, rubbing against him, trying to get into his lap; not wanting to upset the applecart, once in a while he'd sort of slap her off, like a mosquito. And Laura sat in front of him, head slightly bowed, heavy hair shading her smooth brow, and drank from her pint flask. Two or three times, one or another of the men went over and made a halfway pass at her, and on each occasion she made no response, none whatsoever.

Time dragged. His hunger mounted. Finally, conquering his contempt, he grabbed at Mimmy, pulled her close to him, pinched her behind, and whispered to her, "For God's sake, doll, get these kooks *out* of here!" She cuddled closer in, and whispered back, "Honey, you sure do want a little piece of that! You oughta seen *me* when I was her age. Next to me you woulda thought she was an altar boy. Well, I do kinda like you, honeybun. Seeing it's party night, Mimmy'll get your decks swabbed down for you."

In a few more minutes, quietly, to his surprise the room began to clear. One by one, two by two, they drifted out, some bidding him goodnight. Finally, only he and Laura, the sailor, Mimmy, and the small, dark man remained. The sailor was looking at the dark man's pictures, cajoling him, slapping him on the back.

Carse rose. Laura smiled again. Following her smile, he walked across to her. He didn't say a word; no word was necessary. He sat down next to her, his hip against hers. His arm went round her. His right hand touched her breast, continued down so that it rested in the valley between her belly and her thighs.

She dropped her flask. It fell down to the floor. He felt the shudder that went through her and knew that he could have her—

As though responding to his hunger, slowly, very slowly, she turned around. At last, eyes wide, she looked him fully in the face.

"It's almost over," she told him in a small, low voice. "Tomorrow I'll go home." And softly, silently, the tears streamed down from her unseeing eyes.

Carse knew that he could have her any time. But now he knew that he had come too late. Her passion has been raped, her dreadful vulnerability already violated—irrevocably. That which he needed was no longer there.

A single burst of fury brought him to his feet. Then it had passed. Coldly, he looked at them. "Beat it," he said. "I got to take a crap."

It was not true, but he turned his back on them and went into the john. He sat there for ten minutes, for fifteen, finishing his drink, while his fatigue returned a hundredfold.

When he put his glass down on the basin and walked in again, he found them gone. He threw his bathrobe off and sat down on the bed. Abruptly, almost at his feet, he saw the brandy flask. It had no labels on it. It had no cap. It was a quarter full of water, with a little sand, and a thin rag of seaweed hung from its empty mouth.

He stared at it, and felt cold horror stir. He closed his eyes. Instantly, the image of the broken trailer appeared before him, just as it had before his blacking out. And with it came a nightmare suspicion—so hideous that he rose almost to his feet, gasped, forced his eyes wide open.

There was no bottle there.

Carse stood before the mirror, letting the sight of his own splendid body drive the thought away, telling himself that he had drunk too much—that what he'd had was more than twice enough to drop an average man; no wonder he was seeing things. He turned the covers back, snapped off the light, crept in between the worn and mildewed sheets.

A moment later, he heard a creaking door.

He made his head turn round.

"Peekaboo!" Mimmy called. She came out from the closet, onto the bedside rug. "I hid," she giggled. "I had been watching you. Honeybun, you sure are plenty of man—" He heard the terrible hunger in her voice. "—and little Mimmy can use *lots* of that."

She stood there in the moonlight. She let her wrapper fall. She stood there, clothed only in her cerements of sagging, puffy flesh. She got into the bed.

Carse Hannock could not move.

She pressed herself against him. "Last guy I came here with," she whispered, "was Jake. You don't know Jake? He was a dirty bastard, hon." Her arms entwined him. "He strangled me," she panted in his ear. *"You wouldn't do that, would you, lover boy?"*

And it was then the dark, dark night closed down on him.

Melisa Michaels lives in the Bay area of California and has worked at such diverse jobs as ditchdigger and waitress. The gentleness of her writing is deceptive, and it makes no difference whether one is able to pinpoint accurately the source of the story's horror. It's the image that counts and the impact, the difference between the recognition of the scalpel descending and the actual drawing of the blood.

A DEMON IN MY VIEW

by Melisa Michaels

The telephone's incessant ringing kept Carol awake all night, especially in the early months. She would spend hours on the telephone, dialing number after number—sometimes systematically, sometimes at random—and listening to the hollow ringing at the other end.

The first time she got a busy signal, she was nearly hysterical with relief. But after several hours of dialing the same number over and over again, always to get a busy signal, she realized that the phone at the other end must be off the hook. She went back to dialing at random.

Probably those phones that gave busy signals had been in use when it happened, when the people went away. Eventually Carol stopped trying. There was still electricity in the lines. But the phone remained silent, gathering dust. And when she woke in the night to the sound of its ringing, she seldom even reached for it anymore. If she picked it up, she would hear a dialtone. The ringing was only in her mind. There was no one to call her.

"Mommy, are you awake?"

Her son's voice, small and thin in the darkness, startled her. "Yes, love," she said.

"I hear something."

"You're frightened?"

"It's so quiet."

"But you hear something?"

"I hear somebody walking."

"There's nobody to walk, lovey. Come, hop into bed with me." She cuddled her son to her bosom and fell asleep staring at the shadow patterns of moonlight on the bedroom walls.

Where are they? Even in sleep the question plagued her, but she no longer shouted it aloud. There had been enough impotent shouting; helpless rage, and frustration in the early months. She remembered it in dreams: the running, the calling, the weeping, the knocking on doors, the breaking of windows, the crying out against loneliness. No one answered.

Johnny loved grocery stores. He headed straight for the housewares section, oblivious to the stench of decaying food. Even after a year and a half the smell remained, but Johnny didn't remember grocery stores that didn't stink.

While he played, Carol collected a basketful of canned and frozen goods to replenish their supplies. She had suggested the trip more to get away from the house than because they needed anything. But the smell of musty, rotting food reminded her horribly of the peculiar, crumbly heap of rubbish she'd found in the playroom that morning. Johnny hadn't known what it was, although he looked oddly guilty or embarrassed when she asked. It was an enormous thing, bigger than he was, waxy and difficult to sweep up. She'd found the same sort of mess in varying sizes more than once since the people went away—another unexplained phenomenon in a world gone suddenly strange and silent. She shuddered, remembering, and hastily pushed her shopping cart full of groceries out into the morning sunlight. Johnny followed her, carrying a coloring book and a box of crayons.

"Who used to live here?" he asked as they passed an overgrown house on the way home. It was amazing how rapidly the native weeds and vines had taken over the gardens, choking out the delicate cultured varieties, and how soon the houses had fallen into disrepair with no one to paint and panel them.

"I don't know, love."

"You never came here, when there were people?"

"Darling, there were so many people that I didn't know them all." That silenced him. The concept of being surrounded by so many people widened his eyes, and he stared at the house in awe as they passed it.

It smelled of summer sun and the pine tree beside its front door. She wondered what was inside. A dusty television still broadcasting snowy light? A radio left to broadcast static? A kitchen sink full of dishes, beds unmade in the bedroom, toys left out in the children's rooms?

Mostly silence. She used to go in the houses to turn off their utilities, partly out of an instinctive need to save what was left for herself (Can you save electricity? She didn't know, but it had gone out briefly over a year ago, and she'd been terrified of losing it ever since, and so she tried to save it) and partly out of fear that some forgotten gas flame or electrical spark would start a fire like that which had leveled the whole south end of town. But she hated the silence.

It was easier to take, somehow, in the stores than in the houses, and so she tried not to worry about the utilities and stopped visiting the houses. Whenever they needed anything, they went to the stores rather than an absent neighbor's place.

She smiled, remembering some of the early trips. She'd taken money with her to the grocery store and tediously rung up and paid for her purchases for the whole first month. She had stopped going for a long time after that when she ran out of money in her checking account and didn't know how to get more.

Pure hysteria. Any idiot could have realized how silly that was, and yet the habits of civilization persisted until she and Johnny were hungry and her kitchen empty. Only then did she really understand that they were alone. The people weren't coming back, and the things in the stores were theirs for the taking.

She overreacted, tried to take everything. It was like Christmas—all the things she had ever wanted and never expected to have. But now Christmas was over. She took what they needed, or what they planned to use right away, and left the rest. No need to drag everything home with her; the boundaries of home had widened to include the entire city. The stationery store was her office, the toy store Johnny's playroom, the grocery store the larder, the department store their storage room. Everything belonged to them; there was no need to actually hold it all in their hands. They had everything any two people could ever want except the companionship of other people.

"What was in here, Mommy?"

She looked at the store he indicated and then looked away

quickly. "A pet store, lovey," she said. She had thought of the animals too late. Many of them were dead of starvation and thirst by then. She spent weeks driving from pet store to pet store, releasing them. Only afterward had she remembered the zoo.

But she wouldn't have dared release the zoo animals anyway. And she couldn't feed them herself. She did let loose some of the less dangerous species, which had lived in large enough quarters to survive till she remembered them. But the big cats were gone, and the monkeys, and so many others. All the zoos in other cities, all the pet stores she hadn't reached, all the parakeets and hamsters and gerbils and cats and dogs locked in people's houses . . .

"Like dogs and stuff?" asked Johnny. "Can we go in?"

"They're not there any longer, honey."

"Did you let them out?"

"Not soon enough. I didn't remember them in time."

"You mean they're dead? Like the people?"

"Lovey, we don't know that the people are dead."

He looked at her, his wide blue eyes too knowing. "You think they'll come back?"

She met his eyes with difficulty. "I hope so."

"They won't," he said with certainty.

"You sound glad."

He grinned suddenly. "I sure am."

"Why?"

"Because if they came back, they'd get our stuff."

"Our stuff?"

He gestured expansively. "All this. All the stores and toys and food and stuff. It wouldn't be ours then, would it?"

"But we'd be able to buy what we needed. And you'd have friends to play with, like in the books."

"I don't like it in the books. They're always getting mad at each other. Somebody's always sad."

"Sure, but they get happy in the end."

"I know. First they're friends, then they're not friends, and then they're friends again, and everybody's supposed to be glad. But what a lot of trouble. Not like us. We're always happy, without them. Except when you start thinking about what it was like, about the people."

"I miss them."

"They were mean to each other."

"Sometimes. And a lot of the time they weren't."

"I don't like them."

She stared. "How do you know? You don't know what they were like. You don't remember them, do you?"

He shrugged. "I know from the books. I don't want them back. I hate them."

"You wouldn't like somebody to play with?"

"I have you."

"Darling, I'm a lot older than you. People get old, and then they die. Someday you won't have me, either."

He thought about that. "Then I'll get a pet."

She smiled a little. "That's true. You could get a pet to play with." She didn't ask where he would find a tame animal by then. It didn't occur to her to wonder.

"A dog," he decided.

Well, it was a practical attitude for the last man on earth. She wouldn't argue with it. It wasn't altogether comforting to think that she could be replaced by a dog, but it wasn't an entirely novel idea. It would have fit as well in the old world.

"Here's a toy store," said Johnny.

"We can't stay long," said Carol. "The frozen foods will melt."

"I just want a few things. I'll bring them home."

She left the shopping cart on the sidewalk and entered the dusty shop at his side. It smelled of age and silence, and it was cold inside. She stopped just beyond the door, staring at the dust-covered displays, while Johnny selected what he wanted. He disappeared behind shelves while she stared at blue-eyed, baby-faced dolls with dirty blond hair, rows of plastic machine guns and Colt .45's, and little fragile dollhouses and helicopters and horses and coloring books and helmets with blinking lights on top.

There was a Raggedy Ann doll lying on the floor in front of a shelf full of stuffed animals. She picked it up and placed it carefully back among the others.

Johnny came riding out from behind the shelves on a bright red tricycle. Behind it, he had affixed a little red wagon with a length of string. In the wagon rode a collection of games and puzzles and one plastic horse. He never took dolls or toy guns—no substitute people or weapons against them. "I'm ready," he said.

Without knowing why, she picked up the Raggedy Ann again and carried it with her out of the store. "D'you suppose we'll ever find out what happened to them?" She hugged the doll, not realizing that she had spoken aloud till she saw Johnny looking back at her.

"No," he said.

"Don't you ever wonder?"

"No."

Well, why would he? He didn't remember them. He knew them only by their absence, their artifacts. And he was happy. Why would he miss something he had never known?

She tucked the Raggedy Ann into the shopping cart beside a huge canned ham, adjusted its skirt, and pushed the cart away from the store, following her son. It was nearly noon; they ought to get home. She wanted to work in the garden for a while before lunch.

But the next store was a department store, and there too Johnny turned in expectantly. "I want new blue jeans."

She hesitated, fingering the Raggedy Ann. There was something indefinably cold in his tone. "What's the matter with the ones you have?"

"They're getting too small." That was true; the pair he had on was too short. But there was something about the way he looked at her, a distant, indifferent expression like a stranger passing in a crowd. Without awaiting further acknowledgment from her, he got off his tricycle and marched sturdily through the unlocked glass front door.

Most of the stores they frequented were unlocked; the disappearance must have taken place after they had opened for the day. It probably saved Carol and Johnny months of deprivation; she wasn't sure how long it would have taken before she was willing to break into a locked store, even to fill their immediate needs.

Now, facing this department store and her son's unexpectedly forbidding look, she felt the same uncertainty she had the first time she'd left the grocery store without paying. It was as though his indifference to the old laws made them all the more meaningful to her.

He was already inside, holding the door open for her. She followed reluctantly, unaware of the Raggedy Ann in her hands.

"Come on," he said. "You could get a new dress or something. They prob'ly have something you need."

"Thank you," she said as he let the door swing silently shut behind her. Bright sunlight streamed in through the front windows, splashing golden and dancing with dust across the racks of sun-faded clothing that had been high-fashion a year and a half ago. Farther back, the fluorescent lights had nearly all burned out; the back of the store was shrouded in dimness illuminated by a few flickering bulbs. It still smelled of cosmetics and perfumes and expensive bath salts.

She wandered back into the dank recesses, past racks of sweaters and shirts, to the section containing elegant floor-length party dresses and evening gowns. Without thinking, she shed her cotton print dress and pulled a frothy yellow lace confection from the racks.

It was darker yellow on the shoulders and smelled of a year's accumulation of dust, but Carol held it in front of her and examined her reflection in a mirror. The dress looked tarnished, and there was a feverish wild look in her eyes that she couldn't face. She dropped the dress on the floor beside the one she'd worn and went to the storage area to pull out boxes of dresses protected from the dust by drawers and packaging. They were rumpled and creased but smelled fresher than those on the racks.

Her son returned, wearing stiff new blue jeans and carrying an extra pair, while she stood naked in front of a mirror, deciding between a soft blue fluffy affair consisting mostly of nearly transparent ruffles and a simple backless yellow satin gown.

"Get the blue one," he said.

She gazed at him in the mirror. "You like the blue one better?"

"It's happier," he said. But there was nothing happy about his shrouded blue eyes. Where had the laughter gone? Where had that sweet, innocent smile, that beguiling look of mischievous childhood gone?

Carol dropped the yellow gown on the floor and pulled the blue one over her head. "Did you get your blue jeans?"

"Yeah. You gonna get anything else?"

"No; we have to get home soon. The frozen foods will melt."

He was helping her zip the dress when she heard the phone ring. "What's that?" he asked.

She stiffened. "What's what?"

"That ringing sound."

"You hear it, too?" She whirled around, staring wildly across the store and searching for a telephone. "Oh, God, it's the telephone! Where is it? I can't find it!"

"What's a telephone?" Without warning or explanation, the innocent little-boy look was back like summer sun bursting from behind storm clouds. But Carol wasn't looking. She was running down the aisles, her bare feet raising clouds of dust from the carpet, searching for the phone.

There was a row of telephone booths by the door. She burst into the first one, grabbed the receiver, and gasped, "Hello? Hello?"

The ringing went on. She threw the receiver down and darted into the next booth. "Hello?" And the next . . .

Just as she picked up the third receiver, the ringing stopped. She got it to her ear in time to hear the click at the other end, the electronic switching, and the dialtone. In a fit of fury, she threw the receiver through the glass wall.

Trembling, silent, bleeding where tiny bits of shattered glass had struck her, Carol emerged from the booth to face her son. Tears streamed unnoticed down her cheeks. Her mouth twisted in a bitter mockery of a smile. "I didn't get there in time."

"What's a telephone?" he asked.

She contained her rage with an effort. "That's a telephone," she said. "And that, and that. . . ."

"But what're they for?"

"For people to talk to each other." She relaxed suddenly, crushed by bitter, boundless loneliness. "When there were a lot of people, they could call each other from their homes. I don't know how it worked; I only know how to do it. You pick up this part"—she showed him the part she had thrown through the window—"and you push seven of these buttons"—she pushed the buttons—"and then at the house you're calling, the phone rings. Like we just heard. And then the person you're calling picks up this part on his telephone, and puts this part to his ear and talks into this part, and when he says 'Hello,' you can hear him."

Johnny took the receiver from her and listened intently to the hollow electronic signal that meant that a telephone in a dusty, deserted house was ringing. "I don't hear anyone."

"No," she said wearily. "That's because there's no one to hear. But in the old days, someone would've answered."

"How d'you know who'll answer?"

"By whose number you dial."

"Everybody had a number?"

"Each telephone has a number, and each house has a telephone. So if you dial the number of your friend's house, your friend will answer."

"Why wouldn't you just go see him?"

"Maybe he lives too far away."

He handed the receiver back to her, his attention wandering. "I don't like telephones, either," he said. The strange, alien, diffident look was back in his eyes.

Carol replaced the receiver carefully, dusted her new blue dress with her hands, and went to the cosmetics counter to pick up the Raggedy Ann she'd left there on her way in. "You ready to go?" she asked Johnny. The lines of her face were stiff and straight, and her skin felt taut over the cheekbones. The back of her throat ached.

"Yeah," said Johnny. He led the way outside, into the hot noon sunlight, welcome after the chilly darkness of the store.

Carol followed silently. She put the Raggedy Ann back into the shopping cart. She'd forgotten to get shoes to match her frothy blue dress. Pushing the cart patiently down the deserted sidewalk, past dark empty stores and dusty parked cars, she smiled grimly at the image they made—the little boy with his toys and his tricycle, and his mother following obediently behind with her shopping cart and expensive, rumpled dress and bare feet, occasionally patting a Raggedy Ann doll as if it needed comforting, and listening.

But she had missed her chance. The telephone finally rang, and she had answered the wrong one. She tried to remember how it sounded, how she could have made such a mistake. True, the three phones were lined up next to each other. But even in her eagerness, she should have been able to tell which one was ringing. *Why had she answered the wrong phone?*

She looked at her son again. His narrow little back was straight and strong. His hair wanted cutting. His dirty little bare feet, with their toes curled around the tricycle's pedals, went up and down, up and down. He glanced back at her, his sweet baby face flushed with exertion, and smiled.

The next morning when she woke, the long-silent telephone beside her bed was gone. There was only a dust-free rectangle on the table where it had rested. Puzzled, she went to a neighbor's house; there was no telephone there, either. But there was a dust-free rectangle.

She spent half the day searching the surrounding neighborhood, then the downtown area, and then as much of the city as she could reach before the car ran out of gas. There were no telephones. She left the car where it was and walked home. She needed the time to think.

When the electricity went off a year before, Johnny asked about it and Carol explained. The next day it was on again, and it had never faltered since. When the telephone rang, Johnny asked and Carol explained. And the telephones disappeared.

He was waiting for her when she came in. "I like it, just the two of us," he said.

"Well, I don't. Put them back."

He looked surprised. "I can't. I don't know how."

"And the people?"

The cherubic, innocent look was back full force. "I don't know how," he said. His lips curved in a splendid, gentle, blue-eyed smile.

"Then go away," she said wearily. "Leave me alone. Get out. You don't need me, and I don't want you." Her voice was mechanical, emotionless. "I don't like you."

He stared. "You have to like me. You're my mommy."

She smiled thinly. "No, Johnny. That's one thing you can't make happen. I don't 'have to,' and I won't. You're the one who decided the way to deal with things we don't like is to make them go away. So go away. I don't like you."

He thought about that. "I'd be scared at night. I'd hear somebody."

"I don't care."

"You don't care if I'm scared?"

"Why should I? You don't care if I'm lonely, or sad, or scared, or anything else. If you don't care how I feel, why should I care how you feel?" She hesitated, watching him. "Johnny, are the people dead?"

He shrugged. "I don't know."

"Oh, God. Am I going crazy? I hope I'm going crazy. I don't want this to be real."

"I didn't like all the people all the time," Johnny said defensively. "They were always telling me what to do. And sometimes they scared me."

She shook her head. "I don't care. I don't want to know why you did it. If you can't undo it, then I just want you to go away. Leave me alone."

"I didn't know you'd be mad," he said in a small voice.

"What the hell did you think would happen?"

"I thought you wouldn't find out. And if you did find out, I thought you might be scared." He eyed her speculatively, but she had thought of this, and she was ready.

She laughed. It was a hollow, broken sound, but it was a laugh. "Scared? Of you?" She really wasn't; he was still her son, her own sweet, Buddha-faced boy.

He hung his head. His lower lip protruded in a pout. His hair hung across his eyes, a veil between them, like tears. "Don't you love me anymore?"

She resisted the impulse to take him in her arms. "Of course I love you. I just don't like you very much right now. And I'd rather you didn't live with me if you're going to do things that hurt me."

"I didn't mean to hurt you."

"I know. But you did."

"If I made them all come back, would it make you feel better?"

"Yes. Can you?"

"I can try."

You can spend a long time trying to do something without ever learning how, especially if there's no one to teach you. Carol knew that. But what more could she ask of him? "Then do it," she said. Her face was a stiff, angular mask with eyes like glowing coals. "Please, try to bring them back."

He hesitated. "I missed somebody. The one who made the phone ring yesterday. You could find him if I can't get the others."

"How? He could be anywhere. And you took the telephones away. Anyway, it doesn't matter. I don't want just somebody. I want everybody."

He scuffed one dusty foot on the floor. His bare toes curled and fidgeted. "Once I tried to make a . . . um, a toy come back. I wanted it back. It came." He hesitated.

"And?"

He lifted his hooded gaze to hers. A tear trembled on his lashes, broke loose, and slid wetly down his cheek, leaving a clean streak behind. "It got all broken," he said, barely audible.

She stared. Her eyes felt hot and dry. Her throat hurt. She wanted to sit down but was afraid to move, as though by holding still she could maintain some precarious, essential equilibrium in the universe. "All broken how?" Her voice was brittle.

"When it came back, it was like cookies," he said. "All crumbly."

She reached stiffly for the back of a chair for support. Her fingers dug into the upholstery till her knuckles were white.

She remembered the heaps of waxy rubbish she'd found—crumbly, person-sized. "Then start with the telephones. For practice." Her voice cracked. "When you can bring them back all right, you can start on the people." It occurred to her that she felt like cookies, all crumbly. She sat down quickly, before her knees gave out.

He started with the telephones. After the first half dozen waxy little heaps appeared, she knew that it was going to be a long wait.

Beverly Evans makes her living writing commercials for a radio station in an upstate New York community. She is petite, quiet with those she does not know, and absolutely the last person in the world whom you would think has a streak of nastiness in her as wide as her fiction. She also knows that emotional and physical pain often reside on the same side of the coin and that the image can produce just as much horror as the situation that spawns it. A photo album, then, more than a textbook story, and one that will not vanish simply by hiding it in the back of an attic.

IN THE LAND OF THE GIVING

by Beverly Evans

The dayroom was warm, and the afternoon sun was diffused by the opaque yellow panels that blocked the window's view. There were nineteen women in the room, some talking, some napping, some lost in thought or submerged inside the optional postlunch catatonia capsule. In the corner, Mrs. Kendall swayed slightly in her johnny-jumper, resting on the pillows that closed the empty legholes of the canvas seat so that she couldn't slip out. Once, she had rocked so hard that she knocked herself out against the wall and swung gently, unconscious, the entire morning until the second shift noticed her.

"Good afternoon Mrs. Franklin, Mrs. Rogers," the aide said, nodding and smiling with genuine affection. The soft lighting gave a healthy glow to his deep olive skin and left no shadows on his face. "Have you decided what you would like for tomorrow?"

Mrs. Rogers turned her head toward the aide's voice. "Yes, Walter," she said. "I'll take the first finger amputation."

"That's a fine choice, Mrs. Rogers," Walter said approvingly. "And you, Mrs. Franklin, have you decided yet?"

"What are my choices again?" Mrs. Franklin asked in her high-pitched, bewildered voice.

Walter shook his head sadly; it was such a shame about Miriam Franklin. She was losing her mind much too soon, and it was distasteful, even to him. But he patiently replied, "Well, you could have a minor amputation like Mrs. Rogers here, or you could choose between the Biopsy Surprise or induced paralysis in the limb of your choice."

"Oh, dear," Mrs. Franklin fretted, "I don't know. What do you suggest, Walter?"

"Miriam." Mrs. Rogers spoke. "Take the amputation so that we can go in together."

Miriam's eyes widened with pleasure. "That's a good idea, Annabelle. Thank you," she said gratefully. She reached over to give an appreciative pat to her friend's bald head.

"Is that your choice, then?" Walter asked.

"Yes, yes, that will do."

Before Walter left the room, he gave Mrs. Kendall's jumper a friendly little push, and she thanked him with a ragged smile.

"We weren't always so fortunate," Annabelle said, prodding the controls of the motorized wheelchair with her last remaining finger. "My husband couldn't have afforded to send me here five years ago."

Small beads of sweat crept down her forehead and, no longer finding the obstruction of eyebrows, slid into the flattened, closed lids that covered her eyeless sockets. She shook her head irritably, and the silent aide wiped the moisture from her face with a gauze pad.

"Albert has been so patient, and so pleased with me. I want to take advantage of all that I can while I'm here. That's why I won't go home in between options," she said in her tight, proud voice. "When I go home, I want to have lost all that I can."

The aide listened silently; he had heard it all before. Mrs. Rogers had been at the clinic longer than anyone except the woman in 21B. On the second Saturday of each month, Albert Rogers came to visit, spending hours in the visitors lounge with his wife, where they talked and laughed, and listening eagerly to her descriptions of each new removal. Anyone could see that he loved Annabelle dearly and was indeed proud of her. After all, she had chosen to stay and had picked her options with precision and care. Only once had

Albert thought that she had made an incorrect choice, when she had asked for a double radical mastectomy instead of having them done one at a time; but Annabelle had wanted it that way, and he could boast at work that *his* wife had opted for a double.

"Put me on the toilet, George," Annabelle barked at the aide, forcing air back up her throat for each syllable. "I want to take a farewell dump before my colostomy tomorrow morning." She made the dry, raspy noise that he recognized as her laugh as he strapped her to the seat with the safety harness.

"No, I don't miss my hair any more than I miss my teeth, I suppose."

"That's fine, Mrs. Franklin," the young doctor said, making a neat check mark on the list before him on the desk. "How do you feel about major amputations?"

"Oh, they're necessary, absolutely. You can't just stop with cosmetic options like paralysis or clitoridectomy, now, can you? Of course, we all go at our own pace. . . ."

Miriam's voice drifted off as she absently inspected the air just above her wrist stump, as if still checking the condition of invisible fingernails.

"Yes, that's most important. You should only choose what makes you happy."

"Someday, Doctor, I'd like to be like Maura Thompson in room 21B and have my own electric striker frame, not just a johnny-jumper like Mrs. Kendall. Do I have to wait until I'm a double amputee for my jumper, too?"

"Mrs. Franklin, you shouldn't worry about that now. You can have as much done per visit as you can handle, both physically and psychologically. We're very careful about that."

"Has Maura had her lobotomy yet?" Miriam whispered, leaning forward slightly.

"I can't tell you that, Mrs. Franklin."

"She never has any visitors, Doctor. Where is her husband?"

"I'm sorry, Mrs. Franklin; let's continue talking about you, shall we? Now, I see you've chosen both kidneys *and* stomach for your next options. Wouldn't you like to reconsider that?"

Maura had saved her eyes until the end. Room 21B was still dim and looked morning-hazy; she couldn't decide whether she had awakened earlier than usual or whether the day was merely cloudy.

The motorized bed whirred, and the canvas frame tilted her upright, while the linens behind her were rolled around the continuum spool and the fresh portion of sheeting slid into place. Small vibrators in her pressure pad began to massage her back and shoulders and buttocks; her clinical jewelry of wires and tubes jiggled and sparkled in a golden burst of sunlight that briefly filled the room.

I am happy, she thought, truly happy. Herb would have been pleased with me. Dear Herb. He never thought I'd be strong enough to go this far even when he was alive, rest his soul. I've done everything he wanted, down to the last option. Now we'll start burning my memories out cell by cell, and I won't even be able to remember anymore. But it's all right. I'm entitled to as much happiness as any woman here.

NIGHTSHAPES

by Barry N. Malzberg

1 August

Small flecks of blood in her pelt when she returned this evening, the Change a hot and deadly flicker in the dry spaces of the room, the odor sharp, whimpers as she shrugged back into her own form. Then clambering against me in the night, her teeth hot and sharp, the net of her hands drawing me in, drawing me in, and at the end a cry lupine and fierce, my own cry muffled in that desperate exchange of the blood. And now she lies open to the night and circumstance and I sit here and look at her, her body curled in the tentativeness of sleep, the submissiveness of darkness . . . and I do not know, I do not know. She is not the monster, I am the monster. If I were not the monster I would find the cure for her, grant her peace, that most precious gift. I understand this now but to understand is nothing. Nothing. The commission is unspeakable.

2 August

The researches disclose few explanations, the foaming beakers in the shoddy laboratory below stairs yield the most uncertain of formulae. I struggle nonetheless. I must help her.

At one time it all appeared simple, a simplicity: the mystery would open its darkest of hearts and one by one the methods of rationality would provide rational method. I was a fool, of course. I have always been a fool and I understand that too, now. Something about her in her present condition is attractive to me; it is not the wife with whom I am lying on these nights but the wolf, it is not the wife but the wolf whom I penetrate, the image of the beast at the center of all ecstasy. I admit this now; I must always have known it, it must have been the wolf that drove me on or long since I would have made myself free.

I think that I have gone mad.

Nonetheless I believe I have, at long last, devised a potion. I will administer it to her tomorrow night.

3 August

"I'm going out, Eric," she said to me, "I'm going to walk on the fields." Actually they are not fields but rolling empty moors beyond this village in which our house and those of a few stolid neighbors cluster. She is, however, of a romantic turn of mind. Werewolves of necessity must be romantic; it is only this which protects them from the truest apprehension of their being. I allow her these expressions, then. "I wouldn't wait up, Eric, I will be out quite late. I need to think, and I'm restless."

"Yes, Clara," I said. Clara, clearness, clarity. She takes me to be a fool unaware of her condition, her contempt is absolute, but I do not care. For if she knew the degree of my apprehension, what might she do? She might turn upon me. Better to feed her the potion which unsuspecting she drank in her tea at that moment. "Yes, Clara, Clarinda, do as you must." I affected a scholarly bumble, a researcher's detachment, a mild, stunned old man puttering around the ruins of his ambition. "I will not wait up for you."

"I would ask you to walk with me," she said, "but I know what the cold does to your feet, your digestion. Besides, I walk more quickly than you and you might lose your footing."

She is twenty-four, young, graceful, pretty by all conventional standards: What would she want with a man such as me? My own motivations are less mysterious; familiar needs extrude through this uncomfortable shroud of age. But why would Clara, Clarice, Clarinda desire a man with blanket drawn up to his knees, fervidly drinking tea in hot gulps on a cool and penetrating night?

She took another sip from her cup; it clattered against the saucer. Will the potion help her? It is my only hope.

"On the way in," I said, "you might check to see that the fire is still lit. I will be long asleep by then."

"Of course," she said. She came to kiss me with cool and deadly lips, smoothed the blanket over my frail lap. Her features are of unusual delicacy, her bosom soft and fragrant, the taunting secrets which have been revealed to me one by one infinitely tantalizing, leading me to consummation that can never have issue. Of what matter should it be that she is a werewolf? At that moment, feeling her hands light upon me, I came close or closer to the acceptance of my condition.

It is not bad to be here alone with her on the edge of the moors, even though the terrain is already splattered with the blood of another victim. The graves surrounding London know the bodies of more than even I could suspect; they swaddle knowledge that will never be mine. It was necessary for us to leave London in absurd haste and for the flimsiest of excuses. I cannot stand civilization, clutter; we must move, I must have space, she said to me, and I abandoned my position at the university, my domicile, the rounds of my life to move to this place with her.

Some would call this the damp clutch of passion, but I would assay it as sanity. The police would have come sooner or later, and I would have been implicated. Therefore my researches and at last the potion, the potion that must grant her a cure.

"I will return, Eric," she said and left the room, left the fire, the door clattering behind her, then silence. I wondered if the Change would come upon her immediately, as it so often does, or whether the potion would block it. Or whether, more likely, there would be a retarding action and she would retain human custody until she was beyond the village. Once I would have peered through the window to find the truth, but now I have all the truth with which I can deal in the premises of my consciousness.

I do not want to know.

She will do as she must, just as will I, and when she returns we will huddle in the night and from that jumbled mass on the bed will come the cry. The cry that rends me from myself, my own change, the mantle of change descended, and lupine I will scream within her.

In the darkness.

4 August

These notes commenced at month's beginning, when the potion was nearly perfected, to attempt some order: If I could
place on this chaos some sense of progression, string the beads
of the days one by one upon the long, raveled line of life, then
I might have some grasp of what was happening. I thought.
But it was a bad idea. I am a vain man and endlessly these
entries refract upon myself: my pain, my researches, my potion and its administration. Not her pain but mine. I am a
useless man, useless and frivolous to the core. The word,
perhaps, is silly. I am a silly man, Eric the silly, but his Clara,
Clarice, Clarinda matters. She matters.

For she crept in again with blood upon her jaws.

Lying in the bed, my eyes alert to the terrible light of that
first dawn, I saw her slip within, a gray shape, ears pricked,
tail at an angle. And on her jaws, the blood. I feigned sleep,
that sodden unconsciousness with which aspect I have always
confronted her, leading her to the feeling (it is justified) that
she has married a fool who will protect her forever and will
never know what she is; but I was intent on her every gesture.
Slow murmurous whimpers came from her throat. To be a
werewolf is to hurt. The freedom of her nightshape cannot
console. Weeping, she came to the bed.

I waited for the scent and aura of the Change, but it did
not come. She poised, ears down. Why was she not Changing?

The potion?

Was that its effect, a retarded change? Had it worked
against rather than toward her humanity?

Outside, a distant cry. And another and another. It is quiet
in the village at dawn but it was not quiet now: Her latest
victim had been found. Soft growls and the whimpers from
within her. I knew her fear then, shared it, and in that moment saw that if the villagers were to come here, if we were
somehow to be discovered, it would not be Clarice, Clarinda
but we two with whom they would have to deal.

The distant cries faded.

The Change came upon her convulsively.

It came in that next instant and this creature—not my wife,
not a wolf—lay stunned on the floor and wept. I dared not
stretch a hand in entreaty or comfort; were she to see me it
would end for us at once and I would never possess her again.

Had the potion affected her in some way? Would it yet lead to a cure?

After a time she came to bed.

I touched her then and felt the terrible desire raging, and in her way she accommodated me as she always has. On one corner of her mouth, still a small spot of blood, a gangrenous red eye winking as if to lure me home. I lay across her, sunlight in the room. We slept.

And awoke and began the new day. It was an old man, a wanderer on the moors, who died last night. I have heard a fragmentary report from the postman. I dare not go among the villagers to inquire further; unusual interest would only draw attention.

5 August

I have reread these entries.

The only way I can make sense of them now is to see them as done by a man enthralled. And although this is part of it, enchantment is not all. There is something else about me, something about my obsession I cannot reach. The formulae are strong and the answer lies within them; I must believe that. For only when the Change has come to Clara for the last time will I be able to understand the change that has taken place in me.

Yet I still do not know if the potion has worked or not. I must understand the truth; if I have not helped her I cannot . . . to improve the formulae is beyond my means. Also I am much agitated. The last murder was unspeakable. Its details cannot be communicated in the journal of Eric the silly; I have no taste for horror, nor can I convey it. I was made for idiosyncrasy: brandy and badminton, conundrums in the eventide, little tales for infants as conceived by my equally frivolous colleague Dodgson.

I still do not know.

6 August

"You must not go out tonight," I said to her this evening, when she was already pacing and I could sense the need inside her. Yet her aspect was merry. "You must stay here."

"Eric," she said with that strange and solemn gaiety, "you mustn't tell me what to do."

"There was another murder three nights ago. This is no time for a young woman to walk alone on the moors."

"You know the conditions, Eric," she said. "They were made quite clear at the outset, when I agreed to marry, that you would never interfere with me nor I with you. What we do alone must never be questioned." She was smiling. Her eyes were joyous. Was it the potion, which I had again administered in her tea? Or was it anticipation of the night's hunt which made her seem so happy?

"You must not go out," I said again. Fear gave me the force of determination. "Not until the murders are solved."

"I am not afraid, Eric." She walked to the door.

I followed her. Seized her wrist. "I have been searching for a cure," I said. "I know your pain and I can help you find its release."

Her eyes shone with that solemn gaiety. "What are you trying to say?" she said. "Eric, what are you saying?"

"The truth." Grief lent me strength. "We can no longer conceal the truth from each other. Clarice, Clarinda, I have known, I have always known—"

"Known what?"

"About your affliction," I said. "About the Change."

She broke away from me. Still that strange gaiety. "You've given me something, haven't you. Something from your laboratory."

"Yes. But I—"

"Then you understand everything," she said, "but you understand nothing." She spread her fingers and looked into her palm, gazed into it with an expression of delight. "After such cunning, to show such ignoble stupidity!" She opened the door, little bubbles of laughter coming from her throat. I reached toward her. "No," she said, "don't stop me, you won't like it if you do."

And she was gone.

She was gone and I let her go, I sat here to write these words. But I cannot remain alone any longer, I cannot wait again for her to come home at the dawn light. I must follow her. I must know what I have done.

7 August

She is dead she

Is dead she is dead she

Is dead she is dead she was out there on the moors I saw her framed against the moon, I saw the light shining off her pelt and heard the laughter, oh the laughter, and she reached for her throat, I could not comprehend but she reached for her throat and now

I understand what she saw in her palm and what it is I have done, I understand everything: the nature of my own change and what I secretly desired from the first. I wanted to be what she was, a sleek gray shape running free with her in the night, and I yearn now to take the potion and wait for the Change, sit here upon my haunches in the dying blood of the day waiting for the pentagram to appear in my palm, the pentagram that would mark me as my own victim, waiting for the Change that can never come I

Want to be a werewolf so I can die like my Clara, Clarice, Clarinda, she

Tore her throat she

Tore out her own throat in the moonlight but

The moonlight has passed and the day has passed and the potion made her free, it worked as I could never have dreamed. I was not silly but a genius, a man of spirit but the spirit destroyed her and destroyed me, I was undone by my spirit and

And I needed her

I needed her, I needed the blood

Striking once and striking twice and striking thrice and the villagers are striking on the door, screaming, but I will say this, I will say this as they come with the torches that will burn me away, I will say I am not silly. I was a mind of iron, a will of fire. Silly no more silly no more, nor Eric that great Fool, but my Clara my Cordelia driven here and there alone upon the heath until that great wheel of self turned inward, her claws reaching, and only Blinded Gloucester left to show the way through that serene, that gay and mocking, that rigorous and deadly fire

The fire of the shapes of the night.

Chelsea Quinn Yarbro's visions of horrors do not always include the immediately grotesque or the blatantly shocking. Many of her stories, such as the one that follows, rely on the aftertaste, the afterimage, the potential that the reader knows will be realized. It is, in many ways, the most horrific of fiction because the reader has an opportunity to work with the writer. All you need are the directions, and Yarbro knows well how to give them.

SAVOURY, SAGE, ROSEMARY, AND THYME

by Chelsea Quinn Yarbro

She was known as the Herb Woman, and everyone on the mountain was afraid of her, though few were willing to admit it. She had lived in her shack above Lizard Creek for as long as anyone could remember, and no one knew for certain how old she was. Less than a dozen people in Candy had made the rigorous trek up to her place, but it was tacitly believed that more than one girl with a yen for a particular boy had sneaked away to get her philtres and, when they were successful, went again to be rid of what their desires had got them.

Amy Macklin had heard about the Herb Woman but was not sure that she accepted all the stories. Unlike most of the girls in Candy, Amy had stubbornly continued on in the little two-room school over in Pageville, eagerly listening to Mr. Houseford tell her everything he could dredge up from his long-ago college days of poetry and history and botany and art. If Ellis Houseford had been a younger man with prospects instead of disappointments, Amy's family might have encouraged her, but as Ellis Houseford was nearing fifty and was possessed of an ailing wife, Amy's mother actively discouraged her second-oldest daughter's scholastic ambitions.

"What do you think will happen to you, child?" she demanded more than once. "You're getting so's you hardly want to talk to anybody here. Another few months and you'll be like Tom Gosling over in Sandy Hollow, going off to the city, thinking you're too good for the people here. You know how he came back. I don't want that kind of shame brought to this house! Lord between me and evil."

At the time, Amy had set her pretty jaw rebelliously and wished she had nerve enough to answer back, even if it got her the flat of her father's hand for sassing. She continued to bring books home with her, to read them, and to write in one of three looseleaf notebooks Ellis Houseford had given her.

Then Jemmy Howard drifted into Candy, and for Amy everything changed.

Jemmy Howard was twenty-four years old, almost six foot two, with big eyes bluer than a clear summer sky. He had brown hair that streaked out in the sun, a smile that was better than anything Amy had ever seen in the movies, and a voice as warm and coaxing as a sandbank by a swimming hole. Amy Macklin was dazzled. From the first time Jemmy had given her his lazy smile and said, "Now, this is purely the nicest thing I've seen in many a day. I could make a bouquet of you, girl; buttercups for your hair, cornflowers for your eyes, and wild roses for your lips," she felt she had drowned in light. The breath caught in her throat then, and with the baffled ardor of her fifteen years, she had plunged into love with Jemmy Howard.

Three love-fraught weeks later, after Amy had found more excuses than she knew existed to go into Candy for a glimpse of her deity, she caught Jemmy kissing Georgina Taylor. Her dreams dissolved as if dipped in acid. Georgina was nineteen, with hair so thick and dark that no one doubted it when the Taylors said that they were descended from an Indian princess. Her eyes were darker than chocolates with raisins, and her mouth made voluptuous promises when she spoke, even if it was only to say hello.

At home Amy had wept and then become oddly silent, sitting by the window of the room she shared with two of her sisters and staring out at the mountain as if listening for one particular sound. Lucy teased her, and Caralou was worried, but their mother, who knew enough about men like Jemmy Howard to guess what had upset Amy, shooed the other girls out of the house and went about her chores, giving Amy a chance to talk if she wanted to but pressing nothing on her.

"Ma," Amy had said as sunset came, "what do they want? What is it?"

Amy's mother sat down at the dull, well-scrubbed table where she had served family meals for more than twenty years. "I can't tell you exactly, child. There are those who like one thing and those who like another. Some men, if they're good-looking and sweet-tongued, like to keep a lot of silly girls on the string so they can sample a bit of this or a bit of that, as they fancy. Men like that, they think all a woman's good for is kissing. They don't know about the kinds of things that count in this life. There's no faith in them, child. The Good Lord put a special burden on Eve that He didn't give Adam, and not many have the sense to know." She studied her second-oldest daughter, who was so unlike her other children, and wondered whether she had paid any attention.

"Isn't there a way to make them know?" Amy asked in a small, tense voice.

"They say there's always something you can do, but that's not the way for a Christian woman. If the good Lord wants you to have this man, then you'll have him; if not, then all the mooning and sighing and wishing in the world won't bring him to you." She got up from the chair. "Your pa'll be home soon. I've got things to do before then."

Amy shook her head in a daze. "You need help, Ma?" she asked in an abstracted way, her eyes straying toward the door and the sight of the mountain beyond.

Ordinarily, Amy's mother would have accepted the offer with thanksgiving, but knowing how her child felt and the depth of the shock she had received, she changed her mind with a wistful sigh. "Not tonight, Amy. Caralou can set the table this once. It won't hurt her to do it."

Amy murmured a distracted thanks, still preoccupied as her mother got up and went to prepare the evening meal. She listened to the familiar sounds of the pump and the unmelodic clang of the grate in the wood-burning stove and then called out, "When you met Pa, what was it like?"

Mrs. Macklin did not answer at once. "I don't rightly remember. I think I must have been about fourteen the first time he came to the house. It wasn't to see me; he was buying a couple head of hogs from us, for sausage."

"How did you feel when you saw him?" Amy was more forelorn, thinking that no one had ever been struck as she was and been treated so shabbily.

"I don't think I felt much of anything. Why should I? He was just a man coming to buy stock. There was nothing in that. It happened all the time." She had the fire going now and was searching for kindling in the wood box. "You tell Willy when he comes in that I need more cut wood here. There's not enough for doing breakfast."

"Sure, Ma," Amy responded listlessly. It was apparent that her mother, for all her kindness, did not know how she was suffering. She was too proud to weep, but her eyes ached as if the lids had been starched.

There was the sound of a horn and a motor. A battered '48 Dodge lumbered down the road toward the house.

"That's your pa already, and supper not on the table. Give a holler for Caralou, Amy. She's down at the rabbit hutches."

Amy got up slowly and went out the door, paying no attention to the greeting her father gave her or the shouts of her brothers. There were dark shadows on the mountain now, deepening to night in a special way. As she looked up, she shivered, thinking that the shadows were more massive and colder than anywhere else in the world. The pines trembled in the breeze and whispered among themselves as if afraid to raise their voices. Somewhere up past Lizard Creek the Herb Woman lived, spending her days making God knows what mischief. Sally Gibbs swore that the Herb Woman had given her a secret perfume that caused her to be irresistible to men with dark hair. That was why, she insisted, that Hank Patterson was forever chasing after her, and Bobby Huggins as well. Boys with dark hair, that's what the perfume was good for. Idly, Amy thought about that. Everything she had learned from Mr. Houseford taught her that such things as magic perfumes were nonsense, but it was true that boys with dark hair took to Sally Gibbs in no uncertain terms. Perhaps, if it could be made to work with dark hair, there would be a way to do something with light-brown hair with sun fingers through it. She was not aware that she had crossed the field and was at the edge of the pines that sighed like the ocean. Lizard Creek was a good four miles up, maybe more. In the dark there was no telling how she could find her way. It was foolishness, anyway, the desperate gesture of a lovesick girl.

Amy stepped into the trees.

It was more than half an hour before her family missed her; when her father asked why Amy was not at table with the rest of them, his wife nipped the sudden comments of the other children by saying, "Amy is feeling poorly, Sam, and needs time to herself."

Sam Macklin didn't hold with indulging children, but he only grunted, trusting his wife to know what was best where daughters were concerned. Even when Caralou tried to say that she thought Amy might be in trouble, out there by herself in the night, he merely pointed out that she was a sensible girl and would come home when she was good and ready. "No use fussing about her, Caralou. That's one female with a mind of her own. Leave her be."

Caralou fell silent, and Joey claimed the family's attention by announcing that he was going to set up some traps for coons as soon as he got together enough money.

About the time Caralou and Lucy were clearing the table, Amy was wishing she had never started out for Lizard Creek. Her legs were scratched with brambles, mosquitoes had made a feast of her, there was a rent in her thin blouse, and she was not at all sure she was going the right way. She had stumbled twice and once had rolled a fair distance before getting to her feet, and she was disoriented.

There were skitterings, cracklings, and smells in the brush around her, and she tried to forget all the tales she had heard of the poor souls who got lost on the mountain and were found again only as white bones, often marked with the gouges of gnawing teeth. The recollection goaded her on. She had not come this far to let herself be killed by a bear or raccoon. She was going to see the Herb Woman.

With that decision, her way seemed easier. She walked along the narrow trails left by deer, always climbing, her senses tuned to the night with the acuity of long knowledge. She no longer slipped, and her fear of the quiverings and muted grunts around her faded. The Herb Woman would protect her; there was no reason to worry.

For more than an hour she climbed, stopping now and again to peer through the moon-dappled trees up the slope. Twice she crossed large meadows, and she saw deer grazing in one of them. She stopped, reluctant to startle the beautiful animals into flight. The nearest doe raised her head, ears turning, and then lowered it again. Amy smiled with satisfaction and continued on.

On an outcropping of boulders, she missed her step and turned her ankle. She bit back a moan and heard a dry slithering from where she had almost put her foot. Her tongue turned to flannel in her mouth as she realized how close she had come to the reptiles. When she tried to walk, she stumbled, and for several minutes she stood terrified, her teeth chattering, as she thought of herself lying senseless while all the wood creatures with sharp teeth assailed her flesh until she was another anonymous skeleton. She had started to cry in her misery when she remembered the way that Jemmy had kissed Georgina, and that drove her on.

It was close to eleven o'clock when she reached Lizard Creek. By this time, she was light-headed with fatigue and hunger, and her sense of triumph had a muzziness to it, very nearly like a moment in a dream. She bent down and drank eagerly, thinking of the time her father had told her that the sweetest water on the mountain was here in Lizard Creek. He had also mentioned that the Indians who had lived there long ago—dead for almost a century now—had said that the place was haunted by a powerful force that could drive a sane man mad and restore the senses of the possessed. Sam Macklin did not believe such talk, and the pastor at the clapboard church ranted against superstitions, but neither man went willingly to Lizard Creek when the sunlight was not full upon it. Amy wiped her hands on her torn skirt and continued up the mountain.

She stumbled upon the place by accident. Her ankle was paining her, there was a stitch in her side, and she had seen an owl fly past her, which she knew was bad luck. The hollow offered a respite, and she thought that if she found a well-protected spot, she could crawl into it and sleep a bit. She might even wait until morning and then make her way home. Chagrin was fast taking hold of her, mocking her hopes. So intent was she on finding a safe place that she did not at first notice the wink of firelight, or if she did, she decided to ignore it and its worrisome implications. Gradually the brightness drew her, and then she recognized the cabin for what it was.

Ferns grew out of the roof, and other plants clung close to its sides so that even in daylight it might be possible to mistake it for a hummock in the undergrowth. But there were small, square windows neatly divided into four parts with thick, old glass in them, and a low doorway.

She stood staring, giddy with relief that she had found the place though wondering whether it was real. She took a few tentative steps toward it and then asked herself whether she dared to call out. Her mind was not made up when the door opened and a small, shapeless figure stepped out.

"Come on in, girl. No sense skulking out there in the dark."
The voice was old, no doubt about that, but vigorous and
hearty. The figure raised an arm and beckoned. "You come
all this way to see me, you might as well come in."

"You the Herb Woman?" Amy's voice trembled, and she
flushed with embarrassment.

"Of course I am. Who else you think lives up here but me?"
She gestured again and held the door a little wider. "Come on,
child."

Amy allowed herself to be persuaded. By the time she
stepped through the door, she had begun to feel grateful.
"Thank you," she murmured, not knowing what else to say to
her benefactor.

"It's the least I can do," the old woman said with a chuckle.
"It ain't too often that I get company of an evening, no, not
too often." She had gone over to the hearth where the fire
crackled. She was almost a head shorter than Amy and wore
so vast and enveloping a dress that it was difficult to know
whether she was fat or thin. Her face was seamed and wrinkled as a dry creek bed, and her hands, though large and
square, were mottled with spots and ridged with veins like
blue twine. Her eyes were a clear, arresting green, bright
with amusement and something less pleasant. "Here, girl, sit
down, why don't you? There's two chairs at the kitchen table
and a bench under the window. Take whatever one you want.
The rocker's mine."

"Oh, yes. Thank you." Amy chose the bench and sat on it
carefully, poised on the edge as if she wanted to run away.

"Give me a couple of minutes and I'll let you have something for your ankle, and then you can tell me what brought
you up here." The Herb Woman had been stirring a pan by
the fire, and as she spoke she went to the sink and began to
work the handle of the pump.

"How'd you know my ankle's hurt?" Amy demanded, oddly
frightened.

"Good Lord preserve us! I heard you thrashing about out
there, and when you came in, you were limping. The skin
there's all tight and swollen, if you'd trouble yourself to look.
It's what I did." Although her tone was exasperated, she was
not angry.

"Oh." Amy twitched aside the hem of her skirt and looked
down. Yes, her ankle was swollen, shiny-looking, and now
that she realized it, quite sore. "I stumbled."

"That's not surprising. Anyone fool enough to come up

here in the dark, they got to expect to get ruffled up some."
She added the freshly drawn water to whatever was in the
pan. "Now, I want you to put your foot in this," she said as
she came across the room to Amy. "I'll add hot water, and
it'll take care of you in no time."

Amy nodded, wishing that she had enough courage to bolt
for the door. She knew—knew—there was something awful in
the pan, and it would do terrible things to her. Mr. Houseford
had said once that there were chemicals that would just
dissolve whatever you put into them. She closed her eyes as she
placed her foot in the pan. A few minutes later hot water was
added and a pungent, mossy secret smell rose up on the
steam. She blinked.

"You keep your foot in that until I tell you to take it out,"
the Herb Woman said as she sank into the rocking chair.

"Okay," Amy promised. She was feeling better now; the
ache was fading, and the variety of scratches, cuts, and
bruises she had got during her climb seemed less terrible. To
her languorous amazement, she was beginning to feel sleepy.

"I'll give you a little broth in a while, but before that, you
tell me what brought you up here." The Herb Woman rocked
slowly, her chair creaking. "Must be something to do with
love. You're too young to worry about money yet, and it don't
look like you want to stop bearing kids. Unless you got a
drunken daddy who beats you or brothers who want into your
drawers. . . ."

"It ain't like that!" Amy protested, shocked out of the gentle lethargy that had taken hold of her. "My pa's a good man,
and none of my brothers would try anything like that. Ma
makes sure they listen to the pastor." She was dimly aware
that Mr. Houseford would be disappointed in her if he could
hear how she was speaking now. For the last year she had
been talking like a city girl, not a half-educated girl from the
hills.

"Love then," the Herb Woman sniffed. "Thought so. What
is it about you pretty ones that always drives you to this?
Ain't it enough that most girls'd give their eyes to have hair
like yours?"

"But he don't like yellow hair. It's dark hair he wants,"
Amy burst out unhappily. "He can't see me at all, he's so busy
with Geo—" She stopped at once, not wanting to say her
rival's name.

"Oho! Georgina Taylor, is it?" The Herb Woman made a
rattling sound that might have been laughter. "Georgina Tay-

lor. Well, well. I've heard that name before now, what with one thing and another."

Amy repressed the urge to ask to hear more. Instead, she remarked, "She's had other boyfriends."

"Indeed she has," the Herb Woman agreed. "Dark-haired and dark-eyed, isn't she? Like Solomon's lady in the Bible."

There was nothing Amy could say to that; she felt utterly defeated, and so she was silent while the Herb Woman rocked and stared at nothing in particular, her splendid green eyes brooding.

"What is it you want of me, girl?" The question came so quickly, when Amy had been lulled into a wistful drowsiness, that she gasped before answering.

"It's Jemmy, Jemmy Howard. He's new in Candy. He said I have eyes like cornflowers, but that was before he saw Georgina Taylor. I saw them kissing," she went on in a desperate rush. Now that she had admitted her plight, she had nothing left to hide. "There wasn't anything I could have done about it. I don't . . . didn't plan to see. They never knew I was there, either of them."

"I see," the Herb Woman said when Amy stopped talking. "And you want what?"

"I want him to notice me, to kiss me!" Amy cried out. "I want Jemmy to hold me and put his tongue in my mouth." She blushed, anticipating what the pastor would say if he ever heard her confess such desires. "He's not right for her; it's me he'll want. Ma said that men don't always know what will do for them. I know I'm right for Jemmy." She almost knocked over the pan her foot was soaking in as she half rose in her determination.

The Herb Woman waited until Amy was seated once more. "You're kind of young to be saying those things, child."

"I'm not." Amy tried to sound dignified but was afraid that she was being sullen. "Georgina Taylor, she doesn't want Jemmy the way I do."

This time the Herb Woman's laughter was raspier, and there was a tired cynicism in her well-used face. "No, she certainly doesn't. What do you think I can do for you, girl? Do you know?"

Amy faltered. "Well, I want. . . ."

"You've told me what you want," the Herb Woman interrupted brusquely.

"Isn't there something you can do? Maybe a thing I can wear around my neck or some drops I could put in his coffee?" What else was there? She knew that she was willing to do a great deal. After all, she had walked up the mountain at night to ask for the favor. "Tell me."

"Well, first, you better know that nothing's free in this world, especially not my kind of help. You want me to fix these things for you, there are things I got to have in return. If you fail me, then it'll go badly." She paused, looking toward the ruddy logs on the hearth. "This ain't quite the usual situation, however, and if I demand my price of you, I got to tell you now that you don't understand what you're asking."

Amy bridled at that. "If you tell me that Jemmy is a useless man and that he won't take care of me. . . ."

"No, that's not it, although it's true enough." She gave a short, impatient sigh. "You see, I've already taken a hand in these doings. . . ."

"What!" This time Amy did stand up, and the warm, scented water sloshed over the floor. "Did that Georgina Taylor come up here already? Why'd she do that? Or was that how she got Jemmy? Did she try to get him because she was afraid he might like me too much? Was she scared of me?" Amy could not entirely conceal her pride in the thought that she might be threatening enough to beautiful Georgina Taylor, to cause her to seek out the Herb Woman for help, just as Amy was doing now.

"No, no, child, it wasn't like that." The Herb Woman stared down at the dark shine of the spreading water and sighed. "You're looking to the wrong place."

"The wrong place?" Amy echoed, her satisfaction deserting her.

"I've never seen Georgina, just heard about her." The green eyes were hard on her.

"From other girls?" Amy asked, not wanting to examine the suspicion that had begun to grow in her.

"Yes, but not this time. This time," the Herb Woman went on with rough gentleness, "the person who described her to me was a young man, tall, good-looking in a weak-willed way, with a too-ready smile and a tendency to flattering speeches. You recognize him, girl? Do you?"

"Jemmy?" Amy said the name so quietly that the low sputter of flames in the fireplace was louder. "How. . . ?"

"He came up here one afternoon—and brought a lantern with him, too, by the way—and said that he'd met a girl who did more to him than any female he'd ever laid eyes on in all his life. He said she didn't give ant's piss for him, and he was ready to do anything to get her. He'd tried presents and conversation and doing chores for her daddy so's he'd be asked into the house to talk with her. None of it worked. Miss Georgina Taylor wasn't having anything of his, that was plain. So he told her that if she didn't love him, he'd go away, maybe join the army, maybe get killed. Georgina said that was fine with her. That was when he came to me, to find a way to make her want him. He paid my price, and I did what I could. If what you saw is any indication, it must've worked pretty good." She leaned back, thinking for a moment. "You know, it ain't many women, not even those who know herbs and other things, who could have done that."

Amy had listened in growing anguish to the Herb Woman, and she seized on her last reflection. "Does that mean you can still help me?"

"Not exactly. I already accepted a fee from Jemmy Howard." She turned swiftly toward Amy. "If I go back on my bond, there'll be trouble."

"Then there's nothing left," Amy sobbed, at last giving way to the tears that had been building within her. There was no Jemmy Howard for her, would never be.

"He's not worth your tears, girl," the Herb Woman said quietly. "Not after what he did to you."

Amy shook her head, letting her weeping claim her and taking solace in the abandon of her grief. "Never," she was able to say, but nothing more.

"Oh, yes, girl," the Herb Woman went on a bit later, with less warmth. "Yes. You don't know what kind of a man you're dealing with." She got out of her rocker and went to open one of the square windows. A cool rush of wind came through the house. "That's more like it. It was getting close in here. That's the trouble with houses. They protect you, but they shut out a lot." She went on in this aimless way until Amy had calmed herself, and then she came back to the rocking chair. "You know, girl, you're blinded by that man. You want him to kiss you, and cuddle you, and put his hands all over you. It's no use denying it"—she raised her hands to prevent Amy's protests—"and at your age, it's not surprising. But a man like Jemmy Howard, who'd give you away with no more thought than he'd show a line of fish, there's no reason for any woman to cry over the likes of him."

"But it wasn't like that," Amy wailed when the Herb Woman broke off. "Jemmy cared for me!" She shrieked her conviction. "He did!"

"So much that he asked me for a potion to get Georgina Taylor." She stared down at Amy. "So much so that he paid my price for her. Don't you want to know what it was? Aren't you the least bit curious?"

Amy was struck by the remarkably sinister tone of her last remark. "What did he pay?" She did not truly want to know, but she admitted to herself that she would rather learn from this odd old woman than from Jemmy, which would be devastating, or from Georgina, which would be unbearable.

"Why, he gave me his word that a virgin would come of her own free will to me, ready to endure anything required of her on his behalf. You came tonight, and his price is paid. By you."

"What did you say?" Amy had been wiping the wetness from her face and did not hear what the Herb Woman had told her. "I paid the price? But how?"

"You came here." The Herb Woman's face was decidedly nasty now as she folded her arms on the back of the rocker and swayed gently with the chair. "You came here freely, on behalf of Jemmy Howard. When you started up the mountain tonight, Jemmy was able to breathe easy. Nothing can stop him from getting his Georgina after this."

"No!" Again Amy lurched to her feet, thrusting her hands out in front of her. It was not possible. "He wouldn't do that!"

"He did." The Herb Woman gave her a long, impassive stare. "I won't lie to you about that. You see, the thing is," she added more craftily, "I was kind of hoping that he was just being cocksure and that no one would come, so that when the moon was full again, I would be able to claim my price of him since he had not paid his to me." She chortled. "Yes, that was what I wanted. I see a boy like that, strutting his way about, crooking his little finger so that every girl for miles around swoons for him, and I don't like it. There're too many of them. And too many girls, silly creatures that they are, suck up their charming words; and when it's too late, and there's unhallowed loaves in the oven, they find that their lovers don't want a thing to do with them. Most women haven't the gumption to get mad when they've been scorned, girl. They lie back and weep and hurt and let their lives be blighted. Jemmy Howard will have his Georgina for a day or

a week or however long it takes him to get tired of dark eyes
and stolen kisses; then he'll be off to Pageville or Five Roads
or Oak Mountain, looking for another silly girl to charm. I
know. I seen it before, too long."

Amy had listened to less than half of this, trying to shut out
the implications of what the Herb Woman was saying. She
pictured Jemmy, his smile, the way he moved when he
walked. There was nothing of treachery in him. She refused to
accept what the Herb Woman was telling her. "No," she
announced quite calmly. "Jemmy's still feeling his spirits is
all. He doesn't care about Georgina, not really. . . ."

"Probably true," the Herb Woman agreed at once. "That
kind, they don't care about much of anything but what
catches their eye at the moment. It don't seem like that to you
now, but mark my words, girl, when you've lived as long as I
have. . . ."

"Maybe," Amy interrupted carefully. She told herself that
Mr. Houseford had been right and that there was nothing to
spells and magic but a lot of stupidity. It was not possible that
Jemmy would *give* her to this person or would imagine that
he could. Amy all but laughed with uneasy relief. She would
tell Jemmy, and he would be amused, and that would make
him realize how foolish he had been. It was ridiculous to
suppose that Jemmy would actually *do* what the Herb Woman
had said. Not Jemmy, never Jemmy. And when she told him,
he would know that she loved him enough to go up the
mountain to Lizard Creek in the dark for his sake, and Georgina Taylor would be a thing of the past. For the time being
she had to get away, find her way back home. The sorrow that
had filled her faded away to nothing as she tried to imagine
how Jemmy would respond to what she would say. His eyes
would get that glisteny look to them, like dew on leaves, and
he would give her a look that would make her think she was
with the heavenly choir.

"You have to find out for yourself, don't you, girl?" the
Herb Woman asked in a voice both sharp and sad. "You don't
trust me because you're caught by a grinning rogue. What's
an old woman with half her teeth gone compared to his stolen
kisses?" She shrugged. "Go on, then. You won't be satisfied
until you do. You'll have to be disappointed before you
understand."

"I won't be!" Amy declared staunchly.

"And when you know," the Herb Woman went on as if she
had not heard Amy's interruption, "come back to me, and

there are a few things I might teach you. I think there are ways our ends can be served." She stood back from the chair, giving it a gentle shove and watching it rock slowly. "You know the way now, but it'll be easier if you come in the daytime."

"I won't be coming back." Amy's chin went up, and if it were not for her foot in the pan, she would have looked very brave.

The Herb Woman half smiled. "That's as may be, girl. You should have the chance to learn for yourself, I suppose. But if it should happen that it's as I've told you—*if*, mind you—then my door is open. I can take no action; I've told you that. You, though, that's another matter, and there's no reason I shouldn't tell you how to do it. That isn't contrary to my bargain." She stared down at Amy's foot. "I'll get you a length of cotton to wrap up your ankle. And if you want an easier walk, go over the crest and bear to the right at the rock with a sign on it. There's a trail there that leads to the Foley Mine Road, and that will bring you into the outskirts of Pageville. You can get Mrs. Fountains at the hotel to call your folks. That was the way Jemmy came up. He didn't want to make the climb."

"And I don't want my family to know I've been gone," Amy countered at once. "Ma'd be furious, and Pa'd want the pastor to come talk to me about my duty. I'll go the way I came and say that I stayed out in the shingle maker's shack. They'll believe that, and there won't be trouble for anybody." Her indignation was apparent, but it evoked no derision from the Herb Woman.

"A man like Jemmy don't deserve the likes of you," she muttered as she went to rummage in a chest under the open window.

"I don't deserve him, but I want him," Amy said, chiding her companion. "He won't forget about this. He'll know what I did for him, and that will. . . ." She could not see beyond that overwhelming moment when Jemmy would know that he had been wrong about Georgina. Why, she told herself, it was almost like Jemmy was testing her, making sure that she was the right kind of girl for him. And she would prove it beyond any doubt. Georgina Taylor would never go up the mountain in the night for Jemmy or any boy. Everyone knew that. Georgina thought that all she had to do was give one of her smoldering smiles and the thing was settled. Well, now little Amy Macklin would show her how wrong she was.

The Herb Woman brought the cotton and bent to help Amy wrap it around her ankle. As she worked, she said, "When you come back, miss, you bring something he wears: a shirt if you can get it, but a piece of it will do, and some of the dirt he's walked on recently. Don't need much, just a handful. You bring those up to me, and we can do something."

Amy nodded, not wanting to argue further with the Herb Woman, confident that in the next day or so she would have Jemmy Howard in her arms and all this would be behind her. "Okay." It was easier to sound as if she agreed.

"With a shirt and the dirt," the Herb Woman crooned to herself, "he'll plow a hole that's six feet deep and put on his last shirt. It's all in the song, all in the song. When Enoch Parker went away, he went to plow a place for himself."

Amy looked up at the name. "Enoch Parker?" She remembered that her pa had mentioned the name once or twice. The man had been a friend of his father's who'd gone off to the city or to war, he couldn't remember which, and had come back with a high-spoken woman from far away. Nobody in Candy spoke well of either of them, or at least so her pa had said. Then Enoch Parker went away, and while he was gone, his lady friend disappeared. When Parker came back, he had gone back to his old rounder's ways, but they hadn't lasted long. According to Amy's pa, it wasn't more than six weeks before Enoch Parker was laid out at the undertaker's, horribly dead, his flesh shrunken on the bones, loamy, as if he had been in a dry grave for a long time. His clothes were wound tightly about him in spite of his slightness.

Amy's pa had warned his children not to believe all that they heard about that time in Candy. "There's lots of folk hereabouts who don't have nothing better to do with their time than go about scaring honest men with bogie tales and made-up horrors. My pa went to the funeral, and he said that even then the gossips were busy." He admonished his whole family to be sensible, and that, for the time being, was the end of that, except for Joey getting under Amy's window and howling about how he was going to chew up her bones.

When the Herb Woman stood up, there was a sly smile lingering on her lips. "Enoch Parker is dead. You remember that. A shirt and the dirt." She went over to the window. "It's past midnight. You'll have to be careful going down the mountain. I figure you'll be back at your family table in time for breakfast. But you got to keep in mind what I've told you.

I need the dirt and the shirt or there's nothing either of us can do."

Amy shrugged. Her ankle felt better, she had to admit. She wasn't quite so light-headed as she had been when she stumbled upon the cottage. Now she was eager to leave.

"I'll get you a cup of broth. I don't want you hurting yourself again," the Herb Woman said as she bustled toward the stove. There was a kettle simmering on it, as there was in so many country houses. She opened the lid and peered into the pot. "Lamb and rabbit, for the most part, but occasionally a little venison finds its way in as well. I think you'll like this." She ladled out a good-sized portion into a large mug, which she held out to Amy.

"That's kindly of you," Amy said as she had been taught to respond. She did not want to accept anything from the Herb Woman, but there was no way she could refuse without being unforgivably rude. The flavor was strong and hearty. "I like it," she said, a little surprised.

"Good. I don't have much call to cook for anyone but myself. It might be different if I had company more often, but as it is. . . ." She shrugged. "I don't make coffee, but there's lots of herbs that make good drinking teas, so you can have a cup of that, if you want it."

"No, this is fine." In fact, she thought, it was really *good*, full of tastes she had never encountered before and nice on the tongue. She had the last of the broth and handed the mug back. "It was real good."

"I like it too," the Herb Woman confided. "Most people don't, but then, why should they? Why should they?" Her green eyes flashed. "You'd better get moving if you want to be back by sunup."

Now that she was about to go, Amy felt strangely sad. She had enjoyed the time here, but for the terrible lies the Herb Woman had told about Jemmy. The old lady was interesting, and Amy had the unaccountable feeling that she owed the Herb Woman something. Well, when she was married she would invite the Herb Woman to visit, and she wouldn't pay any mind to what the neighbors said. "I'll see you later," she promised.

"Yes," was the Herb Woman's answer as she opened the door.

As Amy made her way down the mountain, she found herself thinking again of all the things she had heard about Enoch Parker. Much of it was made up, that was certain. But the man had been something of a rounder, and he had left that woman of his alone. At Lizard Creek she had another drink and asked herself whether Parker deserved such a death, and at the next moment she giggled uneasily since it seemed to her that she was being unwise to think about such things.

Her climb was so uneventful that she was worried. It was as if someone or something had cleared the way for her. Brambles as well as animals fell back as she went on, and the brush was silent. Yes, she felt that she was being watched. She saw a brightness in the trees and hoped that what she had seen was eyes.

When she reached the edge of the field, the sky was turning rosy. She could hear her pa out in the shed, getting ready to milk their two cows. He was singing a hymn, as he often did first thing in the morning. Amy walked across the low-grazed grasses toward the voice, calling out "Pa!" as she got nearer to the song.

Amy's Pa fell silent, and then the shed door swung open. "Amy! Where in tarnation have you been? Your ma's been up more'n half the night, worried sick about you." For the taciturn man, this was remarkable volubility, and it showed how much he shared his wife's worry. He folded his arms and waited for an explanation.

"I went to the shingle maker's place. It's empty. I wanted time to myself," Amy said as she drew nearer, faltering toward the end when she saw the look on her father's face. "I . . . I. . . ."

"Don't you *never* do a thing like that again, Amy June. Your ma was ready to call Hammond and have them send one of the rangers over. And I won't have any tales about the shingle maker's cabin; we looked there and didn't find you. If it turns out you were off with a boy, you'll have to learn to fend for yourself. I won't have a daughter of mine catting." His face darkened, and there was a nervous vein on his forehead that jumped and quivered as he talked.

"I *did* too stay at the shingle maker's cabin. I went and walked. Look at me if you don't believe it." She had not seen her face or her clothes, but she was reasonably sure that there were scratches and bruises enough to make her statement believable. It shocked and upset her that her pa should be so insensitive as to think that she might meet a boy and put her family to such worry. "No boy's going to do this to me unless he does it against my will." She folded her arms.

"Why'd you do such a fool thing, Amy June?" His expression had softened a bit, but he was still forbidding. "It ain't like you, girl."

Amy stared at him, her mind in turmoil. She had always supposed that her parents were stern but understanding, ready to be sensible judges and dependable allies, but here was her father, questioning her as if she were a trollop and accusing her of all manner of things. "I had to, Pa," she said, pleading with him to sympathize. "I didn't think you'd all worry. You know how I was feeling."

"Mooning all over about that Howard boy. Your ma told me. I want you to know that I won't tolerate it. I'm not going to see any daughter of mine taking up with a ne'er-do-well like him. Just you keep that in mind when you start wasting time on him." His anger had subsided somewhat, but there was still a feeling about him as if he were waiting for a wild animal to break from cover.

"Don't you talk that way about him, Pa. Not to me." She waited for the rebuke and the blow and took them with resignation when they came.

"Who'd you see when you were walking?" her pa demanded.

"Nobody."

"Then who put the bandage on your foot?" His voice was rising again, and he was getting red in the face.

"I did." Amy was becoming angry now as well. If her pa was not willing to give her any comfort, she would not make concessions to him. Had he shown compassion, she might have told him more about what she had done during the night, but now she had no more intention of doing that than of making friends with Georgina. "I found a couple rolls of cloth in the Cottermans' hay barn. I was going to put a couple extra rolls in for them, later." How easy it was to lie, she thought, once you get the hang of it.

"Then you apologize to them. I want to you tell them that you snuck into their barn and took their bandages. I want you to ask them to forgive you. And I want you to have a talk with the pastor as soon as he can spare the time." He turned away. "I got to get to the milking. The cows need proper care, girl."

"I know that, Pa," she said quietly, and because he did not see her face, he thought she was being properly submissive.

"You go on in and talk to your ma. She needs to be thanked for staying up most of the night on account of you. And you're to stay in today. You'll have to do chores for your ma so that she can sleep some." He closed the door of the milking shed as clear indication that the conversation was over.

Amy made her way back to the house, thinking. There were a lot of things she had to do at once. She had to talk to Jemmy Howard so that he could see how much he loved her and what she thought of him. She did feel a little sorry for her ma, but after what Pa had said to her, she wanted nothing more to do with him. He had failed her, and she would not forgive that.

Caralou was up, making biscuits. She gave a startled cry when Amy walked in the door and almost dropped the bowl in her lap.

"Shush," Amy said, beginning now to feel tired. Until her meeting with Pa, she had not felt as if she had been up all night. Now she was as exhausted as if she had been awake for a hundred years. "I don't want to wake the others."

"You're back," Caralou said. "Where've you been?"

"Out." She no longer wanted to explain. "I slept at the shingle maker's cabin, but that wasn't till real late. I'm worn out."

"You're all scratched up," Caralou said, as if afraid to mention it. "Did anything . . . you know, happen to you?"

"Not that kind of happen," she said, sitting down on the couch and tucking up her legs. She was not aware of falling asleep, but the next thing she knew her father was shaking her and demanding that she get up and take over her ma's chores for the day.

It was not until midafternoon that Amy was able to get away from the house. She said that she wanted to go into Candy to get the bandages to put back in the Cottermans' hay barn, and her father reluctantly gave his permission.

"Just make sure that you spend your own money, Amy June. I don't want your ma giving you her pennies for this." He folded his arms and looked down at her.

"It's my own money," she said wearily.

"And don't be too long about it. I want you back here before sundown. Hear?" His own stern parents had taught him by example that it was necessary to make harsh rules for children. One of his sisters had ended up in the city, at a fancy house, which proved that her parents had been lax. He could see that Amy was by far the prettiest of his daughters, and therefore he knew that she would have to be watched closely for any signs of waywardness.

"I'll be back, Pa," she said quietly.

"See that you are." He walked a little way down the road with her, but neither of them spoke.

In Candy she went through the motions of buying two rolls of heavy cotton gauze, and then she started toward Mr. Houseford's place, knowing that she would have to pass the Taylors' house. She thought she might find Jemmy there. Her plans were hazy beyond that. She knew that she could not simply run up to him and tell him everything, but there had to be a way.

As she came around the bend in the road, she looked down toward the creek and saw Jemmy fishing. It was so easy. "Hi, there," she called out.

Jemmy turned. "Why, hi yourself, Amy. What are you doing out here?"

"I'm going over to Mr. Houseford's to borrow a book." She had done it often enough in the past.

"You're surely the readingest girl I ever knew," he said ruefully. "Don't you ever do anything else?"

Amy decided that she would never have such an opportunity again. "I done something else last night. I went up the mountain to see the Herb Woman."

There was a look in his eyes that was gone faster than the flick of a bird's wing. "You did what?"

"I went up to the Herb Woman's. She said you'd been there. She said you wanted something from her and promised her something in return." Amy had folded her arms. "I wanted her to give me a potion to bring the boy I love to me but she couldn't do that." She wished he would figure it all out.

"Why'd you do a thing like that?" He pulled the line out of the water.

"Because I wanted you, and after you met Georgina Taylor, you never came to see me or talked to me at all. So I went up the mountain in the dark and saw the Herb Woman. She said you'd promised her I'd come if you got the thing you wanted. I figured that was just a test." She waited for him to tell her she was right, that he loved her after all, that he thought she was the bravest girl in the whole country.

Jemmy Howard threw his head back and laughed. "Christ almighty, girl, you do give yourself airs, don't you? Hey, Georgina, d'you hear that? Amy thinks I went to see the Herb Woman." He laughed again, and his laughter was joined by another voice. "Why'd I want to do that, Amy, when I had everything I wanted? Besides, the Herb Woman ain't so much, just a crazy old lady living all by herself up beyond Lizard Creek. You're a fool to go up there at night."

Georgina Taylor came along the bank and put her arm possessively around Jemmy's shoulder. "Amy, how do you figure any herb or spell could take him away from me? There ain't no magic can fight what I got, right, Jemmy?"

Jemmy grinned down at her and patted her fanny. "Righter than gospel, Georgina."

Amy watched them in petrified fury. Her face had been scarlet; now it was white. She glared down at them. "How *could* I love you? How? You're worse than she said you are. You're vain and cruel, both of you." Their renewed laughter humiliated her the more, and she started to run down the road, wanting only to get away from the terrible scorn of their mirth.

"Hey, Amy," Georgina called after her, "you tell that Herb Woman that we don't need her at all."

"Yeah," Jemmy agreed. "You tell her thanks for nothing."

Amy pressed her hands over her ears as she ran, blocking out the rest of their taunts. Only when her ankle began to hurt so badly that she stumbled did she slow down. She had paid little attention to where she was, but now she looked about and saw that Ellis Houseford's place was about a quarter mile away. She began to plod toward it, knowing that she could rest there, get a drink of water and an aspirin tablet. Maybe, she thought, longing to escape her suffering, she really would borrow a book.

Houseford opened his door on her third knock and smiled. "Amy, this is an unexpected pleasure. Come in. Do come in."

She went into the shabby house gratefully, trying to smile at the kindly, harassed teacher. She made her way, out of habit, to the back room that had been a sun porch and later had been converted into an office and library. "I hadn't been here much, so . . . here I am."

Houseford was not an unobservant man, and he knew there was something very wrong with Amy. That grieved him, for she was one of his few students who had shown a capacity for scholarship and a little of the glimmer of real intellect. Amy Macklin was intelligent, and he dreaded what would become of her if she remained here in Candy. He had spoken once with her father, but that had proven a fool's errand. With an effort he kept a calm expression. "It's good to see you. I'm glad you stopped by. I had a new load of books just last week, and I was thinking you might want to have a look through them."

"Sure," Amy said with little enthusiasm. As he brought the large cardboard box out from under the desk, she asked politely, "Is Mrs. Houseford well?"

"No, unfortunately not. She's over at the hospital in Hammond. I won't keep you long," he added, knowing how little it took to harm a girl's reputation in a town as small as Candy.

"Oh. I hope she's better soon." She peered into the box Houseford had offered her, glancing over the titles. Most of them were about Greeks and Romans, but there was one that caught her eye: *Folklore and Shamanism: Celtic Magic in British Song and Story.* Amy stared at the book. Her tongue was suddenly dry. "Mr. Houseford, would you mind if I"— her newly discovered craftiness asserted itself—"if I borrow a couple of these? I need something to get my mind off things."

Houseford was aware of Amy's crush on Jemmy Howard. Who in Candy was not? He also knew that Howard had taken up with Georgina Taylor. Secretly, Houseford was glad because he knew that this was his last chance to instill academic ambitions in Amy. "Why, certainly. Take whichever ones you want. I won't be getting around to them for at least two weeks. Perhaps when you've read them, we can discuss them."

When Amy left, she had four books with her: three on Greek myths and the book on shamanism. She read as she walked until she got near the place in the road where she had seen Jemmy and Georgina. She faltered, dreading another exchange with them.

There was a splash and a whoop, followed by a giggle. Amy listened, thinking that if she ran by while they were swimming, they would not see her. And then another, darker thought occurred to her, and she hid herself in the brush by the road as she crept nearer. Sure enough, there were two piles of clothes on the bank. Amy put the books down and crept nearer. She parted the branches carefully and stared toward the swimming hole.

Jemmy and Georgina were farther down, near the old railroad trestle where the water was deepest and the most still. As Amy watched, she saw Jemmy reach out and fondle Georgina, saying something in a voice suddenly low and husky. Georgina's answering murmur was ripe as August melons.

Knowing that Jemmy and Georgina were not paying attention to anything but themselves, Amy slid closer to the piles of clothes, reaching out with care for the shirt Jemmy had worn and scooping some dirt into the cloth. She drew the garment back into the bushes and wadded it tightly. Then she made her way back up the bank, picked up the stack of books, and headed for home.

A week later, Amy returned the books to Mr. Houseford, and he noted with amusement that the book on shamanism had been very well thumbed, as had the book on Diana and Astarte. He wondered whether he ought to offer her the text on comparative anthropology in the near future.

He might have been more concerned about her interest if he had been able to follow her home, for Amy would periodically stop and pick the blossoms and leaves of various plants, singing quietly to herself as she went. There were three of the necessary plants, and she made sure that she got plenty of them, just in case.

That night she was more quiet than usual, and her pa began to think that the worst was over for a while. The pastor had told him that teenage girls were tricksy creatures, but a firm hand and prayer would keep them in the path of righteousness. At least, her pa had told her ma the night before, she wasn't chasing after that no-good Jemmy Howard any more.

Late that night, Amy pulled the shirt, the dirt, and the sprigs of sage, rosemary, and thyme from under the mattress where she had hidden them. Carefully she rolled them up and stuffed them into a grain sack, along with her own meager collection of eleven paperback books. Certain that her two sisters were asleep, she let herself out of their bedroom, stopping in the kitchen for a slice of ham and a half dozen hardboiled eggs before going out the front door forever.

The woods were friendly, and she climbed up the mountain with greater strength. With each step, she recited a little of what she had learned. There were ways to be revenged. With the shirt and the dirt, there were many things she could do. It was only a question of making the best choice. She might make the skin tear off his body in strips. She might blind him, like that Greek king, and leave him to make his way alone, for Georgina would want nothing to do with a blind man. She might give him a constant thirst so that he would bloat up like a balloon and still not be satisfied. She might wither him up like a leaf on a dry vine. She might cause him to be consumed with carbuncles and sores so that there was not an inch of his body that did not fester. She might wreck him as a man by causing his thing to grow so that it dangled lower than his knees, giving no one any pleasure. There were an endless number of things she might do, assuming she found winter savoury.

Considering what had happened to Enoch Parker, she was confident that the Herb Woman would have some. Her joyous bloody anticipation gave her renewed speed. She was happy now that she had thought to bring along one of her pa's shirts as well.

In the hollow, the little cabin waited, ruddy with welcome.

Alan Dean Foster, in real life and in most of his fiction, is an unassuming and gentle man. His fictional visions are expansive and often Romantic, but every so often he turns that vision inward and illuminates with dark light those interiors of the soul and the mind that are sometimes better left unexplored. Take a stock fictional situation, then, and a classic case of revenge, and never let it be said that horror is only a matter of will.

THE INHERITANCE

by Alan Dean Foster

". . . my home, Trenton, its contents, and the sum of $550,000, after other and all taxes have been paid."

Every eye in the pecan-paneled room turned to Mayell. She remained composed in her green sleeveless dress and pumps, and she managed not to grin.

"There are two 'conditions,'" the lawyer continued, his tone indicating disapproval of the manner in which the deceased's secretary's skirt had crawled an indecent distance up her thighs. "You must remain in residence at Trenton House for six months to enable the staff there to make gradual transition to other employment."

"And the other condition?" Mayell asked with the chiming notes of a gamelan, displaying a voice sweet enough to match her appearance.

The lawyer harrumphed. "There remains the matter of Saugen, the deceased's cat. You will henceforth be responsible for the animal's care. Full transferral of the aforementioned sum occurs six months from today, provided that Trenton remains home to its present staff for that length of time, and provided that Saugen appears happy, healthy, well-fed, and content at that date."

"That's all?"

"That is all." The lawyer evened the mass of paper by tapping the double handful on the desk. "This reading, ladies and gentlemen, is concluded."

Mutters rose like flies on a hot day from the small group from disappointed distant relatives and modestly rewarded servants, from hopeful acquaintances and somber-faced business associates. Some had received more than they'd hoped for, others considerably less. None had fared nearly so well as the late Hiram Hanford's "secretary," the delectable Mayell.

Of the servants, none seemed as satisfied as the gardener Willis. None had reason to. For while Hanford had left him only a slight sum, Willis was heir to much more than was indicated in the will. He had inherited Mayell.

As she rose and turned to leave the lawyer's chambers, their eyes met in silent mutual congratulation. They had each other. In six months they would have the money and Trenton House. Soon they could live as they'd wanted to these past miserable five years.

"Nice kitty, kitty. Sweet Saugen-mine." Mayell knelt in the foyer of Trenton and cooed to the yellow tomcat. It slid supplely around her ankles, meowing affectionately.

Willis's gaze was appreciative, but it was not wasted on the cat. Instead, he was luxuriating in the landscape provided by Mayell's provocative posture: kneeling, inclined slightly forward. It highlighted her burnished blond hair, the regular curve of delicate shoulders and hips, the cleavage better described in terms geologic than physiological, resembling as it did other remarkable natural clefts such as the East African Rift.

She stood, cradling the sleek feline in her arms. It purred like a tiny stove set on simmer. "See, he likes me. Saugen sweet always did like me."

Willis noticed the cat staring at him. It possessed the penetrating, hypnotic gaze of all cats, magnified in this particular instance by overlarge yellow eyes. The black slits in their centers glinted like cuts. He shook himself. All cats stared like that.

"Good thing he does, too. That parasite of a lawyer will be around in May some time to check on the house and his furry nibs there. Keepin' the house and roses lookin' good is going to be my job. Keepin' the cat the same'll be up to you."

Mayell hugged the tom close to the warm shelf of her bosom. "That won't be any trouble, Willis. He doesn't seem to miss Hiram much." She gently let the cat drop to the floor. It made a moving, fuzzy bracelet of itself around her left ankle.

"That's something we have in common." Her perfect face twisted into an unflattering grimace. For an instant Willis had a glimpse of something less attractive hiding behind the beauty-queen mask. "Five years of my life, gone." She nestled into the gardener's arms. "Five years!" She clung tight to his rangy, sunburned form. "Only you made it bearable, darling."

"We're gettin' fair pay back. One hundred and ten thousand for each year of hell." He glanced around the massive old house, at the garish neo-Victorian decor and wealth of antiques. "Plus what this mausoleum will fetch. And no one suspects."

"No." She showed cream-white teeth in an oddly predatory smile. "I didn't think anyone would, not as slowly as I altered his medicine. Ten months, a fraction at a time. Otherwise, the old relic might've gone on for another twenty years." She shuddered from a distant cold memory. "I couldn't have stood it, Willis." Her voice and expression were hard. "I earned that half million."

"Six months and we'll leave this place forever. We'll go somewhere sunny and warm, as far from Vermont as we can get."

"Rio," she murmured languorously, savoring the single soft syllable, "or Cannes, or the Aegean."

"Anywhere you want, Mayell."

They embraced tightly enough to keep a burglar's pick from slipping between them, while Saugen slid sensuously around the perfect ankle of his new mistress.

"Willis?"

"Yes, Mayell?"

They were sipping coffee on the heated, enclosed veranda of Trenton, watching bees busy themselves among the spring flowers of the garden. It was Saturday, and the remaining servants were off. They could indulge in each other without gossipy eyes prying.

"Do you think I look any different?"

"Different? Different from what, darling?"

She looked uncomfortable. "I don't know . . . different from usual, I guess."

"More beautiful than ever." Seeing that she was serious, he studied her critically for a moment. "You might've lost a little weight."

She half smiled. "Seven pounds to be exact."

"And it troubles you?" He shook his head in disbelief. "Most women would find that a bit weird, Mayell."

She ran slim fingers through the tawny yellow-brown coat of Saugen, a puffball of fur asleep in her lap. "I haven't changed my eating habits."

He smirked, leaned back in the lounge. "Could be you've been taking more exercise lately."

She laughed with him, seeming relieved. "Of course. I hadn't thought of that."

He looked at her in mock outrage. "Hadn't *thought* of it?" They both laughed. "I guess we'll have to work at making it stick in your memory."

A concerned Willis led the scarecrow called Oakley up the curved stairway.

"If she's as ill as you think, man, why didn't you call me sooner?" Grit and Yankee stone, the elderly doctor mounted the steps without panting.

"She didn't call me. I told you, Doc, I've been in New York all week, making arrangements for the sale of the house and land. I didn't know she was this bad until I got back yesterday, and I called you right away."

"Kind of unusual for a gardener to negotiate sale of an estate, isn't it?" Oakley had a naturally dry tone. "Down this hall?"

Sharp old birds, these country professionals, Willis thought. "Yeah. She trusts me, and she's suspicious of lawyers."

That struck a sympathetic nerve. "Got good reason to be. Sound thinking."

"This is her room." He knocked. A faint voice responded. "Willis?"

They entered. The expression that formed on Oakley's features when he caught sight of the figure in the old plateau of a bed was instructive. It took something to shake an experienced general practitioner like Oakley, and from his looks he was badly shaken.

"Good God," he muttered, moving rapidly to the bedside and opening his archaic black bag. "How long has she been like this?"

"It's been going on for several weeks now, at least." Willis looked away from the doctor's accusing stare. How could they explain that they wanted no strangers prowling the house, generating unwelcome publicity and maybe dangerous second-guessing questions? "It's gotten a lot worse since I've been away."

He took the chair on the other side of the bed. The hand that moved to grip his was wrinkled and shaky. Mayell's formerly satin-taut skin was dull and parchmentlike; her eyes bulged in sunken sockets. Even her lips were pale and crepe-crinkled, though neither dry nor chapped. She looked ghastly.

Oakley was doing things with the tools of the physician. He was working quickly, like a man without enough time, and his expression was grim, a dangerous difference from its normal dourness.

A fluffy fat shape landed in Willis's lap. "Hello, cat," he said, absently stroking Saugen's ruddy coat. "What's wrong with your mistress, eh?"

The tom gazed up at him, bottomless cat eyes piercing him deeply. With a querulous meow, he hopped onto the bed.

"Is he in your way, Doc?" Willis made ready to move the animal. Mayell put a hand down to stroke the tom's rump. It meowed delightedly, semaphoring with its striped maroon tail.

"No." Oakley hadn't paid any attention to the cat. He was intent on taking the sphygmomanometer reading.

"Good Saugen, sweet Saugen," Mayell whispered. Willis was shocked and frightened to see how broomstick thin her arm had become. She looked over at him, and he forced himself to meet her hideously protruding eyes. "He's been such a comfort to me while you were away, Willis. He kept me warm every night."

"You should've called the doctor yourself, Mayell. You look terrible, much worse than when I left."

"I do?" She sounded puzzled and oddly unconcerned, as though unable to grasp the seriousness of her condition. "Then I must get better, mustn't I?"

Oakley rose, looked meaningfully at Willis. They moved to a far corner. "I want that woman in the hospital at Montpelier. Immediately, tonight. It's criminal that she's still in this house."

"I told you, I was in New York. I didn't *know*. The last of the regular servants left three weeks ago, and we were going to do the same at the end of the month. She wasn't nearly this bad when I left." Despite the reasonable excuse, Willis still felt guilty. "What's wrong with her?"

Oakley studied the floor and chewed his upper lip before looking back at the bed and its sleeping skeleton.

"I don't know that I can give a name to any specific disease, or diseases, since I think she's suffering from at least three different ones. She's terribly sick. Can't tell for certain what's wrong until I get her into the hospital and run some tests. Acute anemia, muscular degeneration of the most severe kind, calcium deficiency probably caused by reabsorption . . . that's what's wrong with her. What's causing it I can't say. She can't have been eating much lately."

"But she has been," Willis protested. "I know. I checked the refrigerator and pantry this morning when I made my own breakfast."

"That so? Then I just don't know where those calories are going. She's burning them up at an incredible rate. Daywalking, maybe. People don't consume themselves by lying in bed." He checked his watch.

"I'll want to travel with you to the hospital. It's after five. You have her ready by eight. I'll want to prep the ambulance team. We're going to put her on massive intravenous immediately, squirt all the glucose and dextrose into her that her system will take. You try to get her to eat something solid tonight. A steak would be good if she can keep it down. And a malted with it."

"I'll take care of it, Doc. Eight o'clock . . . we'll be ready."

It was hard to keep himself busy while he waited for the ambulance to arrive. He checked the window locks and the alarms. If they were going to be away for a while, best to make certain no one broke in and carried off the furniture. He was still worried about Mayell but took some comfort from the fact that Oakley had told him on departing that she would probably recover with proper medication and attention. She *had* to recover. If she died, his own hopes for an easy life would die with her.

Not unnaturally, his overwrought mind turned to thoughts of some sinister plot against them. Could someone, some disgruntled relative left out of the will, be poisoning Mayell in a fashion similar to the way they'd polished off Hanford? That was crazy, though. The house had hosted no visitors who might qualify as potential murderers while he'd been there, and Mayell had begun to deteriorate well before he'd departed for New York.

Besides, if he recalled the will correctly, in the event of any recipient's death, her portion of the inheritance was to go not to others but to several of Hanford's favorite charities. He remembered the faces present at the reading of the will and could not consider one capable of killing solely out of spite.

Saugen tried to keep him company, meowing and hovering about his legs as he kept an eye on the steak. He glanced irritably down at those fathomless feline eyes. Gently but firmly, he kicked the sable shape away. It meowed once, indignantly, and left him to his thoughts.

Some plot of Hanford's, maybe? Had he suspected what was being done to him, there at the last, and hired a killer to exact a terrible revenge?

There was the dinner to fix. Potatoes were beyond him, but he did all right with the meat, and heating the frozen peas was easy enough. Recalling that honey was supposed to give you strength, he dosed her tea liberally.

As he mounted the stairs toward her room, the clock chimed seven times in the hallway below. An hour would give her enough time to eat.

"Mayell? Darlin'?" She didn't respond to his knock, and so he balanced the tray carefully in one hand and turned the knob with the other.

It was dim in the room, lit only by early moonlight and the single small bulb of the end-table nightlight. She was still asleep. He moved toward the other side of the bed. There was a pole lamp there. As he fumbled for the switch, he noticed a familiar shape on her ribs. It meowed, an odd sort of meow, almost a territorial growl.

Saugen moved, lifting to a sitting position on his mistress's chest. Willis thought that he saw something glisten; he looked closer, one hand on the light switch.

The carpet muffled the clang of the tray when it hit, but it was still loud. Peas rolled short distances to hid in the low shag, and the juice from the still-steaming steak stained the delicate rose pattern as Willis stumbled backward. He fell into the lamp, and it broke into a thousand glass splinters when it struck the floor. Funny, half-verbalized noises came from his throat as he tried to give voice to what he had seen, but he could do no more than gargle his fear.

Eyes bright and burning tracked him as he staggered toward the door. A penetrating meow started his vertebrae clattering like an old woman's teeth. He could still see the fur on Saugen's stomach wriggling of its own accord as dozens of the thin, wormlike tendrils reluctantly withdrew from the drained husk of what once had been Mayell. They reminded him of tiny snakes, all curling and writhing as though possessed of some horrible life of their own. The hypodermic-sized holes they left in the wasted skin closed up behind them. Willis thought of the spiders he'd seen so often in the gardens, liquefying the insides of their victims and sucking them empty like so many inflexible bottles. The glistening he'd seen was caused by moonlight reflecting off the myriad drops of red liquid still clinging to the tip of each hair. He retched as he finally found the door and rushed out, thinking of how many nights the cat-thing had spent seemingly asleep on the girl's chest, when all the while it had been silently feeding.

"Keep him contented and well fed," the will had stated. Ah, damn the old man, he'd *known*.

Nothing in the house looked familiar as he half fell, half stumbled down the stairs. His thoughts were jumbled and confused. The full bowls of cat food left untouched in the kitchen these past weeks, the privacy whenever Hanford had fed his pet, the regular visits of poor women from the city who came expecting to fill one normal desire and who left, their eyes darting and fearful, never to return.

Somewhere in the gardener's shed there was a pistol he kept to ward off thieves and trespassers. He sought the front door. Oakley would be there soon with the ambulance and its crew. They wouldn't believe, but that didn't matter, wouldn't matter, because he would get the gun first and . . .

He stopped in midbreath, frozen as he stared forward, paralyzed by a pair of deliberate, mesmerizing yellow orbs confronting him. He tried to move, fought to look elsewhere. He couldn't budge, could only scream silently as those fiery flavescent eyes held his swaying body transfixed.

Its encrimsoned belly fur flexing expectantly, the tawny cat left its place by the door and padded deliberately, plumply, forward.

Award-winning author Lisa Tuttle is well known for her gentler stories in the field of science fiction. However, when I first read the following piece, I was literally unable to forget it. It illustrates a dark side of Tuttle that few of her many fans know and one that is, in the best sense of the word, horrid.

DOLLBURGER

by Lisa Tuttle

When she listened hard, Karen thought she could hear the men downstairs searching for dolls. Although she didn't know what they looked like, she thought of them as hairy troll-like men with the large square teeth of horses. She glanced at the attic door. All her dolls were safe in there. Surely the men would never come upstairs into her room.

The thought made her clutch the blankets to her chin, her body rigid with the effort of not breathing. The bed was safe, it had always been a sanctuary, but she didn't know the powers or limits of these doll thieves and could only guess at protection. She'd learned about them just that morning, from her father.

"Daddy, have you seen Kristina?"

"Let daddy read his paper, sweetie—he doesn't know which doll Kristina is," her mother said, flipping pancakes.

Daddy dipped a piece of toast in his coffee and looked at it thoughtfully before biting. He replied with his mouth full.

"Did you leave her downstairs?"

"Yeah—I think."

Daddy shook his head. "Shouldn't have done that. Dangerous. Don't you know what happens to dolls that get left downstairs all night?"

Karen glanced quickly at her mother. Catching the half smile on her mother's face, Karen raised her eyebrows skeptically.

"No," she said, in a tone that dared him.

Daddy shook his head again and consumed the last of the piece of toast.

"Well, if you leave your doll downstairs, you can just expect that when those men come looking—"

"What men?"

He looked surprised that she should need to ask. "Why, the men who eat dollburgers, of course!"

"Dollburgers?"

"Just like hamburgers. Only, of course, made out of dolls."

"No."

"No?"

"People don't eat dolls, and dollburgers are just tiny hamburgers, like what mommy made on my last birthday, which you feed to dolls."

"But dolls don't eat—people do."

"You *pretend*," Karen said, exasperated with him. He was shaking his head.

"I don't care what you call little hamburgers—but I happen to know about dollburgers. People eat them, and they're made out of dolls. There are people who just love them. Of course, they're illegal; so they have to sneak around, looking for houses where little girls have forgotten to put their dolls safely away. When they find abandoned dolls, they pop them into a sack until they collect enough to grind up into dollburgers."

"That's a story," Karen said.

Her father shrugged. "I'm just trying to warn you so when you lose a doll you'll know what's happened to it and maybe you'll be more careful in the future."

Her mother came to the table. "No dollburgers in *this* house. Pancakes, though. Karen, get your plate if you want some."

Karen suddenly remembered where she'd left Kristina. Of course—last night before she went to bed, she and Kristina had been lost in the wilderness and had crawled into a cave to rest for the night—Kristina must still be in the cave.

"In a minute," she said, and went purposefully into the living room.

The bridge table was the cave, but there was no doll underneath. Karen dropped to her hands and knees. Kristina was gone. Something gleamed in the corner by a table leg, and she picked it up.

A blue eye gazed impassively up from her hand. There were some shards of pink plastic on the carpet. Kristina?

"Karen, do you want pancakes or don't you?"

"In a minute," she called, and carefully picked up each tiny piece and put it in her pocket. She looked at the eye again. Kristina's eyes were blue. She put the eye in her pocket.

"Daddy," she asked over pancakes, "do the people—the people who eat dollburgers—do they ever just, you know, eat dolls? I mean, right where they find them?"

Her father considered. "I suppose sometimes they get so hungry that they might just crunch up a doll right there, with their teeth," he said. "You never know what they'll do."

"I'm sure Kristina is perfectly safe," said her mother. "I'll help you find her after I do the dishes."

After breakfast Karen went up to her room and examined the eye and the pieces of pink plastic, the last remains of Kristina. What daddy had said about the dollburger eaters was real, then, and not just a story like the grizzly bear in the cedar closet.

Karen had the attic room. Her closet was actually the attic itself—without wallpaper, beams bare overhead, and decorated with bits of discarded furniture and boxes of old clothes. She kept her toys there, and it was home to all her dolls. She took Kristina's eye there, climbed onto a rickety chair, and put it in a secret place atop a ceiling beam. It would do better than a funeral, she thought, since there was so little of poor Kristina left.

The dolls watched her steadily from their places. Karen looked around at all of them from her position atop the chair, feeling queen of all she surveyed, giant queen-mother to all these plastic, rag and rubber babies.

Hard-faced Barbie sat stonily beside doltish Ken in front of their dreamhouse. Her clothes spilled out of the upstairs bedroom; two nude teenagers (Barbie's friends) sprawled in the kitchen.

The bride doll sat next to Princess Katherine, where she'd sat for months undisturbed. There was dust in her hair, and the shoulders of her white gown looked grimy. Princess Katherine's crown was bent, her green dress stained, and her lower right leg secured to the upper leg with Band-Aids and masking tape.

Raggedy Ann, Raggedy Andy, Aunt Jemima and Teddy-bear slouched together in the rocking chair. The talking dolls, Elizabeth, Jane, and Tina, sat grimly silent. The babydolls had been tossed into one crib where they lay like lumps. Susan, bald and legless, had been wrapped tenderly and put in the blue plastic bassinet.

Karen looked at the top of the old dresser, where Kristina used to sit with Beverly. Now Beverly sat there alone. Karen felt tears in her eyes: Kristina had been her favorite. She suddenly felt uncomfortable standing above her dolls, felt that they were blaming her for Kristina's disappearance.

She felt guilt, a heaviness in her stomach, and thought she saw grim indictment on the still, staring faces.

"Poor Kristina," she said. "If only someone had warned me." She stepped down from her perch, shaking her head sadly. "If only daddy had told me before—then I could have protected her. When I think of all the times I've left some of you out—well, now that I know I'll be sure to take good care."

She looked around at all the dolls, who had not changed expression, and suddenly the silence of the attic became oppressive.

Louisa, Karen's best friend, called that afternoon. "Would you and Kristina care to join me and Isabella in having a tea party?" she asked in her best society-lady voice.

Karen assumed a similar voice to reply. "Oh, my deah, I would love to, but Kristina has been kidnaped."

"Oh, how dreadful, my deah."

"Yes, it is, my deah, but I think I shall bring my other child, Elizabeth."

"Very good, I shall see you in a few minutes. Ta-ta."

"Ta-ta, my deah."

Elizabeth was one of the talking dolls, always her favorite until golden-haired Kristina had come as a birthday gift.

Louisa's little sister Anne and her ragdoll Sallylou were the other guests at the tea party, treated with faint disdain by Louisa and Karen for their lack of society manners.

"Why don't you let Elizabeth eat her own cookie?" Anne demanded as Karen took a dainty bite. Elizabeth had politely refused the cookie.

"Be quiet, silly," Louisa said, forgetting her role. "Dolls don't eat cookies."

"Yes, they do."

"No, they don't."

"Uh-huh."

"They do not."

"Well, if they don't, then what *do* they eat?"

"Nothing."

"Pretend food," Karen amended. "They have to eat pretend food because they only have pretend teeth and pretend stomachs."

"Anne shook her head. "Sallylou has *real* teeth, and so she has to eat real food."

"Oh, she does not," Louisa said. "All you do is mash cookie in her face so she gets crumbs all over. Show me her teeth if she has them."

"I can't, 'cause her mouth is closed," Anne said smugly. "You're just stupid."

Later, when they were alone, Karen told Louisa what had happened to Kristina and watched her friend's eyes grow wider. This was no story; it was real and immediate, and the proof was the blue eye now lying on a bed of dust and staring unceasingly at the attic roof.

Karen's ears ached from trying to hear movement downstairs. She always lay awake at the top of the house, feeling silence and sleep wrap the house from the bottom up until it finally reached her and she slept. But now every distant creak of board, every burp of pipe, made her tense and listen harder. She'd left no dolls downstairs, of course, but what if those men should not be deterred by stairs but were lured on by the scent of dolls up in the attic?

She thought of Louisa across the street and wondered if she too lay awake listening. Louisa, she knew, had put all her dolls under the bed, the safest place she could think of.

Karen suddenly thought of her own dolls, more frightened than she, sitting terrified in the dark attic, listening to the sounds as she did and wondering if the next creaking board would bring a dark sack over their heads, labeling them dollburger meat. It was her duty to protect them.

She went on bare feet to the attic door, the full moon through her window giving her light enough to find her way. She opened the attic door and thought as she did so that she heard a movement inside, as if perhaps a doll had been knocked over.

She had to go inside the attic several feet to reach the light cord. Her bare foot nudged something as she did, and when the light came on, she looked down to see what it was.

Poor, bald, legless Susan lay naked on the floor, and Karen noticed at once that Susan now was not only legless but armless as well. When she picked her up, small shards of pink plastic fell from the arm sockets.

Karen felt an almost paralyzing fear. They were up here, somehow in the attic without having come past her bed, and already they'd begun on her most helpless doll. Holding Susan to her, she began to gather all the other dolls into her arms. She lifted the skirt of her nightgown to make a bag and tumbled the dolls in there. They were scattered around as if they'd been thrown, none in their right places: Barbie on the floor, Ken in the rocking chair with Raggedy Andy and the bride. Every time she bent to pick up another doll, she was sure she could hear the muffled breathing of the hungry dollburger eaters and feel the pressure of their eyes against her back.

She began to pray, whispering and thinking, "Oh, please, please, please, oh, please."

Finally she had all the dolls together, and she stumbled to the door and closed it, leaving the light still burning in the attic. For safety she pushed her chair in front of the door.

Then she went to bed, arranging all the dolls around her, lying down, falling asleep sandwiched by their small hard bodies.

She may have dreamed, but she never woke as they began to move closer to her in the night, and she didn't see the crumbs of plastic that fell from Elizabeth's open, hungry mouth.

J. Michael Reaves has written what Edward L. Ferman, publisher of The Magazine of Fantasy and Science Fiction, *calls one of the most terrifying stories he's ever published. Introduction enough from the best editor this field has.*

SHADETREE

by J. Michael Reaves

Before the day that Shadetree killed his great-uncle, Colly Sue would come and sit with the two of them almost every evening and listen to the old man tell stories about ghosts, witches and haunts. She had done this ever since she was a child. Great-Uncle Arlie's house was an old unpainted shack with a breezeway—a wide, open corridor through the middle of it—and a rusty tin roof. Colly Sue would sit cross-legged in a straight-back chair during the stories because the gray wood floor had ragged, inch-wide cracks between the planks, and if she put her feet on those cracks, a haunt might reach cold hands from the darkness beneath and grab her. But Shadetree sat right on the floor. On occasion he would make Colly Sue cry by shoving his hand into one of the cracks and shouting that a haunt had him by the fingers.

Great-Uncle Arlie—which Colly Sue called him as well, though she was not related to him—was a thin and gaunt thing, hairless and shirtless, with suspenders stretched like cables over leather. His dry whispery voice telling stories of the haunts never failed to terrify the six-year-old child, but she came again and again, not only to hear the stories and to see Shadetree but also to get away from her mother's house and the constant wailing of her baby sisters. Even at that age, a child's wailing wound all her muscles tight inside her.

She requested the story of Daisy and Walker over and again. She could almost mime the old man's creaking words as he told of how haunts were born of the dead, crawling maggot-small from the nose and mouth of a corpse as it lay rotting in its grave, and digging their way down to the underground caverns and tunnels that honeycombed the earth. A haunt was hollow inside and could not stand the sun; it looked quite normal except for its eyes, which were like black well-holes in its face. They lived on the insides of corpses and, after scooping them hollow, laid their eggs in the shell. A haunt never stopped growing during its lifetime, but mobility was difficult after it grew past twelve feet. They hibernated in the ground then, until their flesh merged with the ground and they died.

One day—so his story went—while walking in a ravine, a girl named Daisy found a cave and entered it. It was actually the nostril of a gigantic haunt, huge enough to have an entire community of haunts living inside it. They took her to eat and bury, and so breed more haunts. Her beau, a boy named Walker, searched for her all day. He wandered into the graveyard at sundown and, stopping to rest, heard laughter from within a grave and dug into it with his bare hands. There he found a haunt feasting on a corpse and forced it to tell him where Daisy was. He then led rescuers into the underground world to battle the haunts and save Daisy, and they lived happily ever after. That was Colly Sue's favorite story.

Shadetree's favorite was about the "swapchilds." They were small haunts exchanged for human babies, full of cunning and guile. Their task was to gradually lure everyone in the community into caves and graveyards, where they were dragged, screaming, into the dark below. When Colly Sue and Shadetree were ten years old and Shadetree walked her back to her mother's house, he told her a secret. On her mother's porch he leaned close to her, his green sunglasses shining in moonlight like the wings of June bugs. "I'm one," he told her.

"One what?"

"One o'*them*. Them swapchilds. But don't you worry," he assured her as she drew away from him, "I won't hurt you, Colly Sue. I'll never hurt you."

He turned then and left her, walking quickly down the packed red dirt of the road, which the moonlight darkened to a river of blood.

The next day Shadetree told their classmates at school that he was a haunt and that his merest touch would be enough to lure them down into the richly shadowed caverns that they all believed honeycombed Shadman County. The children believed him and avoided his touch as they would have a leper's. Colly Sue knew that this alienation was exactly what Shadetree wanted. He was a frail and moody child, with a skin condition that made him quite ill if he stayed in the sun more than three hours. It affected his eyes, and quite early in life he began wearing dark glasses constantly. His nickname grew from this illness, for during recess he always stayed under the old elms and hickories on the school grounds. He was uncomfortable in crowds and preferred to be alone, yet there was something about the pale, quiet boy that attracted and fascinated others. Only Shadetree could have declared himself a social outcast and, by doing so, become more popular than ever. One child, recently moved from Tennessee, tried to achieve similar status by pretending to be a witch-boy who had ridden eagle-back across the crags of the Great Smokies. The other children quickly put him in his place. Only Shadetree they believed—they came to him in terrified fascination for tales of the Underworld, and his refusal to speak of it only whetted their appetites for more.

Colly Sue, however, remained his only confidante. Only with her would he play children's games, and only because she shared his morbid turn of mind. They played tag on rocky slopes, where the slightest misstep would result in death; they would meet in the graveyard at midnight to topple tombstones, while horrific dinosaurs and behemoths made of trees and creeping kudzu vine brooded over them. She felt herself to be a misfit no less than he. For as long as she could remember, she had thought of the sprawling, two-story farmhouse where she lived as her mother's home, not hers. She knew that it was expected she marry upon leaving school— under no circumstances should she wait past twenty—and spend the rest of her life bearing babies and keeping house. That was not for her, she told herself firmly. Even as a child herself, she was repulsed by babies—their constant wailing, their soiled diapers and unceasing demand for attention. She loved everything else about life in Shadman County, but if she stayed, she knew she could not escape this fate.

Although Colly Sue believed for several years that Shadetree was a swapchild, she had no fear of him. Not then. Not even when it became popular opinion that Shadetree was crazy—that only drove her closer to him.

Most people came to that opinion after Shadetree killed Great-Uncle Arlie, even though the death was an accident. When he and Colly Sue were fifteen, her mother bought a four-wheeled riding lawn mower for the hired man to cut the yard. It was difficult to cut the tough Bahia grass around the old man's shack with a push mower, and so Shadetree began borrowing the machine. Great-Uncle Arlie hated the roar and smoke of the engine and would often follow Shadetree as he rode the mower around the property, shouting and waving his wooden cane. One day, as Colly Sue sat on the butane tank and watched, Shadetree rode the mower too near the pebbled arc of the dirt driveway. The spinning rotary blade scooped up a stone the size of a cotton boll and shot it with great force and precision right through the old man's left temple. The *crack!* of the splintering bone was audible even over the roar of the engine. Colly Sue happened to be watching him at the time; she saw the dark red puncture appear as if by magic, saw Great-Uncle Arlie stand as if puzzled for a moment before folding, joint by joint, into a weathered and angular pile of clothes. Shadetree had not seen it; he continued riding the canopied mower around the house. Colly Sue did not scream. That was what the other women who lived in Shadman County, the brainless ones, would have done. Instead, she approached the crumpled old man and forced herself to touch the corpse, lift the head, check for a pulse. Great-Uncle Arlie was dead. There would be no more stories of haunts.

When Shadetree came around the house again and saw what had happened, he stopped the mower and joined Colly Sue. In the sudden buzzing silence they carried the dead man to the breezeway. John, Arlie's old bluetick hound, crept out from under the porch and began to howl. Shadetree threw a stick at him, then looked at Colly Sue.

"You got to tell your cousin E.A. something important," he said. His voice was quiet and soft, showing no signs of grief at all as he squatted holding the man's head.

"Tell him what?" Colly Sue decided that she would be damned if she would show any more emotion than Shadetree did. To prove she was strong, she pinched the dead eyes shut, but the head lolled at such an angle that they fell open again.

"You got to have him promise that he won't embalm Uncle Arlie." Shadetree released the corpse and put his hands on Colly Sue's shoulders—his right thumb left a spot of blood on the crisp white cotton.

Her cousin was the local mortician. "Whatever for? E.A. could go to jail for that!"

"It's not against the law," Shadetree told her. "Say it was Uncle Arlie's last request."

"That waren't never no request of his," Colly Sue said slowly.

"It's a request of mine," Shadetree said. "That old man ain't gonna be embalmed." He hesitated, then explained, "The haunts need him, is why."

Later, people labeled his increasingly solitary ways as madness and dated it from his great-uncle's death. He did not seem changed to Colly Sue, however, save for his insistence in clinging to his fantasy. She did as he requested, and the old man was laid to rest intact. It would make no difference to Great-Uncle Arlie, and it meant much to Shadetree. Other people's mutterings about him made her worry, though. She knew that Shadetree was gentle, if morbid, that he would never harm anyone and only worried that others might harm him.

In due time, they graduated from high school. It had been assumed by everyone that Shadetree would marry Colly Sue, an arrangement that Colly Sue's mother was not happy with. Neither was Bubba Colbin, a redheaded burly farmer's son who wanted Colly Sue. Colly Sue's mother approved of Bubba. She was a small, sour woman, slowly dying of a lung disease, and her one desire was to live long enough to see her grandchildren. Colly Sue's younger sisters were already married; if she wanted to inherit the farm and land, she was expected to follow the pattern.

Her virginity had been troubling her. In Shadman County, most women remained virgins until married, or at least married the first man they bedded. To do otherwise was to gain a reputation. The unfairness of this was obvious to Colly Sue— still, she had to decide if she wanted to defy convention for its own sake and to satisfy her growing desires at the expense of needless trouble for herself. It is always hard to be a pioneer. Added to that difficulty was the fact that no man she knew, including Shadetree and most especially Bubba Colbin, appealed to her sexually.

Bubba, however, wanted Colly Sue, and what Bubba wanted he was accustomed to having.

He took her to a movie at Beatriceville one night, and on the way back he attempted to seduce her. Outspokenness and independence in women had always been equated by the men of Shadman County with looseness, and so he was surprised at the strength and desperation with which she fought him in the cab of his old Dodge pickup. Seduction quickly escalated into rape. She was stronger than he thought a girl could be, and at last, knowing he would not enjoy it this way, he told her he would tell her mother that she had been sleeping around unless she let him have his way. Her mother believed anything Bubba said, and Colly Sue knew her condition was such that this lie could kill her. Though she had always felt a stranger in her family, still she loved her mother. And so Bubba had her, but he did not enjoy it. Colly Sue spread her legs and fixed him with a terrible glare which she kept on him like a lantern while he groaned his way to climax. She did not move an inch during the act, not even when he broke her hymen, and he bruised his lips on her tight-set mouth. Nor did she move afterward while he drove her home, but lay there in that same awkward and accusatory pose until he threatened to hit her.

She still met Shadetree in the graveyard on occasion, as they had done when children, and this time she told him what Bubba had done. "There ain't no way," she cried, "that I'm marryin' him. God blast him dead at four o'clock in the morning, that—"

"Marry him," Shadetree said.

She stared at him, stunned. "Shadetree, you can't mean it!"

He pulled a length of Spanish moss free from a crumbling cross and stroked it. "Oh, I do," he replied. "I do. The pressure's on you to get married. Cain't inherit the farm till you do. Well, then, get married, and leave it to me. I guarantee you'll have your respectability and your freedom."

"Just what you plannin'?"

"Folk feel sympathy for a woman whose husband deserted her," he said.

She stared at him, half hidden in the shade of a curtained oak, and slowly smiled.

And so the wedding came to pass, on a lovely spring day at Burnt Bluff Church. People whispered approvingly that the bride appeared a proper lady for once in her life, scrubbed and set in lace, and smiling obediently as the pastor gave her to a sweating, tight-collared Bubba in holy wedlock. She wondered if anyone noticed the clawlike set to her fingernails as Bubba kissed her.

Afterward was the reception, which was held at Colly Sue's mother's house—though she was now named in the will, she still could not think of the place as hers. Her mother was too ill to come downstairs, which was just as well—Colly Sue did not know what Shadetree had planned, but she knew the way his mind worked.

Pictures were taken of Colly Sue and Bubba feeding each other cake and posing in front of the wreaths. There was an impressive stack of presents from Bubba's side of the family, mostly for him, tools, new coveralls, and the like. Shadetree had not come to the reception, and though Colly Sue knew it was a good idea, still she felt alone and alien in the midst of these familiar strangers. Bubba kept leering at her and pinching her while people watched. She hated him more each moment—the thought of frightening him out of Shadman County by whatever terrorist campaign Shadetree had devised had her trembling for its start.

At last the bottom of the pile was reached, and the last present—a small square box, wrapped in coal-black paper, with a ribbon of glossy black. A red card, like the hourglass on a black widow, said simply "Bubba Colbin." When Bubba lifted it in his calloused hands, the laughter and light banter trickled into silence, as all the guests and in-laws stared at the ominous present.

Colly Sue stared too, with mounting excitement. This, then, was the beginning. Bubba was too bull-stupid to feel anything other than annoyance that the party had been spoiled, and so, in dull anger, he ripped the package open. A rending of cardboard, the cold rustling of tissue; Bubba leaped back with a curse, letting the torn box hit the floor, letting its contents roll free of the wrappings: a skull, yellowed bone gleaming under the chandelier, bits of rich graveyard loam still packed in eye sockets and jaw joints. A clot of earth broke open on the carpet, disclosing a writhing worm which burrowed into the shag.

The screams began.

As the crowded room began to empty by all exits, women holding handkerchiefs to their mouths and collapsing in the arms of pale-faced men, Bubba tore his glare from the dead staring thing at his feet and fixed it upon Colly Sue. He was also pale, but there was such anger in his eyes, such a swelling of his shoulders that she held her face like a stone, knowing that the slightest confirmation of his suspicions in her expression would surely cause him to strike her dead.

That was the beginning of Shadetree's campaign to scare Bubba Colbin away from Colly Sue. But Bubba did not scare easily. He was a stubborn scion of dirt farmers, burrowing deeper and deeper. He did nothing about the first incident, though it was common opinion that Shadetree was responsible. There was, after all, no real proof. Subsequent happenings, all quite grisly but essentially harmless, had no more effect. It was apparent that Bubba could not be frightened away by such childish tricks. Colly Sue was disappointed in Shadetree—she had expected a campaign more complicated and subtle. It did have results, however. After a few days Bubba's patience wore thin, and he correctly guessed that the best way to put a stop to this harassment was to beat Colly Sue. This remedy was partially successful—it did stop the juvenile stunts.

The next day Shadetree sat on the porch with Colly Sue, waiting for Bubba to return from the barn.

Colly Sue had tried to talk him out of a confrontation, but Shadetree was adamant. "We gave him hints aplenty," he said. "He should've taken 'em."

"You got no idea what he's like, Shadetree! He's not playing games, he'll *kill* you!"

"You just watch," Shadetree said complacently as Bubba's pickup jounced into the driveway amid a cloud of red dust.

Bubba stepped onto the porch, shoulders set and head lowered. "You got no business on my property," was his greeting.

"You had no business marrying Colly Sue," Shadetree replied.

Colly Sue saw Bubba glance at her. She said nothing, merely stared back with one eye, the other being swollen shut as a result of her beating. She knew he was looking with pride upon his handiwork.

Bubba looked back at Shadetree and smiled lopsidedly. He leveled a finger like a weapon at the thin, pale man. "So you want me run off," he said. "You think you can scare me away from my woman and all that property she's set to inherit. Well, you gonna have to do way under better than you been doing to make me scat."

Shadetree smiled then, suddenly and somehow most frighteningly. "No," he said softly. "You're pure wrong. That ain't what I want at all."

Bubba hesitated just an instant before asking, "What, then?" His voice was just a trifle too loud, and Colly Sue realized with amazement that he was nervous. She, too, was uneasy; she had never seen Shadetree act like this before.

"You," Shadetree said to Bubba. "Dead."

Bubba looked the length of Shadetree's pipe-like frame, barked a note of laughter, and swung his fist. He outweighed Shadetree by almost a hundred pounds. His fist was the size and shape of a large eggplant. The blow never connected. Shadetree caught it in midcourse and held him by the wrist, impossibly, without a tremor of his thin arm. Colly Sue watched in shock as he seized Bubba's neck, which was bigger than Shadetree's thigh, and *lifted* him off his feet. He shook Bubba as a hound shakes a weasel, though in this case the proportions were reversed. Then he dropped him. Bubba landed heavily on the stone steps, rolled over, and stared up at Shadetree.

"Run," Shadetree suggested.

Bubba ran.

Shadetree leaped from the porch and followed. Colly Sue stood paralyzed, watching the events happening with dream slowness. Bubba, with mouth working around terror, leaped into his pickup, twisted the key and stamped the pedal almost before he was touching the seat. The tires spat gravel, and the truck leaped forward, door still open, Bubba hanging onto the wheel, fighting for control. Colly Sue watched Shadetree running with long, somehow *elastic* strides that rapidly closed the gap between him and the speeding pickup. Bubba stared over his shoulder—Colly Sue could see his eyes shining with fear like the eyes of slaughterhouse cattle. The truck hit a patch of soft dirt and fishtailed, the left rear fender slapping Shadetree away like a bothersome insect. He landed, rolled, and sat up, staring expressionlessly. Bubba was hugging the wheel as the truck spun completely out of control and collided with the butane tank.

The explosion knocked Colly Sue off her feet and brought blood from her ears and nose. A brief geyser of flame enveloped the truck, and then there was a second slamming thunder as the truck's gas tank blew up. Colly Sue lay dazed, watching the orange and black column climb up the curve of the sky and beyond the porch roof. When it finally began to subside, she found her feet and stumbled shakily over to where Shadetree stood beneath the shelter of a magnolia tree, staring at the pickup's blackened metal skeleton. She stood beside him, numbly. And after a time he sighed, shook his head, and said sadly, "Hardly a bone left to bury. Ain't that a goddamn shame."

And she knew quite clearly that his regret was that the haunts would have no cold flesh to gnaw, no swollen body in which to incubate their foul brood. She thought of old Arlie's tales of them crawling, wormlike, in the caverns below the land, perhaps beneath her very feet. Any other woman of this county might have screamed and fainted, and so Colly Sue would not let herself do that. What she felt was anger, overwhelming anger at Shadetree for daring to think of his fantasy at a time like this, after a human being, even one deserving of death, had met such a horrible end. In a sudden fury she turned to him and struck, clawed four fingernails down the side of his face. He stepped back, one hand going to his cheek as though to hide it, then stopping, for she had already seen the results of her attack.

He was not bleeding.

And then, with a rushing soundless roar in her head, the last of the numbness dropped from her, leaving her free to remember how Shadetree had lifted Bubba with superhuman strength, how he had chased the pickup with those hideously long strides, and every one of the times since they were ten years old that he had told her what he was.

She turned and ran from him then. And as she ran, through the sharp slashing corn away from Bubba's house, she heard him call again, softly: "I'll never hurt you, Colly Sue."

Colly Sue told no one that Shadetree had been responsible for Bubba's death. It was easy enough to put the blame on drunkenness. There was some talk, but, again, nothing could be proved. She was a widow now and not expected to seek another husband until after a proper time of mourning. Time enough to worry about that then. Her mother had assured her that the farm would be hers, since it was evidently God's will that she be alone for a time.

She avoided Shadetree for the first time in their lives. She did not know what to do about him. No one would believe he was one of old Arlie's scare-stories; as time insulated her from that day, she did not know whether or not to believe it herself. She had heard that insane people possessed fantastic strength. The more deeply committed to their delusions, the more they entered the role, even to the point of controlling autonomic bodily functions such as bleeding if it suited their purposes. Shadetree must be mad then, totally and completely insane. She had never seen him hurt anything before, but now there was always the possibility that he might turn on her one day. And yet, she could not bring herself to tell anyone he was dangerous.

Though she had escaped her marriage and was now assured a farm and income, there was no happiness in her life. Her break with Shadetree was not the only reason for this. The week after Bubba died, the doctor confirmed her suspicions; she was pregnant.

The news stunned her. Happiness had been so close, and on its eve her best friend and her body had both betrayed her. There was no alternative to having the child. An abortion was unthinkable. No local doctor would perform one, and the stigma attached to it would make her anathema in Shadman County. To put the child up for adoption would also cause talk. The community was too isolated, too dependent upon itself for her to safely flout its strict morals and mores and not make trouble for herself. She did not know what to do. Her confidant and advisor was lost to her now. To her relief, when they encountered each other on roads and in stores, he never tried to force recognition. He merely watched her with what some thought was sadness and what Colly Sue feared was something more sinister.

As the months passed, she watched her body swelling with this alien lifeform, this other; a usurper who would control and dictate her life for the next twenty years. She did not want it, and yet there was no way she could rid herself of it.

Her mother, ailing for longer than she could recall, began to sink slowly, finally, toward death. She remained in bed constantly, soiling the bedsheets, plastic tubes in her nose bubbling softly as her lungs rotted. Yet she clung to the shreds of her life, grimly determined to keep her pledge and hold her grandchild in her flaccid arms. She failed. Weeks before Colly Sue's time was due, the bubbling stopped, and her mother expired quietly in the night.

Colly Sue still did not believe the stories of the haunts—had never believed them, she told herself. Yet she spent quite a lot of the family money to have a special mausoleum built for her mother—she would not see the old woman lie in the ground. The farm was now hers, and yet she felt no sense of triumph. The child was imminent, the tiny intruder who would make life miserable for her. What could she do?

It was winter now, the ground hard and frozen and lightly dusted with frost. The first heavy snowfall was threatening. Colly Sue spent her days in dreadful expectation. The hired hands did the chores, and she stayed in her room on the second floor, where it was always cold. Coldness now seemed right to her.

The child was born.

It arrived exactly seven months from the day the doctor gave her the bad news. The doctor was there to perform the delivery, summoned at six-thirty on an icy-clear morning. The delivery was a painful one. The child was a boy, with Bubba's large shoulders, and Colly Sue had a narrow birth canal. At last there were the shattering sounds of a slap and the baby's cry—the first of many, Colly Sue thought. The doctor laid the wizened monkey-form on the bloody quilt beside her. She turned her head away from it and stared out the window at the brittle sky.

The next day, as evening was beginning, the door of her room opened and Shadetree entered.

Colly Sue looked at him without surprise, and without fear. She realized that she had somehow been expecting him.

He looked down at the infant nursing at her breast, at the resigned expression on her face. "Strong-looking boy," he said.

She sighed. All feeling, all terror, had been leeched from her. "What you want?" she asked this stranger she had known for a lifetime.

He pointed. Again, she was not surprised.

"It'll be so easy," he said. He seemed nervous, ill-at-ease, his eyes wide and intense. "Say you was sleeping, the window open. Someone clumb up the trellis. You never saw who it was. You'll never see the boy again, won't be troubled by it no more. Give him here, Colly Sue. Please. You owe me this much."

It would be so easy. She felt a great tiredness as she asked, "What for you want the child, Shadetree?"

"You know what for," he whispered. His gaunt and ridged form was trembling. "For the haunts, Colly Sue, the haunts . . . for to swap."

"What makes you think I'd want a holler-eyed night-thing when I can't even stand a human child?"

"It don't have to be you what takes the swapchild," he assured her. "We'll put 'im in somewhere else. But a balance's got to be kept, don't you see? We got to have a human child to swap for."

She was suddenly too tired by far to play this game with him again, ever. "Stop it, Shadetree. Almighty God, please stop it."

"You hate the child," he hissed, and terrible eagerness

shook his voice. "I'm offering you release! You'd gladly have had it aborted, wouldn't you?"

She nodded wearily. She could not put into words how she felt. She still loathed the child, yes, but conditioning was too strong to ignore. She knew a few months on either side of the womb made no real difference. This was not yet a thinking creature; it had only the most rudimentary self-awareness. It was no greater sin to kill it now than to have aborted it in the womb. But a child at her breast, however unwelcome, was not the same as a fetus, and she could not give it to Shadetree.

"Go away from me," she said.

He straightened, his knuckles whitening like unearthed roots on the brass bed railing. "Colly Sue, you got to," he said desperately. "Listen—I was raised too human—I couldn't never bring myself to lead folk down under. I'm in trouble, Colly Sue. I bought time by giving them whole corpses, un-embalmed, but they ain't satisfied with that no more. They want a child, and I mean them to have yours!" And with that he bent over her and scooped the baby from her breast, then was out the window in one long stride. She ran to the window and watched him go, like a spectral scarecrow across the darkening fields. With him went her last obstacle to the life she wanted to lead, a life completely her own. All she had to do was let Shadetree take the child and—

—bury it alive.

She did not call for help. The hands had all taken off for the night. Instead she took her rifle, loaded it, and started after Shadetree.

She struck out in the direction she had seen him take, across the south forty towards the hills. It was quite dark now, but a full moon had risen, white-shining like the skull that had been Bubba's wedding present. By this leprous light she soon saw him, crossing the second in a series of ridges like rumples in a blanket. It had snowed that day, and the mantle gave back the moonlight, fluorescent, dead light for a dead world. The only sound was a distant howling, like a dog caught on a barbed-wire fence. She neither lost nor gained on him. Shadetree moved swiftly across the lunar-colored landscape under the grasping skeletal trees, and Colly Sue followed.

The baby was not crying. She wondered if he had killed it already. The possibility aroused neither hope nor fear. It might have been a rag doll Shadetree carried. She wondered why she followed, and had no answer.

Either Shadetree slowed his pace or she quickened hers, for she began to gain on him as he picked his way up the scattered talus of a ravine. The child was crying now, a thin, wailing cry that touched no heartstrings within her. She saw his destination and quietly cut across a ridge to meet him there. When he came around a shoulder of rock, she was standing before the cave, rifle pointed at him.

When he saw her, a look of utter despair filled his face. "Why did you come?" he cried.

"Give back the child," she said. Her words frosted in the waiting air.

He ignored her words. "I won't let them take you," he said, and at that she felt a sudden, freezing fear that the cave behind her was the nostril of a giant haunt and that *they* were coming—

She whirled, and Shadetree struck.

Though he was over twenty feet away, he seemed to cover the distance instantaneously and had the rifle barrel in his free hand. He twisted it—the barrel bent, and the stock tore from her grip. But in the moment before he could cast it away, while both hands were full, Colly Sue leaped at him. They fell backwards down the slope, the shrieking child rolling free, Colly Sue clawing at Shadetree's face. Her thumb hooked the wire earpiece of his sunglasses, and she tore them from his face.

What she saw affected her like a blow; she fell away from him, scrambled to her feet, seized the baby, and ran. The bloated moon spotlighted her as she tumbled her way down slopes and through copses. She glanced behind her once and saw Shadetree close behind her, running noiselessly as a lizard. She had seen him overtake Bubba's truck and knew he could have her in a moment if he tried, but he did not. Breath scorching her lungs, she ran . . . then they were in the woods, her face whipped by branches, the child's voice a constant keening. And Shadetree was always close behind her, Shadetree, smiling at Arlie's stories, alone and aloof at school, holding Arlie's body, telling her "marry him," holding Bubba aloft, hiding his bloodless scratches . . . a thousand images of the horror close behind her as they broke free of the trees and she stumbled over a gravestone and fell.

Silence. The baby lay stunned, twitching feebly.

Colly Sue rolled over, felt blazing pain in her hip. She stared at the graves about her, stark in the moonlight, and recognized where Shadetree had herded her.

He stood at the edge of the graveyard, sobbing. "They made me do it, Colly Sue," he cried. "I never wanted to hurt you." The agony in his face was made hideous and mocking by the empty black holes of his eyes.

She heard then the scrabbling sounds beneath the ground, all about her. They grew louder, the sound of earth being ripped and clawed. Beside her, a pale clawlike hand broke through a grave. Another, near her feet, seized her ankle.

She would not, could not, scream.

Craig Gardner is a relatively new writer in the fantasy field; but unlike many others on the same plateau, he views his material with a freshness that, were it not for the subject, might be described as springlike. For a man so young to have a streak so nasty bodes well for the field.

KISSES FROM AUNTIE

by Craig Shaw Gardner

It was the punch that did it.

We decided that afterward, of course. There wasn't time to think of anything else when it happened, which was funny. At Auntie's we usually had more time than we could ever use.

"Give us a kiss, loves," Auntie said, and she smiled with her big red lips. Both Bruce and I closed our eyes and waited. We knew what was coming. If you kept still and didn't squirm, you'd get it over with right away.

I mean, it was bad enough when I had to put on one of my smelly old dresses and then had to let Mom brush out my hair before we went to Auntie's party. And Auntie had parties *every* week! And then, first thing, right when we got there, Auntie always had to kiss us. A big wet one on the cheek. Absolutely blech!

Auntie had this smell—lavender water, Mom said when we asked her about it. Bruce and I decided that she had to pour it all over herself to smell that bad.

"Oh, you're my special children!" Auntie said when the kissing was over. "If only Uncle were here to see you now. You know, I've watched you grow since you were knee-high to a grasshopper. But you probably wouldn't remember that, would you?"

Bruce and I both shook our heads. "Be polite!" Mom and Daddy always said. For a while we tried.

But I was talking about the punch, half ginger ale and half

cranberry juice. It tasted much worse than either one tasted by itself, I mean, absolutely blech. We got it when the grown-ups got their wine or liquor or whatever it was that grownups drink. Auntie would go around and ask, "What would you like to drink, Tom?" And Daddy would say, "I don't know, Alma. Maybe a Manhattan." And then Auntie would ask Mom the same question, and Mom would say, "Oh, whatever Tom's having is fine with me." And then she'd ask Gramma and Gramma's other sisters. But never, never did Auntie ask us what we wanted. She just brought us the punch.

Something had to be done about it. Bruce and I both stared at our glasses and frowned.

"Oh dear," Auntie said, bending close so that we could really smell the lavender. "It looks like poor Bruce and Laura have the fidgets. You don't have to stay here, dears, and be bored. Why don't you run upstairs and play until dinner?"

So we did.

Bruce and I decided that everything about Auntie couldn't be that bad, because upstairs was a special place, particularly the door right at the top of the stairs, the place Auntie called the back bedroom. It was full of all sorts of things; Daddy called it junk, but Bruce and I knew better. I mean, there were a lot of dusty green books with gold lettering that nobody would ever want to look at, but there were also three big brown photo albums with pictures of Auntie when she was my parents' age, standing in all sorts of places with some man Bruce and I figured must be "Uncle." And there were piles of old *National Geographics*, some of them with pictures of people without any clothes on. There was a big box of old toys that sat in front of the closet door with a lot of dolls and a red metal fire engine and a big bag of crayons, half of them black. When we could get away from the grownups, Auntie's back bedroom was all right.

But this time, when we reached the bedroom, the box of toys was gone. I frowned at Bruce. We'd have to look at the pictures again.

"Maybe," Bruce said, "Auntie put it behind the door." He walked over to the closet, with me close behind. Bruce turned to me and grinned. It was a door we had never opened!

He pulled the door open as quietly as he could. We were wrong. It wasn't a closet; there were stairs going up.

"Should we?" I whispered. Mom and Daddy might get mad if we didn't come down in time for supper, but I'd never seen a real attic!

Bruce hit my shoulder. "C'mon! It's better than going back downstairs to drink Auntie's punch!" The first stair creaked when he put his foot on it. He went up anyway.

I climbed right behind. I had to lift up my dress a little so that it wouldn't get dirty on the old steps. They were narrow and spaced wide apart, more like a ladder, almost. It was dark. Something brushed my forehead—a piece of string. I grabbed at it and pulled the light on.

We were in the attic, and we saw the skeleton.

I had turned on two light bulbs with the string somehow. We were under one of them, and the skeleton was under the other—a human skeleton. Bruce grabbed my arm. It got to me too, but I wanted to explore.

"Don't be a scaredy-cat!" I whispered. "Bones can't hurt you." I took a step toward the skeleton. Bruce stayed close behind. It was my turn to be brave.

The walls of the attic were full of shelves, and the shelves were full of jars, all sizes and shapes of jars, each one labeled with tiny handwriting that was hard to read. Bruce squinted inside a particularly big one.

"Aren't those eyeballs?" he whispered.

Honestly! My big brave brother. The first time we get into a strange place, he gets the creepies.

I thought the attic was great. We crept down a narrow path left between the jars on one side and the piles of old furniture and boxes on the other. Bruce started to slow down, but I pulled him after me. We were walking toward the skeleton. The bones hung from a hook in the ceiling, and there was an open space on the floor around them. It was the only open space in the whole attic. On the other side of the cleared place was a big desk, with the biggest book I'd ever seen on top of it. In between the desk and the bones, I could see something written on the floor.

I bent down to take a closer look. There was a big yellow circle painted on the floor, with some kind of black marks scribbled next to it. I tried to see whether the marks said something, but the floor was much too dusty. I rubbed the dirt off one with my thumb, but the shape underneath didn't look like any letter I'd ever seen.

I dared Bruce to step into the circle, but he wouldn't do it. He just froze in one spot and stared at the skeleton. What was he afraid of? Brother Bruce, always teasing me, daring me to go places?

I stepped into the circle.

I felt like I was going downhill in a roller coaster, swinging up in a swing, and flying through the air all at the same time. I giggled and danced. I could dance, or jump, or somersault, or fly, or do anything I wanted to. That's how I felt.

My hand hit the skeleton when I jumped.

"How dare you!" I jumped again, and all the happiness left me. Auntie stood on the stairs. "What are you children doing?"

Bruce and I looked at each other. Bruce blurted out something about looking for the box of toys.

"Well, come down from there right away. You could get hurt."

Mom and Daddy were waiting for us in the back bedroom. Daddy looked angry, like he was ready to yell.

"Now, Tom," Auntie said, as she led us both by the hand past our parents. "Don't be too harsh. They're still only children, and I never told them they couldn't go up there. If I move a couple things out of the way they might get hurt with, they can go up there every time you visit."

"Mommy!" Bruce blurted out. "There was a skeleton!"

Auntie laughed. "That's something I'll definitely have to move. Uncle was very fond of it, you know. Part of some research or other. I really never understood it." She steered Bruce and me down the staircase to dinner.

That night, after I got home, I wanted to go back to Auntie's again. I wanted to find out all about the attic and stand inside the circle again. Who cared about my uncle's old skeleton?

Anyway, we went to Auntie's almost every week for what Daddy called "family dinner parties." Daddy called them other things too, but Mom told us never to repeat those. And so we went back to Auntie's pretty soon, even though it seemed like forever to me.

I barely waited for Auntie to kiss us to run upstairs with Bruce before she even got to the punch.

"I don't know if I want to go!" Bruce said as I pulled him up the attic stairs. But he calmed down when we got to the top and he saw that the skeleton was gone. He still looked around nervously, as if he expected it to jump out from the shadows or something. But I told him that Auntie had probably locked it in one of the trunks in the back of the attic or hung it in a closet somewhere, and that seemed to make him feel better.

I dragged him straight to the circle and pushed him in. He

looked afraid for a second, but then he smiled. I stepped in after him.

Things started to happen. I mean, first it was the same feeling I had had the last time, the flying and all that. Except this time Bruce was flying with me. But then . . .

Bruce and I looked at each other, really looked at each other so that I saw right inside Bruce's eyes and saw blue lightning deep down. Bruce told me that he saw orange fire deep in mine. And the lightning flashed from Bruce's eyes, the fire jumped from mine, and they hit each other halfway between us. And where they hit, something grew.

I couldn't see what was growing there, not exactly. But I knew that it was there just the same. It grew and rose toward the ceiling.

Then I had an idea. I looked around the room. Jars shook on their shelves; something rattled in an old crate pushed into a corner. Then I saw the book on the desk, that heavy, heavy book that looked like the biggest dictionary I'd ever seen. I pointed to it. Bruce nodded. We stared at it, lightning and fire. The book took off all of a sudden and flew just above our heads. We shrieked and ducked, and the book crashed to the ground.

Bruce and I looked at each other. The lightning and flame were gone. I was happy and scared at the same time.

We heard Auntie's voice calling us to dinner.

The trouble started just as we pulled into Auntie's driveway.

"Laura, darling," my mother said, "and you too, Bruce. Your father and I have been talking. We think you should stay downstairs and talk with the relatives tonight."

"What?" Bruce yelled. "But we have to go into the attic!"

"You don't have to do anything, young man," Daddy said with a frown. "A good part of the reason we come to these silly dinners is for your grandmother and her sisters to see you. So I think you can be polite enough to stay away from the attic for once and talk to everybody."

But we couldn't do that! We had to go to the attic and fly and make everything around us fly! We always went to the attic!

Bruce started to wail, but I shook him and shook my head. Wailing never did any good with our parents. I whispered in his ear.

We ran upstairs before Auntie could even kiss us. We ran

into the circle. Jars shook. The crate r tiled and bumped. We'd do what we wanted! We'd show our parents!

Bruce stopped and stared behind me. I turned my head. Auntie was there.

She smiled her big red smile.

"My special children. Your father's very angry at you, you know."

"So what?" Bruce demanded. We were in the circle. We could do anything.

"I told them you'd get tired of your game and come down to dinner eventually. You're both very special to me. I don't want to see anything happen to you."

She walked toward us on old, shaky legs. The smell of lavender filled the room.

"Give us a kiss," she said. For some reason, we let her.

"Now be careful," Auntie said as she walked away. "I don't want to worry your parents."

And she left us alone.

We were still in the circle, and I still felt the fire. It warmed my fingers and toes and ran hot along my spine. Cold lightning flashed in the dusty air, and the fire from my eyes mixed with it, and the thing that came from part of Bruce and part of me grew.

It wanted something. It wanted to be free. It would make us free. We'd never have to do anything we didn't want to again. No more being polite for our parents, no more kisses from Auntie, no more homework, no more early bedtime. We just had to let it grow, and it would show us how.

The cloud moved away. We heard Daddy's voice echo up from the back bedroom.

"Come on, kids! Time to go home!"

I looked at Bruce. He shook his head. We couldn't go home now, not now! Neither of us made a sound.

"Come on, you little devils! Don't be so stubborn! You've already missed your dinner! I'm not going to let you miss your bedtime, too!"

We heard Daddy's feet on the stairs.

"Go away!" I screamed. He couldn't come up!

"Nope! Time to go home!"

Blue light flashed in my head. I looked at Bruce. He was right. We couldn't let Daddy get us. Not u til we knew.

I concentrated too and could feel the fire meet the lightning, and it grew again. It was stronger than ever this time. I could feel it throbbing in the air.

We pushed it down the stairs.

Daddy said a dirty word. Something fell, bumpity-bump-bump. "Tom!" Auntie screamed.

It was quiet after that. We were scared. What had we done? We only wanted to stay a little while and play.

Bruce went down the stairs first. I came down right behind him. There was no one in the back bedroom. We walked out onto the landing. Daddy lay there, very still. I could hear Mommy on the phone downstairs. She sounded upset.

We walked into the living room as the siren whirred outside. Mommy flung the door open to let in two men carrying some poles. They walked up to where Daddy lay. One of the men felt Daddy's body.

They undid the poles into some sort of stretcher while one of the men talked to Mommy. She nodded, and they put Daddy on the stretcher and carried him outside.

Mommy turned to us. I could tell that she'd been crying.

"Daddy's broken his leg and maybe something else. I've got to go to the hospital with him. Auntie's been good enough to volunteer to take care of you overnight. Don't give her any trouble."

Mommy grabbed her coat and ran out the door.

Auntie smiled her big red smile. "Now, Bruce and Laura, don't be frightened. Give us a kiss."

She put her big wet lips on my cheek and hugged me tight. I almost choked on the lavender smell. She went over and did the same to Bruce.

Blue flashed in my brain. I blinked. Maybe we could do it now anywhere in Auntie's house. Maybe we could do it any-place we wanted.

We could do anything we wanted.

"You're Auntie's special children." She patted Bruce on the head. "Come into the kitchen. I'll give you some punch."

Bruce and I looked at each other. Absolutely blech.

"And then we can play some games. I imagine you children have lots of games you like to play. We'll have such a good time. And you can stay forever and ever."

Lightning flashed. I could feel the fire. We'd do what we wanted. Nobody—not Auntie, not our parents, nobody—would ever tell us what to do again.

"Come into the kitchen, children. Your punch is ready."

Bruce and I looked at each other. No more cranberry juice and ginger ale!

It grew.

No more kisses! No more boring games!

The cloud filled the room over our heads. I could really see it now. Spots of orange flame flashed in the darkness. Blue bolts of light stretched to the carpet. No more! No more!

"So soon?" It was Auntie's voice. She could see the cloud too.

The cloud moved toward her. Auntie stumbled against the refrigerator. "Bruce, Laura, you were always my special children. So gifted. When Uncle made his plans, I knew. . . ." Her voice trailed off as the first flashes of blue light snapped at her outstretched hands. She closed her eyes and let the cloud cover her.

The cloud vanished, and Auntie was gone too.

I felt like I hadn't slept in a month. It hit me just like that. The cloud had been too big; it had used up too much of us.

Bruce had fallen on the floor, his eyes closed.

What had we done? What would Mommy and Daddy say when they couldn't find Auntie?

"Bruce?" I whispered, even though there was no one around to hear. "What can we do?"

My brother opened his eyes and smiled. "It's a shame it had to happen so young."

"Bruce?" I asked. What was he talking about?

He rolled over and pushed himself up. He swayed when he stood.

"Still, Uncle will be here soon, and we'll be together for ever and ever."

"Stop talking like that!" I backed up toward the kitchen door.

He walked toward me like he didn't quite know how to use his feet. He stretched out his arms to touch me. The smell of lavender was in the air.

"Give us a kiss, love," he said.

In horror fiction, the author often simply takes an ordinary situation, household, or employment and brings it to a conclusion many of us fantasize but dare not act upon. The most common of these deal with children and parents, those two major groups most in love and most often in conflict. Steve Rasnic Tem knows this well, to the shuddering delight of his readers.

MORNING TALK

by Steve Rasnic Tem

"I tell you, there's something *wrong* with the boy!"

Once again the noise from the kitchen had awakened Michael, who now had his small body stretched out from the bed, leaning precariously over his toy chest in order to put his ear against the door.

Again he heard the raised voice of his father, and in the background, silence. His mother never said anything during these early-morning conversations. Michael imagined tears, protestations, trembling entreaties for his father to be more reasonable, to be more loving, but he never heard them.

"I can't put up with it, Clara! And I'm *not* going to put up with his craziness any more!"

It was generally the same conversation every morning, the same lecture, the same little talk. There were only slight variations in the wording, and the event that set off his father's anger was a little different each time.

This time Michael had built a fort out of old bricks in the driveway. He had forgotten to tear it down before his father got home from work the previous night. His father had run into it, and the new Cadillac had a small scratch.

But his parents had these conversations every morning. Michael had gotten used to it.

The puzzling thing, however, the really disturbing thing,

was that the kitchen was right off Michael's bedroom. His parents *had* to know that he could hear them when his father talked so loudly. Michael was only ten, but he knew everything that was going on in the house that way. He had come to believe that this was the way his parents let him know things they wanted him to know.

Again, his father: "I don't care! He's bleeding me, Clara!"

Again, his father: "He's killing me, Clara!"

Again, his father: "Things could be a lot easier around here if. . . ."

Sometimes his father's voice trailed off at just the right moment, before Michael could find out what he had planned for him. But his parents only let Michael know what they wanted him to know.

Early morning, every morning, it was the same. Michael had several questions he wanted answered, suspicions he had; and every morning he tried to listen as closely as possible to discover those answers.

But he never could listen quite carefully enough. Always his father's voice would trail off, and Michael could not catch it.

"I don't know why we ever. . . ."

Michael listened carefully each morning to see whether he was really adopted, to see whether they were planning to get rid of him, to see whether his mother too hated him.

But his father's voice always trailed off, and his mother never spoke.

"You're too *easy* on him, Clara. You coddle the boy. I don't know why I put up with *either* one of you! I'm just going to have to. . . ."

He heard noises out near his door; he sneaked back under the covers, as he had many times before, and pretended to fall asleep.

He'd die. . . .

Michael woke up confused and disturbed. It had never happened that way before. He'd pretended to be asleep when he heard his father approaching his room, and he'd actually fallen asleep.

He wondered what time it was. It was still dark outside, or dark *again* outside. Had he slept through until night?

He'll be dead. . . .

But there they were in the kitchen, talking, no, whispering this time. And that couldn't be right, what he'd thought they'd said; they were whispering purposely so that he might misunderstand, so that it might worry him.

We kill. . . .

He crept out of his bed and put his ear against the door.

Better off dead. . . .

He shivered in his pajamas. But it was summer, and they couldn't be saying this.

Go to the door and. . . .

Of course, he must be dreaming, and he must be about to wake up now. He *must!*

Go to his door now. . . .

He began to cry, bringing his feet up and down in time to his small wails; in horror, he saw that he had wetted himself, that the pool of urine was spreading around his feet. They'd *kill* him for this.

Now, do it, now. . . .

He must be imagining it. He must be dreaming.

Open the door. . . .

He burst through the door screaming, running through the kitchen, crying out in terror as the hands clutched at him. If he could only make it to the back door, if he could only run fast enough!

Michael . . . Michael . . . Michael . . .

The two shadowy forms had trapped him; there was no more room to run. His father stepped out of the darkness, his face pale, lips white, blue-tinted, reaching out to Michael.

He handed him the knife, the hammer, this man who was going to kill him, and pointed at the corner where they had their kitchen table.

His mother sat in a chair, her face drawn and her eyes wary. She seemed to have been crying; her eyes were deeply etched in red. She wore her prettiest pink nightgown.

His father gestured again and pushed Michael toward her with a sour-smelling hand.

It was then that Michael noticed his own hand: the exposed blue veins, the white skin, the tattered pajama sleeve. And then his feet, the broken toenails, the raw red places. Just like his father.

Michael. . . .

His mother began to weep again, her voice a high keening wail, as he first looked back at his father and then approached her slowly with the knife pushed forward in his frayed-looking, little-boy hand.

Richard Houston, like several of the authors in this volume, lives and works in Texas. I suspect, then, that it's something in the air down there, or maybe in the water. Whatever the reason, Houston has taken the ordinary and given it just the necessary twist to produce a horror that stems not from the supernatural but from something all of us have done countless times in our lives. And what's so harmful about petting a pet?

THE MAN WHO WAS KIND TO ANIMALS

by Richard Houston

Randall lived in his mother's house, which had been built at the turn of the century. Its decor was a hodgepodge of Federal and Victorian, all inexpensive revival work of the type that passes for antique among people who don't know the difference and couldn't afford it if they did. Mrs. Church had lived in the house for fifty years until her death at the age of seventy-eight. It was still very much the old woman's house, dark and ornate, ripe with the fusty air of age.

Gary stayed with Randall, in his mother's house, whenever he traveled to Barclay, which was usually at least once a month, because his job demanded it. He worked for Engleberry Industries, manufacturers of a host of plastic products, among them the first childproof cap. Until three years ago, Gary had lived in Barclay too, where he had met and befriended Randall through the intermediary of Mrs. Church.

"You're the only person I know who drinks beer from a glass," Gary said, deferentially filling his own glass with care, lest the explosive head spill over the top. They sat in the parlor.

"Old habit. If you like, I'll take it straight from the can, like a man."

Gary ignored him and took a foamy sip.

"How are Joan and the kids?" Randall asked.

"Fine, just fine."

"Oh, I don't think I've told you the news."

"What's that?"

"I have some new neighbors across the street."

Gary picked up on his tone. "Not your favorite people, huh?"

"I'd like to kill them."

They played cribbage, as genteel a way to pass an evening as Gary could imagine. He had never even heard of the game until Randall taught it to him. Randall pegged the score on a large cribbage board that his grandfather had carved, a beautiful slab of polished teak with pegs of birch and cedar.

Randall was tall and almost delicately slender. His hair was neatly trimmed in the styleless manner of men's hair before the 1970s. He wore dark horn-rims and even smoked a large-bowled briar pipe. He was the senior account representative of the Barclay First National Bank, and his standard attire was a neutral gray suit, selected with care from a large closet full of neutral gray suits. The cuffed and pleated pants were held up by suspenders or a skinny black belt. Around the house, Randall exchanged his suit jacket for a cardigan sweater with worn, bulging pockets.

Gary spent most of his time in jeans and flannel shirts with the sleeves rolled up. In warm weather, he wore shorts and T-shirts. He was shorter than Randall and far more solidly built. His sandy hair varied in length with his mood, but not since his tenth birthday, when he told the barber that he was too old for the little-boys' cut, had his hair been as short as Randall's.

"Fi'teen two, fi'teen four, and two pairs make eight," Gary said.

"You won't catch up that way." Randall pegged the score.

"My crib." Gary spread out the four new cards and couldn't resist a smile.

"Your luck is changing," Randall said with a raised eyebrow of discontent.

"Let's see now. Fi'teen two, fi'teen four, six, eight, ten, and twelve. And six pairs make it twenty-four." He sat back with a sigh.

"I couldn't have said it better myself." Randall jumped Gary's peg far ahead on the board. "You're ahead now by three points."

They were interrupted by the roar of a powerful automobile engine straining in deceleration. It revved a couple of times, winding up for a tire-squealing start. The sound grew louder as it approached the house, and it seemed to stop right in front. Gary noticed Randall's glum expression.

"The neighbors," he said simply.

"Sounds like some of my old friends."

"The neighborhood. . . ." Randall held his hand high above the level of his head. The hand spiraled toward the floor like an enemy aircraft in a John Wayne movie, complete with sound effects. "Right in the toilet."

Even through the thick walls of the old house they could hear the commotion Randall's neighbors were causing just by getting into their house. Loud music soon followed.

Randall won the first game, and they proceeded to a second.

Later, in the bathroom, while admiring the free-standing tub with its scrolled feet and the porcelain faucets all around, Gary saw something small and black run across the floor.

"I spotted another roach!" he called to Randall. "I bet you still haven't talked to an exterminator."

"I really can't see why it's necessary for a couple of roaches."

"They'll be crawling all over you if you don't get 'em quick." He went to the kitchen and opened the refrigerator. "Want another one?"

"No, not for me."

"Well, I'm not fin—damn, there's another one!" The shiny black bug skittered across the counter and disappeared behind some bottles. "You really ought to do something about this, Randall," Gary said as he returned to the parlor.

"They don't bother me."

Gary picked up the game again, drinking unceremoniously from the can by this time. "Look, an old house like this, you got to be careful. Your mother used to have it sprayed regularly, I remember her telling me. Termites get in here, and the whole thing's likely to come down around your ears."

"All right, I'll do it. Now let's play."

While he shuffled, Gary said, "I know you, Randall. You just don't want to see the poor little bugs die."

They played and talked, stopped playing and talked, and in the end went to bed much later than Gary felt they should have. He had to be on the road early in the morning.

He awoke less than eagerly to the sound of Randall busying himself downstairs in the kitchen. Very domestic, that guy.

Joan had never asked him not to stay at Randall's, but her back stiffened and her voice went a little cold at the mention of his name. From their first meeting six years ago, she had always been aloof around him. Their insurance agent, a former college all-American fullback who hadn't made it into the pros and who had been Randall's agent for many years before Gary ever thought of needing one, had been quick to make insinuations when they first met.

"How long you known this guy?" he asked when Randall was out of the room.

"A couple of years."

"You ever think he's kind of strange, you know what I mean?"

"No, what do you mean?"

"I mean living with his mother, and you know." He winked and nudged Gary with his elbow. "You've never seen him with a woman, I bet."

"No, I don't think I have."

"I'd be kind of careful around him, if you know what I mean. You never can be too sure about these guys."

Somehow—perhaps because Gary had been buying a policy to cover himself and his new, pregnant wife—it had never occurred to this insurance salesman that Gary might be every bit as "strange" as Randall. And Gary didn't really know *that* about Randall, even after all this time. There were apparently no women in his life, but there were no conspicuous relationships with men either. If Randall was indeed a homosexual, it was something he had never felt the need to make Gary aware of.

Gary staggered into the kitchen, where a disgustingly bright Randall was making breakfast for the two of them.

"I scrambled the eggs with some milk. I trust that's the way you still like them."

"Yes, thank you. Is there any coffee?"

"Have a seat."

Gary sat down with his head in his hands and heard the sound of coffee trickling into the cup, smelled its aroma, and only when it could no longer be avoided, uncovered his eyes and took a sip.

Randall placed a beautiful dish of eggs, ham, hash browns, and toast before him, poured a glass of juice, and went to the front of the house to get the paper. Five minutes later, Gary was awake enough to be concerned that Randall hadn't returned.

As soon as he stepped out the door, Gary heard the shouting. Across the street, Randall had a boy of seven or eight by the throat and was shaking him vigorously. The child was terrified.

"Randall!" Gary yelled, already halfway across the street. "What the hell are you doing?" He tried to force himself between Randall and the kid, but his friend was determined. "Let go of him, Randall! You're going to kill him!"

At that moment a plump woman in her late twenties came out of the house. "Billy! Oh, my God! You let go of him!"

"Come on, Randall, get hold of yourself," Gary pleaded.

"Jim! Jim, get out here. That man's got Billy!" She flew at Randall.

The woman's husband appeared after her on the porch. "Hey! What you think you're doing? Let go of my kid!"

Gary finally pried Randall's hands off the child and tried to drag him back across the street. The woman swung at them with her open hands before stooping to her child. Randall struggled to get free, but Gary had him firmly.

"You're crazy, man," the husband said, standing between Randall and his wife and child. "I'm calling the police on this one. You can't go around attacking kids."

"You should teach your kids some respect!" Randall shouted.

"I'll show you who needs teaching," the man said, coming toward them. Gary whirled Randall around and gave him a strong shove toward his house.

"Look, I'm sure it's all some kind of misunderstanding," Gary said, palms out in a calming gesture. "Your kid's okay. Why don't you take him inside?"

The husband was heavier than Gary, somewhat younger, and decidedly meaner-looking, but he did not advance any farther. "You some kind of friend of this guy?"

"Yeah, I am."

"Well, you better tell him to keep his hands off my kids." He shouted past Gary to Randall, menacing with an emphatic index finger. "You leave 'em alone, or you'll wish you had! You got that?"

Randall wouldn't let it pass. "If I see any one of your kids mistreating an animal again, they'll regret it."

Gary pulled him toward the house, looking back to see the husband glaring but standing his ground. He didn't breathe freely until they were inside and the door was securely shut.

"What the hell was all that about?" Gary demanded.

Randall was still too agitated to speak. Gary had never seen him like this. Randall rarely even raised his voice and never became physical.

Finally, Randall spoke. "That's the second time I've seen that child attack an animal. He shot a cat with a pellet gun."

"I didn't see any gun."

"It's in the grass. He dropped it. You can go back and look for it if you don't believe me."

"All right, I believe you. But for God's sake, Randall, do you realize what you were doing? You could have really hurt that kid."

Randall had nothing more to say. Gary tried to eat some of his cold breakfast but had little stomach for it. He finished the coffee and debated about leaving with things in the state they were. He could hear Randall above him on the creaking floorboards. At least he knew where the man was. There was also a rattling, scratching sound from somewhere, faint and irritating. Then he heard the meow of a cat.

When Gary opened the back door, he found a black and white cat lying on the floor of the porch, panting. The entire area was screened in, but he saw where a flap had been pried up. He bent down to look closer at the animal and saw that it had been wounded on its right flank.

"Randall, get down here! Your cat's on the back porch!"

Above, there was the abrupt change of sound from feet pacing to feet running. In a moment, Randall was beside him. Without a word he scooped up the cat in his long-fingered hands and took it inside.

Gary was through Barclay again three weeks later and was told by Randall's embarrassed secretary that he was in jail. The police wouldn't let him see Randall, but a lawyer was already posting bail. Later that evening, they talked about it.

"You were asking for this, you know," Gary said.

"What am I supposed to do? Those little monsters roam the entire neighborhood, terrorizing any living thing they can find. They shoot at birds with their pellet guns and don't always miss. I saw them tending the fires of burning anthills the other day. A little gasoline, and up they go. I don't know what they do to flies, but I know they pull the wings and legs off beetles and grasshoppers. Somehow they got hold of a cat long enough to tie a rope to its tail yesterday, and they were swinging it around their heads."

"You've got to report these people. There has to be a law against this sort of thing."

Randall was quiet for a moment. "I've called everybody I can think of, and so far, nothing. Nobody's interested unless a pet owner complains. I'm not a pet owner, so I don't count."

"What about the owners? Aren't they complaining?"

"Those kids are still at it."

"Have you talked to the other neighbors?"

"They don't believe me, or they don't care."

Randall disappeared into the kitchen and returned quickly with a bottle of Johnny Walker Black.

"You still haven't told me why you were in jail," Gary said as he sipped the liquor.

"I had this scheme. I bought a Polaroid camera yesterday. I was going to get some pictures of them in the act. That way somebody might believe me." He went to a table in the corner, returning with a small stack of snapshots. "Unfortunately, they aren't very definitive from a couple of hundred feet away."

Gary saw a series of pictures that showed three scruffy children—two boys and a girl—and a dog. The older boy he recognized as the one Randall had fought with. The dog seemed to be playing with the children in a few of the pictures, and in a few others it was tied to a tree. The children were doing something to the dog, but it was impossible to tell what. He looked up uncertainly at Randall.

"They slit its paws with a razor blade."

Gary could not speak, and Randall gestured for him to follow. They went upstairs to one of the three rooms on the second floor. Gary noticed a rancid smell even before the door was opened, and it became much stronger as they entered the room. Randall switched on a light. On the floor was a dog, the same one as in the pictures. Its feet were in bandages.

"I'm not much at first aid," Randall said, "but I did what I could to clean the wounds."

The dog lifted its head toward the two men but showed no sign of welcome or pleasure. Gary had never seen a dog's eyes so cold. Another dog was in the corner behind them, a large German shepherd. It didn't seem injured, but it too lay still and watched them. The floral-pattern rug was stained in several places.

Randall closed the door when they left the room, and as they walked past his bedroom, Gary noticed the black and white cat lying on the bed. It watched them pass. Randall continued the tour to the back porch, where he had at least six birds with damaged wings, and then to a small back room that contained a little dog and two cats.

"What's wrong with them?" Gary asked.

"Nothing that I can determine. They may have some internal injuries I can't detect, but I think they're just frightened."

"You're turning this place into an animal shelter."

"Do I have a choice? I'm trying to keep them confined to areas where they can't do much damage. But they show up here, and I can't just run them off. Somebody has to look out for them."

They went back to the parlor and the scotch.

"So now you've got evidence. Take the dog to a vet or an animal hospital and show them the pictures you took. That should start something."

"I certainly hope so."

In what seemed like a very short time they polished off half the bottle, and Gary refused to budge from the sofa. He half remembered Randall covering him with a blanket. Then nothing.

Gary woke up in the dark with no idea of what time it was. His mind sorted the subtle noises of the old house to determine which one had awakened him, and he settled on a clanking sound coming from the direction of the kitchen. He got off the sofa and stumbled to the nearest lamp. From its glow, he could see down the row of rooms to the back of the house. His shadow grew shorter as he approached the kitchen. He heard the sound again.

At the kitchen door, he reached into the room and flicked on the light. First he saw insects—dozens, perhaps hundreds —crawling madly on the floor, scrabbling for cover, afraid of the light. But the bugs were not making the sound.

There was a movement at the extreme edge of his vision, and his head jerked toward it. A cat was standing on the stove, licking grease out of the drip pan beneath the burners. When the cat changed position, the slightly warped grate jiggled and clanked.

Was it one of the cats from the back room? he wondered. How had it gotten in? It paid him no attention, licking furiously. The audacity gave him an eerie feeling of violation, of being used.

"Well, cat, I don't care if this is an aid station for distressed animals, you're going outside where you belong." Gary moved to pick up the cat, and the animal burst into a fit of savage anger. Gary jerked his hands away from the flailing claws and backed off. The cat calmed somewhat but still glared at him with smoldering fury. A few seconds later, the cat sensed its victory and went back to licking the grease.

Gary left the kitchen slowly, closing the door behind him. His arms and back tingled as he returned to the parlor. Something was going on that he couldn't quite grasp. He had never seen a cat react like that before, never seen an animal show such ferocity without serious provocation. He lay on the sofa for a while with the lamp still on, but it hurt his eyes. The darkness was not that comfortable when he lay down again, but it was the only way to get back to sleep. He wondered whether he should wake Randall and tell him about the cat, and then he realized how foolish he would appear. He pulled the blanket up tightly around himself, and moments later he was asleep.

He awoke the next time with a feeling of warmth on his chest, warmth and weight. His eyes opened abruptly but functioned poorly in the dark. Comprehension came gradually.

A cat was huddled on his chest.

His thoughts were sudden and jumbled. Was it asleep? Maybe it was looking for companionship. Was it the cat from the kitchen? But he had closed the kitchen door.

The soft hiss of the cat's breath matched his own. He felt the thin column of pressurized air on his neck. When his vision cleared, he saw the glint of the cat's eyes staring at him.

He shifted position slightly.

From nearby in the darkness, he heard the beginning of a growl. Something brushed his foot.

For an unmeasurable length of time, Gary lay still, with the cat on his chest and unseen animals close around him. At some point he must have slept again, impossible though it was for him to believe that. His first memory of the next morning's light found him alone on the sofa, alone in the room.

Eight days later, Gary took an unscheduled swing back through Barclay to check on Randall. At the bank, they said that he was sick and hadn't been in all week.

He noticed the smell the moment Randall opened the front door, the same rancid stench of urine and animal waste that previously had been confined to the room upstairs and the back of the house. Now it seemed to possess the entire building.

Randall looked terrible, with his eyes sunken and his cheeks hollow. Dressed in an old purple silk robe, he led the way to the parlor, threading a path through the animals. They were everywhere: seven or eight in the front room, half a dozen in the parlor itself. Gary would have sat on the sofa, but it was already occupied by a large boxer, which glanced up and casually dismissed his presence. From where he stood, Gary could see that the delicate fruitwood of the furniture had been gnawed, that the upholstery and carpeting had been soiled and ripped.

"What the hell's going on here, Randall?"

"They just keep showing up. I don't understand it." His voice wavered slightly.

"Get a hold of yourself, Randall. Throw these beasts out."

"It's not safe outside." His eyes would not meet Gary's.

"They're ruining your house; hell, they're ruining your life. You've got to do something."

"They burned a cat yesterday."

"Jesus!"

"It was still alive when I found it. Charred and blistered, but it was still alive. I had to smash its head with a rock." So saying, Randall half demonstrated the motion and in doing so revealed his left hand, which had until then been hidden in the pocket of his robe. It was bandaged almost to the elbow.

"My God, what happened to your hand?"

Randall looked confused at first, seeming to understand only after he looked down and saw the bandages. "Oh, that. It's nothing; just a scratch."

"All right, that's it. I'm taking you to the hospital."

"No!" He pulled back from Gary's outstretched hand.

"With the filth in here and your present frame of mind, I'll bet whatever's under those bandages is one hell of an infected mess. You've got to have it looked at."

"It won't be safe for them if I leave."

"God damn it, Randall, you are not responsible for these animals!"

It took a lot of coaxing, but Gary got Randall to the hospital. He sat in the emergency room while his friend was being treated. Afterward, the doctor informed him that the hand had been bitten and clawed seriously by an animal. There was some question of whether Randall would have full use of all his fingers again, and the issue of a possible rabies infection was discussed. They were going to keep him in the hospital for a few days.

Randall seemed more lucid when Gary went to see him in his room. "They won't let me out of here, you know," he said.

"It's for your own good."

"So they tell me."

"Randall, I wish I could stay and help you take care of this mess, but Joan's expecting me home tonight, and I've got a meeting in the morning."

"I know how it is. Don't worry, I'll be all right."

"You know, you have to take the animal that bit you in for examination. You'll do it, won't you?"

"Yes, I suppose so."

"And you'll use your head and get rid of the rest of them too, won't you?"

"Yes, I will. Maybe I can find some of their owners."

"Just do it." He studied Randall's face for a sign of commitment but couldn't find one. "God, I hate to think of what they're doing to that place."

The following weekend, Gary took his children to the park; while there, he witnessed an odd incident.

He saw a group of kids beating a dog. They had the animal trapped in a fenced compound and were throwing rocks at it and swatting it with sticks. The dog ran frantically from corner to corner, each time coming up short against another fence, giving the children much entertainment. Finally, the dog found a gate in the fencing and slithered through. The children chased after it but quickly tired and went on to other games.

A half hour later, the dog was back. It seemed foolish, but Gary had never pretended to understand the psychology of animals. The dog cowered when people passed it, slinking as much as walking. Then a boy—not one of the children who had tormented it before—stopped to pet the animal. Gary could see the dog regaining some confidence and spirit as the child played with it. A happy ending after all, he thought.

Then the dog bit the boy—a cruel, vicious bite. The child fell to the ground screaming, and the dog stood over him. In that moment, though he realized it was a totally subjective observation, Gary saw what looked almost like . . . like *satisfaction* in the dog's eyes.

He ran toward the child, as did several other people who

had heard his cries. When he got through the crowd, the dog was gone.

Gary tried to dismiss the event, but it bothered him through the rest of the day and into the night. He knew that there was something in what he'd seen that should have solved a mystery rather than deepened it, but it eluded him. All he knew was that it had something to do with Randall.

He woke up in a sweat in the middle of the night, sitting bolt upright in bed. He had to get to the phone.

"What is it, honey?" Joan asked sleepily.

"Randall," was all he said.

Randall's number rang and rang, but nobody answered. Gary's hands trembled as he held the phone. After the twentieth ring, he jammed the receiver down. He considered calling the police but realized that they would think he was a kook. Nobody would believe it. He wasn't sure he believed it himself.

He apologized to Joan as he threw on some clothes, and then he was off into the night. The hours of driving the tediously familiar route to Barclay were agonizing—hours to worry, and ache, and question his concern. Perhaps it was stupid. He was attributing a lot to one simple event in the park. No one really knew how much animals thought, if they thought at all. Sure, they had to think, but it was instinct, not reasoning. But that was part of it: instinct. At that base level, they were survivalists, the ultimate pragmatists: bend, give in, surrender, submit. But under extreme duress, when taxed beyond limit, what then? They wouldn't bite the hand that fed them, no. But they wouldn't bite the hand that beat them either. It was too great a risk. No; if they needed to bite something, to lash out and devour something, it was the hand that petted them, that caressed them, the kind hand, the safe hand, the hand that bore no threat.

The front door to Randall's house was unlocked, not even fully closed. Gary pushed it open, and a wall of stink blew over him. Without even stepping inside, he saw the ruin of the front room—furniture overturned, lamps and vases shattered, walls and floor scratched and spattered. He entered the house cautiously, waiting for the animals. It was quiet inside except for the buzzing of flies. Shafts of the dawn's light shot into once-darkened rooms where heavy drapes had been ripped and wood-slatted blinds splintered.

"Randall!" There was no reply, no rustling or stirring, nothing.

Each room, Gary passed through was as ravaged as the last. Randall was not in any of them. He tried to find encouragement in that. Surely the man had seen what was happening and had gotten out in time. Perhaps this wreckage had occurred while he was still in the hospital. *The hospital.* Gary managed to find the phone, but the wires were chewed through in several places. Then he remembered a wall phone in the kitchen that might have survived.

The kitchen smelled worst of all. The doors of the cabinets, the pantry, and the refrigerator hung open; all the contents were spilled in a rotting mess on the floor. But the phone was still on the wall.

He stepped gingerly through the soft mounds of garbage, his shoes sliding on buried slime. Insects were everywhere: roaches, ants, and things beyond his knowledge. He noticed a line of ants carrying small lumps of a reddish substance. The line led out from under the sink and off into a pile of trash. Without fully understanding it, he bent down and scooped up one of the ants. The lump it carried was soft and spongy, rather like meat, and released an oily moisture when he squeezed it.

No, he thought. It couldn't be. It just couldn't be.

The doors under the sink were closed. Something hung out of the bottom on one side. Gary moved to get a closer look. A piece of purple silk was wedged into the base of the door—from the inside. Gary's hand trembled, but it moved toward the knob on the door.

There was a growl from behind him. Gary twisted around to see a huge black Doberman standing in the doorway. There was a long, reddish bone in its mouth. The bone thudded to the floor. Bared teeth glistened in the dog's muzzle; saliva drooled from its lips.

He reached for the knob again. The dog rumbled in its throat but did not attack.

Gary pulled on the knob, but the door was stuck. He pulled harder. The door crackled and gave slowly. A seam of darkness appeared between the doors. It widened, and Gary peered into it, denying what he wished not to see, terrified of what he must see.

Something fell out: a piece of something, a chewed and

shredded piece of something that might once have been the arm of a man. Gary threw up on it.

"No! No, no, no, no, no. No. No. NOOOOO!"

Gary staggered through the kitchen, screaming and stomping. His feet decimated the line of ants with the spongy meat, ground roaches to pulp, kicked mounds of garbage high into the air. When his rage finally subsided, he stood breathlessly at one side of the room near the phone.

The Doberman whined and panted. It moved to Gary's side and licked his hand.

Nicholas Yermakov is one of those new young writers who waste no time making their presence felt right from the start. By the time you read this, his first novel will be out, and he's already had a number of short stories published in the major genre magazines. The following story is typical of his work only in the fine writing and the careful way in which he lays his bludgeon about him.

FAR REMOVED FROM THE SCENE OF THE CRIME

by Nicholas Yermakov

In a dark room on Robben Island, just off the coast of Capetown, a man with no name hung manacled from the ceiling, receiving electric shocks in his genitals. Sweat streamed from his pores, every one of which was open and screaming. His ebony face was contorted as the pain coursed through him and blood trickled from the corner of his mouth. He had bitten through his tongue.

"Tough old *kaffir*, aren't you, one eighty-seven?" said the by-now familiar voice of his tormentor, speaking from somewhere back in the darkness. It was an Afrikaner voice, rather droll and not unpleasant. "Be smart, *kaffir*, make the right decision. Talk to me. Tell me what I want to know and I'll send the nasty man away."

There was no reply. The nasty man grinned and closed the contact. The power flowed. One eighty-seven bucked in the air like a hooked trout breaking surface.

"Sing, *kaffir*!" called the voice. "Da, da, da, da, da, da, dada, da, da, da, *wir leben Südwest!*"

Eyes bulging, one eighty-seven thrashed twice more and fainted. The only sound in the darkened room was that of the rope creaking as the manacled man slowly swung back and forth, suspended in midair.

"Bloody hell," muttered Van Owen. "Take him down."

The nasty man and another, also in uniform, unfastened the rope from its hook, and one eighty-seven dropped like a stone to the floor.

"Gently, now, *gent*-ly," cautioned Van Owen. "I wouldn't want the bastard to crack his skull before I'm through with him."

The others picked him up, one by the hands, one by the feet, swinging him slightly. They tossed him in the general direction of what passed for a cot, propped up in the corner of the room. One eighty-seven hit the wall and bounced down onto the bedding.

"That's your 'free Namibia' for you!" snarled the nasty man.

"Cool out, sergeant, cool out," said Van Owen, lighting up an American cigarette, a Lucky Strike. "This isn't personal, you know. Just do your job."

The sergeant looked as if he was about to say something, but one look at Van Owen's impassive face stopped him. "Yes, sir," he muttered, managing something that looked vaguely like a salute, then leaving the room along with his companion.

Van Owen, alone in the cell with the unconscious man, rose to his feet and crossed the floor; standing by the cot, he looked down at the senseless black man.

"Who are you, one eighty-seven?" he asked softly. "Who in bloody hell are you?"

They called him by a number. The number stamped upon the plastic bracelet welded to his wrist, just like the ones worn by all the other workers. Workers who broke their backs doing the most menial of labor, never to be allowed to attain the rank of supervisor, never to be able to leave their jobs without fear of corporal punishment . . . or worse. Workers who were paid in meager quantities of sugar, fat, and flour, a diet of which was all they had to sustain their families. Workers who were always "on call." Workers who lived to an average age of thirty-one years only to be buried in the dirt with nothing to mark their final resting place except a somewhat tombstone-shaped board bearing the number on their bracelets. Workers who lived and died in the searing sunlight of Namibia. Southwest Africa. Workers who were black.

They had caught him at a rally. He had been the one with the bullhorn. A lot were killed, the rest were scattered. The flags and placards with the SWAPO slogans had been trampled in the dirt. His "name" was one eighty-seven. Only, it wasn't. One eighty-seven was dead. His employer had remembered him very well. They had had to shoot him, for whatever reason Van Owen did not recall. The man they had was someone else. A special someone else.

They had loaded him, along with the others, into a pickup truck, the bed of which was enclosed with wood and steel mesh; then they drove him to the jail. He had been beaten, many times. He had been questioned, many times. They had starved him, tortured him, and threatened him with death. And, despite all that, one eighty-seven had not said one single, solitary word since that day when they knocked the bullhorn away from his mouth, chipping several teeth in the process. Not one word.

Now, he was in the prison on Robben Island, just off the coast of Capetown. Far away, far removed from the scene of the crime. Yes, he was a special man.

"You're mine, one eighty-seven," said Van Owen. "You'll all mine. And, by God, I'm going to crack you."

Van Owen had been many things in his life. Now, he was a mercenary, on and off. Capetown was his home, his place of birth. Southwest was *his* land, *his* country. Without them, the *kaffirs* were nothing. *They* had brought the industry. *They* had brought the organization, the progress, the government. Van Owen would see all the blacks in hell before he succumbed to their majority rule. SWAPO was a threat, but to him, it didn't seem to be much of a threat. A slight annoyance. The Southwest Africa People's Organization, indeed. Something invented by the United Nations. A bunch of meddlesome foreigners. They weren't much of a threat, either. A lot of talk, a lot of noise, but who cared, really? Van Owen had been to America, to New York. His work took him many places. Most New Yorkers didn't even know the difference between the General Assembly and the Security Council. To them, all the United Nations stood for was something that was responsible for all the little children with the orange canisters who collected dimes and quarters on Halloween for UNICEF. No, the UN wasn't much of a threat. But men like one eighty-seven, if there were more such as he, they were very much a threat, indeed.

Van Owen told himself he did not hate the man. After all, it was not his job to hate. And Van Owen was only doing his job. Was only doing what was right. It was nothing personal. Not really.

"Who are you, *kaffir*?" he asked the prostrate form. "Where did you come from? Who are your friends?" He squatted down next to the cot, close to the black man's ear. "When you come around, we'll talk again, you and I. We're going to be good friends, *kaffir*. We'll tell each other all our secrets."

He stood up and flicked his cigarette into a corner of the room, where it lay smoking. He slapped his hand against his thigh, absently.

"Rest well, one eighty-seven. Rest well." He brushed his thick blond hair away from his eyes and turned to leave the room. The door was open. On the other side of the door was a darkened room. In the corner of the darkened room, against the wall, stood a makeshift cot. On the cot, face turned towards the wall, lay a man.

Van Owen frowned. "What the hell. . . ."

He entered the other room. The room where, moments before, there had been a hall.

"Sergeant?"

There was no response. Van Owen slowly approached the cot. He gazed upon the unconscious form of one eighty-seven. He turned around and looked through the door through which he came. There was a darkened room. With a cot. And a man lying on that cot, face turned toward the wall. . . .

He spun around, again. Reaching out, he grabbed the unconscious man by the shoulder and turned him over. The man flopped over, heavily, like dead weight, onto his back. His eyes were closed and bruised. His face was puffy, battered from numerous beatings. His neck was scar-crossed. There was blood on his lips and chin, already drying. His mouth was open, and several teeth were chipped and others missing.

Van Owen ran through the door and into the room on the other side. He raced over to the cot. Van Owen froze in his tracks, stopped as if he had hit a wall. The black man on the cot was lying on his back, his face a symphony of violence, his mouth hanging open, displaying cracked and missing teeth. Van Owen spun around again. The view through the doorway, into the other room, was identical. He ran to the door and slammed it shut, then rubbed his eyes and slapped his face several times.

"Sergeant! *Gerhardt!*"

His voice, in the room, sounded hollow. He opened the door, only to slam it shut once again. What was on the other side had not changed.

"Holy Mother of God," he whispered. "I must be losing my bleedin' marbles!"

Steady, boy, he thought. Steady. It's only the strain, that's all. Only the strain. You've been at this thing for hours now, you must be more tired than you thought. These things never bothered you before. Cool out, now. Breathe easy.

He inhaled and exhaled, deeply, several times. He held his hands out before him. They were shaking, slightly. Damn. The nerves. The nerves were going. The bastard's getting to you, son, he thought. All this time, not one single word, it's bound to shake you up a bit. He's just another *kaffir*, that's all. A bit more stubborn, perhaps, but no different from any of the others. It's late. Go home, now, get some sleep. Tomorrow is another day.

Van Owen counted ten, slowly. He turned around and put his hand on the doorknob. And found that he could not summon up the nerve to turn it. He tried to force his mind to order his hand to open the door. His forearm shook with the effort, the muscles standing out, the knuckles of his fingers white. The doorknob moved slightly. He could not bring himself to open it.

"*Gerhardt!*" he screamed.

There was no answer. He tore his hand away from the doorknob and smashed his fist into the wood. The skin on his knuckles broke. "*Damn!*"

Cradling his bleeding fist in his other hand, Van Owen staggered over to the cot and kicked it, savagely.

"Wake up, you bloody bastard! *Wake up!*"

Van Owen backed away from the crumpled man, who had begun stirring slightly. His blue eyes were wild as they stared from the prisoner to the door. Jesus Christ, Van Owen, he thought to himself, get a grip on yourself. You're going loony. He ground his fists into his forehead, shaking like a stunned bull. His legs were unsteady.

One eighty-seven slowly, painfully, managed to lift part of his upper body off the floor. He squinted at Van Owen through swollen eyelids. One hand wandered, jerkily, to the spot on his ribs where Van Owen had booted him.

"*On your feet!*"

One eighty-seven dragged himself to a sitting position. He was not a big man. Thin. Bony. Going bald. He could have been either twenty-five or sixty. His ravaged tongue poked out of his mouth and licked at his split lips.

"Well," he said, in a deep African voice. "If it isn't my old friend. Mr. Van Owen. And how are you this fine day?" He labored to get the words out, breathing deeply.

"So," sneered Van Owen, "you can talk, after all, you black son of a bitch. You know who I am, do you?"

"You are," one eighty-seven paused, "*Mister* Van Owen."

"I'll mister you, by God. Open that door!"

The black man stared at him. "I take it, I am free to go, then?"

"OPEN THE BLOODY DOOR!"

The scream almost ripped Van Owen's vocal chords asunder. He stood there, holding his damaged fist, shoulders rising and falling with each breath. One eighty-seven looked at him, meeting his gaze. Then, his face like a death mask, he smiled.

"You open it, white man."

Van Owen leapt forward and kicked one eighty-seven full force in the face. Blood spurted onto his combat boot. Van Owen's face was ugly. It was the face of a man who had killed. And would kill again.

One eighty-seven coughed and hacked, spat blood, and tried several times, unsuccessfully, to use his arms to prop himself back up. Failing in this, he turned over on his back and stared at his inquisitor. A large piece of bone protruded from a break in the skin on his nose. He looked barely human.

"You are strong, man. Very strong." He coughed and wheezed. "Why don't you kill me and get it over with?"

"You'd like that, wouldn't you," Van Owen said with quiet malice. "I won't give you that satisfaction. You'll wish you *were* dead when I get through with you!"

"Such a strong man," croaked one eighty-seven, "and, yet, so very much afraid."

Van Owen unholstered his revolver, an American Smith and Wesson Model 66. The stainless steel magnum looked huge in his fist as the bore swung toward one eighty-seven.

"Ever take a couple, *kaffir*?" Seeing the look in the man's eyes, Van Owen added, "I won't kill you, you know. The first one goes in your foot. The next, right in the kneecap. If you think you know what pain is, my friend, I promise you, you've only just begun to learn."

One eighty-seven struggled to rise to a sitting position. After several false tries, he made it. "I don't think I can move any more, Van Owen," he said. "You're going to have to shoot me."

"You'll move, all right. Now, open that door."

"I . . . all right." He sighed, heavily. "All right. I'll try."

Dragging himself with his hands, one eighty-seven began to crawl across the floor.

"Come on, come on. . . ."

It took an eternity, it seemed, for him to reach the door, but reach it he did. His hand raised itself up, limply, moving like the neck of a dying swan. His hand clasped the doorknob. Turned.

The door came ajar. One eighty-seven let go of the knob and dragged himself back a bit. Then, taking hold of the door itself, near the floor, he pulled it inward, into the room, opening it fully. Van Owen stood so that he could not see out through the doorway.

"Tell me what you see!"

One eighty-seven looked at him through the slits of ruined eyes. He was not defeated. Cagey caution prevailed, even while the confusion remained. He answered slowly, literally. "I see the hallway . . . a chair, made out of wood . . . a ceiling light. . . ."

Van Owen rushed to the door. It was true. The hall was empty and silent, save for the muted buzzing of a fluorescent bulb. He stepped outside, uneasily. A light burned at the far end of the hall—his office. There was the halting clicking of a typewriter as Gerhardt stumbled through the latest in the series of reports Van Owen submitted daily, weekly, unceasingly, it seemed, on the heretofore mute one eighty-seven. Van Owen rubbed his hand against his damp forehead and grinned. He could handle it. It was nothing new. Lapses of reality under stress, resulting in hallucinations. He'd slapped men out of them before.

"So much for holier-than-thou, old son," he murmured.

Machine-gun fire didn't faze him, but messiahs are unsettling. An emaciated, battered black messiah. Interesting casting. Up till now, a troublemaking *kaffir*. Up till now. He gazed back at the almost motionless form half sitting on the floor inside the cell.

"You're a wonder, you are, son." He pointed an accusatory finger at the black man. "And you won't sneak up on me, again."

One eighty-seven stared back at him, uncomprehending.

"You don't know what I'm talking about, do you, my little *klonkie*?" There was no answer. "Mmm. It's just as well. We'll dance some more, you and I, only next time, I'll play a different tune."

Van Owen slammed the door on the numberless cell. His last sight of one eighty-seven was that same composed, curious, unblinking stare. No sound came from behind the door.

There was no sound in the hall. The erratic sound of typing had ceased with the slamming of the door.

"All right, Gerhardt," he called, "just leave it on my desk. You can finish it off tomorrow."

There was no reply. The door remained closed.

"Gerhardt! Gerhardt, are you deaf, man?" The fluorescent tube seemed to buzz more loudly. "*Bliksem,*" Van Owen muttered, "bastard." Thirty paces brought him to the door. He wrenched it open. . . .

One eighty-seven was halfway onto the cot. His upper body slumped face-down upon the filthy canvas; his waist and legs trailed behind him on the floor like so much shapeless protoplasm. Mechanically, the head lifted and slowly swiveled in his direction.

It had returned. The same feeling he had known during those nights in the Sinai, in the jungles of Cambodia, in the alleys of Marseilles. It was as though someone or something leaned against him, exerting a great pressure, and his limbs tingled and lost all strength.

His eyes narrowed, involuntarily attempting to shut out the unacceptable reality. It was a struggle to get the words out past the constriction in his throat.

"How . . . are . . . you . . . doing . . . this . . . to me?" Van Owen gurgled. He moved towards the black man, sluggishly. Fingers working with spastic jerks. Fire in the lungs. "Do you think you can play with me like those stupid black animals in the fields? You think I'll fall for your martyr's juju? Your witch doctor shenanigans?"

Van Owen reached forward, grasping the prisoner by the neck and hauling him almost to his feet. "I won't take any more of your shit, *kaffir!*" he screamed, using his full force to hurl the man against the wall.

One eighty-seven hit with a soft thump, like a heavily stuffed pillow. He slid down onto the floor. There was defiant hatred in his eyes.

"*What are you doing to me, goddamnit, what are you doing?*" Van Owen screamed, kicking him in the ribs again and again.

The black man seemed to be beyond pain. Yet not beyond acceptance. "What *can* I do to you?" he rasped, genuine incredulity in his voice.

Van Owen stopped. His face was white. The purest white that it had ever been. His lower lip was trembling. There was an evil weight upon his chest. His eyes began to glaze.

Gerhardt turned the keys in the door, balancing the bowl of slop that passed for prisoners' breakfast in his other hand. The cell was empty. There was no way for the man to have escaped, yet there was no denying the obvious evidence of his senses. Gerhardt gave the alarm.

Van Owen could not be reached. Van Owen could not be found. The guards at Robben Island drew their own conclusions. Only, they never spoke them aloud. Nothing was ever said, no agreement ever reached, no paperwork crossed anybody's desk. Another prisoner was placed into the cell, his number entered onto official records. The matter passed from memory.

In a dark room on Robben Island, just off the coast of the mainland, near Capetown, a man with no name hung manacled from the ceiling. Sweat streamed from his pores, every one of which was open and screaming.

A man sat against the far wall of the cell. Blood trickled from the corner of his mouth. Van Owen had bitten through his tongue.

Jack Dann is no stranger to either fantasy or science fiction. Although much of his enviable reputation lies in the latter field, I believe that his skills are nowhere more apparent than when he hones characterization and situation into a knife edge for the former. He is also one of the handful of writers who understand that delicate is not necessarily a description of fragile, or necessarily a promise of something sweet.

THE DRUM LOLLIPOP

by Jack Dann

The argument had been going on for an hour. It ebbed, rushed forward, then ebbed again—a steady calculated rhythm. The flow began for the last time; it carried an echo, as if it were being mouthed in a whisper somewhere else.

Frank Harris remained a little ball while the rest of him screamed at his wife. "I can't love you like that. I just don't have it. It isn't there." His voice became strident. "You want something I just can't give you. And I won't." A wand lifted him from his seat and pushed him toward the door, into the hall, past the sunken dining room, and through the pantry.

His wife rushed after him, calling, crying, pleading. She overtook him as he fumbled with the screen-door latch. Slipping her arms around his stomach, she dropped to her knees, her fingers wrapped around his belt for support. It would be useless for him to pull himself out the door; she would hang on, crying, and he might hurt her trying to wrench free. It was an old ploy; it had worked before. The argument was over. Whimpering, she would follow him into the den and tell him that she loved him more than anything in the world.

Upstairs, Maureen put her pick-up sticks away in her toy chest, deep inside, past the toys she did not care about, but she could not find space for the drum. The wands were safe, but the drum, she thought, the drum. Hide it in the closet, in the hamper, under the bed.

"Maureen," her mother called from the foot of the stairs. "Dinner will be ready soon. Clean up your room and come down. Everything's all right now, baby. So come downstairs."

It's broken. A rivulet bubbled under the skin, cracking the taut drumhead. Leave it on the bed. It's broken. She centered it on the pillow, controlled her tears, and calmly went downstairs to eat.

They ate quietly. Maureen played with her food, drawing circles in the corn, and thought about her drum. It would be better to leave it there and make something else. She would never touch it again; she would curl around it when she slept and protect it.

She looked at her father, who was ponderously eating a muffin. She never protected him. She wasn't supposed to. He was supposed to protect her. *I want you to love me the way I love you.* "What's that mean, Mommy?" The wands sang in the toy chest.

"What's what mean, honey?" she asked as she stacked the plates. "Give me your plate."

She's cold. She's like that dead lizard. The drum on the bed. The drum is on the bed. "Nothing. Can I go back to my room and play?"

"No, dear. You've been in your room too long today. You should go out for a little while, at least. It won't be dark for another two hours yet."

Her father left the table.

"Okay." Maureen left everything as it was before. The drum was heavy on the bed. The pick-up sticks hovered in their nook. The dolls were faceless, carelessly thrown about the room. They would be all right. But the drum was cracked. The air pushed inside it. She could leave the house, but this time she would not build a bridge as she left. She reconsidered: a very small one without spokes, or beams, or spongy girders.

She could feel the tension grow behind her. She sat down under a tall oak in the back yard and stared at the white stucco house. Dumbly, it stared back at her through its second-story windows.

But I love you. In my own way. I have always thought of our relationship as something beautiful, something sacred. But I can't love you that way. You're like a daughter to me.

Start with a fence, a white picket fence. Draw a fence around the house. No, that isn't any good. Okay. Eight dogs in the driveway with pointed teeth to protect the house. She laughed: she could not visualize a dog. They looked like horned doughnuts. Pointed teeth, not square teeth.

Closing her eyes, she let her thoughts form around the drum, puffing air each time she slapped it. She shuddered. It was not the drum. It was not a wand. She had drawn something she had never seen. It escaped from her. It settled in the living room, hiding behind transparent walls. The fence collapsed and she stood up. She could not see it; she did not want to see it. She took a step toward the house. And then another: it was fun to be scared.

It was not in the pantry. She passed the washing machine and opened the door into the kitchen. The kitchen was empty. The hall, to the right, down three stairs, there it was. A half image of its substance was concentrated in a tiny puddle. It oozed and grew and contracted. It tossed stimuli of coagulation, vomit, and infection at her as it settled into a scarred asterisk. It was brown, then ocher flecked with black. It grew tentacles and digested itself.

Maureen turned away from it. It pulled her back, enticing her, flooding her. She hated it; it grew fangs.

She could not hear anyone in the house. They were probably upstairs. But why didn't she know? The puddle turned her around and began to disappear, leaving only an aura of warmth. It expanded, engulfing Maureen in a thousand pinpoints of heat. She was free; it did not hold her. But she did not want to go. There was no need. She could stay. She was in love. It had changed; it smelled pretty.

She felt warm and concealed. The aura was a fire to protect her and color the room. It followed her, tracing patterns in the air, up to her room. There, it spun a web from the walls and cradled the bed, careful not to touch the drum.

She heard a creak from the next room. It was the bed. She visualized her parents clutching each other and jarring the springs. She had never heard that before. They had not done it since she was born.

She listened and fell asleep. The web thickened, then turned into a cocoon.

She was up early the next morning. Her room smelled musty, as if the warmth pouring through the open window had not yet evaporated the dampness. The toy chest was closed. She counted three dolls on the floor. The fourth was hidden under the bed, its stuffed sunflower head ripped off and lying upside down beside the torso.

Holding her breath, she tiptoed down the stairs and jumped three steps into the living room. She could not make out the image of movement that had held her last night. She concentrated on the wavering lines; they became more distinct. She closed her eyes, allowing it to sketch its form on her dark retinal field.

It was a drum. Opening her eyes, she glimpsed the dank puddle decaying in the rug. It changed shape, became a bubbling star. It vibrated and emitted a thin glint of warmth. It was a drum pounding. She reached out and caught it with her finger, pressed it into her palm, and imbibed it slowly. She was happy. But it passed quickly.

She waited. Ordering it into being was futile; begging, coaxing, singing did not work either. She took a few steps toward it; it dimmed into an outline. She imagined it had grown another tentacle. It had.

The drum, get the drum and cover the pick-up sticks. The drum was on her bed, but she could not touch it. She had promised. It is not a drum anymore. She ran out of the living room and up the stairs. Secure in her room, she picked up the drum and examined the torn head. It could not be fixed. She slapped it angrily. A flood of revulsion cascaded up the stairs and into her room. She threw the drum on the bed and held her palms tightly against her eyes. The smell dissipated.

Tapping the drum carefully, she listened for a pop of air. It was not an old drum. It should not have ripped. A glimmer sneaked into the room, a very tiny ray of warmth. She could not see it, but she knew it was close to her. Tapping her drum, she watched the door; she concentrated; she giggled; she tried not to urinate in her pajamas. She had not made the drum and she could not fix it. Another drum would not be the same; she could never make another one like it.

Another glint. But softer, a bit wider. She shuddered as it passed through her.

They were awake. She sensed her parents' blurred awareness. The sensation dissolved. She put the drum on top of her toy chest and stared out the window as they quietly got dressed. The sunlight splashed on the floor, then escaped into the suspended stiffness of the house. She breathed around the dust motes that floated in the yellow liquid. Invisibly, they dropped into the cracks in the floor.

Her mother was downstairs first. The smell of margarine, a whiff of ozone, then eggs, toast, the clatter of the icebox door, the gurgle of water in the pipes. Maureen could not see any of this, but she was happy.

It was dead. Her drum was on the chest. The puddle in the living room couldn't work without the drum. The drum couldn't work without her. It couldn't work without her. She heard her father swear in the bathroom and a slight odor of nausea swept the room. If you cry it will get worse; it will turn black and gore into the rug. She combed her hair back into a ponytail and admired herself in the mirror. The odor thickened. She leaned out the window to feel the warm air, to see the bright morning. Don't think about the drum. Leave it on the chest. Torn. Leave it alone. It's not there.

She could not smell the cooking odors—they were lost in the heavy waves of nausea rolling into the room. Thicker. Pulling her into the room, stabbing into her mouth and nose, plucking her insides until they strained to vomit. But she could not vomit. She could not take her eyes from the drum, now wavering in sympathy. She could rake the drum, pull its head off, tear the wood into splinters, crack the plastic shoulder strap into red squares.

She lunged toward the toy chest, but found she was still by the window. She was crying, then laughing, then clenching her teeth, dreaming of fangs, and hating everything in the room, especially the drum. She felt her mother forced into her. She could not close her pores; they were gaping holes. She was naked. Her mother. A swill of anger and screaming, a flattened mask of tenderness. A doll yellowed with years, cracking, pulling taut. She screamed at everything that had been taken away. Inside, her mother swelled, tantalizing with promises of depth, promises of emotions yet unfelt, thoughts to tingle her spine, sensations greater than herself. But they were only surface reflections.

Forcing her mother out, she reached for her father. She shrank back, and he did not embrace her. He was heavy; he would have smothered her. She snatched at his face, clawing off a piece of withered skin. She gouged at him, concentrating her hatred into her fingers. Stop it. Go away. She looked at the clawed image of her father and began to cry. Go away. She concentrated on the drum; it reflected the puddle downstairs. Change into something else. She visualized animals, trees, designs on bedspreads, dolls' faces, colored pictures. The clot of substance in the living room remained unaffected. You can't change it; you didn't make it. The clot wavered and distorted the wall behind it. I did, she thought. I made it, I made it. She grabbed the drum and ran out of the room. I didn't make the drum; I don't care about it.

She stood on the stairs, her drum nestled in her arm. She could not make the puddle disappear. Concentrating on its imagined shape, she destroyed it in her mind. It remained unaffected. Have to make it go away. She wanted to scream, cry, run to her mother basking in the smells of the kitchen.

She looked at the drum. She was calm, suddenly very old. It bubbled; she snatched at it and it popped. She was very warm and sad. She sat down on the stairs, her legs extended. A golden thread crawled up the stairs and she caught it between her fingers and imbibed it with a pop.

Thoughts of crying and shouting became remote. It was a game. It was fun to be scared. She was flooded with warmth. Loving threads crawled up the stairs, flashing, protecting her, laughing with her, suddenly sad, but pleasantly sad.

"Call your father; breakfast is ready." Her mother stood in the hall below. She looked relaxed; a slight smile twitched at the corners of her lips and then dissolved. "When did you break your drum? It's almost brand-new, and you've already broken it. Were you banging it with a stick? It's made to be hit only with your fingers, not with a stick. Well, it's not any good now. Take it downstairs and throw it away."

"Okay. But do I have to do it now?"

"Now. This minute. Throw it in the wastebasket in the kitchen."

She could not throw it away yet. It would start all over again: the vomit, the smell, teeth, claws, kicking, pulling, hitting, crying, punching, hating. No, I won't throw it away.

She threw it away, her mother before her, her father behind her. And in a rush.

Nothing happened. She ate breakfast and went out to play under a tree, ate her lunch, studied the puddle in the living room—now a tan stain in the rug—played under the tree for a few more hours, tried to draw things in her mind, thought about the drum and the protean stain. The stain was still there, bubbling unnoticed, but the drum—that was hidden in the garbage.

Maureen waited for something to happen. She spent each day under the tree and watched the house. The stain remained in the living room, unobserved by the rest of the family, including Uncle Milton who dropped over at least once a week. She did not think about the drum anymore; she had not made it.

She forgot about being scared. It was a game, like the others, and she had used it up. But she could not make anything, not even a bridge or a fence. The smear in the living room had taken everything from her. Now she could only work with tangibles. It muffled everything around her; she could not sense words or people.

Slowly things began to change. There were no more marital clashes; her mother and father were falling in love. They held hands, whispered in the bedroom, bounced on the springs, and went out on Saturday night. Even Uncle Milton began dropping in more often; he claimed it was the only place where he could relax.

The laundryman came twice that week. He said he had forgotten that he already collected the laundry.

And the telephone man repaired the wires twice.

And the stain assumed an honest shape. Maureen had been outside when it became active. She had learned to use her hands, but it was not the same. The drum was lost: She had relinquished all control. She was making mud pies in the rain. This would be her last mud batter: she was getting too old for mud pies.

Shouting, "Mother, come and see," she ran into the house, her hands and lacquered boots covered with mud. Through the pantry, kitchen, dead-end in the den, up three stairs into the hall, and there they were in the living room. Why hadn't she looked there first? Because it's there now. It's working. She shrugged off a familiar sensation; everything seemed clearer.

The room was red—she had not noticed that for a long time. A fake stone fireplace was propped against the far wall for decoration. A large mirror hung directly above it, reflecting a fat velvet sofa and an oil painting of the family. A glass table, chairs, a few pieces of crystal, maroon curtains, and a red plush carpet completed the scene.

The tentacled asterisk was visible. It palpitated in front of the fireplace. It had grown four more tentacles, and its black speckles had turned to crusted sores oozing goo into the air. It was radiating long thin yellow spokes of love all over the room. It threw a few wisps at Maureen, but she stepped aside, only to see her mother and father sitting sleepily on the companion rocking chair near the entrance to the dining room. Bathing in love, they held hands across the doorway.

A wisp of yellow settled on Maureen's braid, hung loose, dropped to her shoulder, and disappeared into her crinoline dress. She felt a burst of security, a cushion of warmth. As she stepped into the living room, the doorbell rang.

"Darling," her mother said, "would you get the door?"

Maureen opened the door for Uncle Milton. He marched into the house, beads of sweat gleaming on his bald pate. Skimming a line of perspiration from his barely visible mustache, he said, "How's my Maureen? Jesus, what the hell happened to you? Fall into a hole? You've ruined that pretty dress. Better go tell your mother. Wait a minute. You're getting tall, almost as tall as me." He puffed his stomach out. "Where's Mom and Dad? In the den?"

She shook her head and pointed toward the living room. She stood in the hall; she did not want to go into the room just yet. And the mud was sticky.

"Maureen," her mother said, "go upstairs and take a bath. And leave that dress in the bathroom. You can put your pajamas on when you're done. Then you can come down and join us."

Yes, Mommy, I'm covered with fuzz, closed in the room, I don't care. Into the bath, peel off the mudskin, no bra yet, red dress in the hamper. A few threads wiggled under the door to keep her company and burst in her hair.

She washed quickly, jumped into her pajamas, and tiptoed into the living room. No one noticed her entrance. The room had turned gray, but it was gradually building up strength. She breathed strength into it. She could feel, taste, hear.

"You know," Uncle Milton said, "I don't know what it is, but I feel so comfortable here lately."

"Sure you do," her mother said, her smile drawing back her thin lips.

"Well, there were a few times when I thought I would have to let you sign those separation papers."

Everyone laughed. It did not have to be funny: it felt good. Maureen sat on the rug, her blond hair untied, enjoying the feel of everything and everyone.

Outside, the noises trickled in. Maureen heard them first. *Leggo, oh, here, eat it then. Too warm tonight, doesn't matter —feels good. I don't know why, just felt like coming over. Relax. Get dark in a while. Put that dirty handkerchief away.*

"Mommy, hear the people outside the house? They're on our lawn. Sounds funny. Hey, Johnny Eaton's mother's out there. Johnny's coming too."

"I don't hear anything," Uncle Milton said, staring at the new tentacles growing out of the asterisk. It readied itself for another burst of energy, its suckers grasping for support. It emitted a gurgling noise, but no one seemed to notice. Contracting, it threw off a puddle of phlegm and radiated full force. The yellow bars passed through the soft walls and wallowed in the grass and people outside. Uncle Milton poured himself another drink, spilling a jigger as a strong wisp passed into his throat.

"Four more people, Mommy. Mr. Richardson and his kid Wally and Mr. and Mrs. Allen from Snow Street. Remember them? They gave us all those vegetables last summer."

It grew, then fell back on itself, preparing for another surge through friendly streets and houses.

Maureen closed her eyes and drew pictures. She could see the lines clearly, only a little fuzz where she could not remember a color. Johnny, look in your pocket, fingers around it, matches there too, don't worry how, let it go, under the tree, there. The colors were darker than she imagined. It's getting late.

"That sounded like a firecracker, didn't it?" her father said. "Sounded like a pretty big one too."

"Could have been a backfire," Uncle Milton said. He leaned back into the couch, hands folded, eyes closed. He inhaled a flood of love, soft clouds perspired by the asterisk. He giggled with contentment.

"No," her mother said, standing inside the curtains and peering out the jalousied window into the front yard. "Why, it's that Johnny Whatshisname. He's playing with firecrackers. And no one's even paying any attention to it."

"Johnny Eaton," Maureen said.

"Yes, Maureen's right; there are over twenty people on our lawn. Look, Mr. Logos is waving at me. It's a regular picnic. They've even got blankets and radios."

Maureen watched the slick tentacles growing out of the asterisk. Better not wait, do it now. Be too late soon. Where's the drum?

The room turned yellow with love, thick strong rays that rolled over the carpet, too heavy to float. And out through the walls. Uncle Milton was asleep. He turned over, burying his face in the soft velvet of the sofa.

"Strange we're in the living room," her father said. "Usually I prefer the den."

Sandra Harris sat down on the floor beside her husband's chair, rested her head on his knee and said, "I guess it doesn't matter if they stay on the lawn. I'm too lazy to bother. Frank, I'm glad everything's settled. Better than before. Frank. Do you see something on the rug? There, in the middle of the room, in front of the fireplace. Jesus, it's ugly. Frank. Frank. I think I can smell it. Can you smell it?"

Maureen faced the wall and stared through minute cracks into other cracks that led outside. Don't look or it'll happen. Can't happen behind me, isn't there. Can't see it.

It equalized the pressure in the room and bathed Sandra Harris. She rested her head on her husband's lap and said, "I love you."

He didn't flinch. Stroking her face, he said, "I know you do. And I love you too." He yawned and fell asleep. It was dark outside. A few candles flickered in the yard and the street light glowed dimly.

Uncle Milton stayed the night. He slept on the sofa, clutching a pillow. He said he felt so good he would stay another day. And another night. Until it turned into a week. And the front yard population grew until it covered the back yard. They brought pup tents, Coleman stoves, guitars, a green water hose, and more relatives and friends. They packed themselves into the yard until everyone was in some sort of physical contact with the others. No one minded. It was good. It was pure. It was in friendship and love.

Maureen's mother and father tacitly agreed not to talk about the neighbors that had suddenly moved in. The neighbors pressed their faces against the windows and smiled. Uncle Milton periodically yelled at them in good humor.

Maureen did not like it. She knew the ending, only she did not realize it.

Until the next day. It was early in the morning; breakfast was bubbling in a greased frying pan, sunlight was streaming in the kitchen windows, and Maureen was catnapping in the living room. Uncle Milton had been ordered to sleep in her room, cutting off access to the pick-up sticks and drum, almost grown.

Her mother stepped into the living room as she untied her red apron. The asterisk became active; it stretched its tentacles across the carpet. "Come on, honey. Help Mommy get the food on."

"Do I have to do it now?" she asked. Don't let her look at

it. It wants her to see it. Protect her. But she moves, she walks, she says things. Something's burned out or burned in. Not real enough.

"Is that a stain on the rug over there? What is it?"

Maureen was locked into the room. The asterisk bubbled, smiled at her by raising its tentacles, passed a beam into her, a shaft of glass connecting her to it. She loved her mother now, very clearly. All the fond remembrances became real; they flowed through the beam. A reassuring drum thumped upstairs. Her mother was beautiful. All her age lines were lifted; her fair faded into gray.

"It's ugly." Her mother watched it spellbound. "I seem to remember seeing it last night. Like a dream. Fell asleep with your father. I can't think." She stepped backward and screamed. It drew itself into a ball, squelched half its substance to the side, stank, decayed a bit, and shot a beam of love right into her heart. It thickened and held her by the liver and collarbone.

"Mother, don't touch it. Leave it alone." She changed the picture. Nothing happened. She could not move. Mother is beautiful, she thought. Long beautiful hair. "Mother, you are beautiful. I have long hair just like yours. Yours is prettier. Daddy loves your hair. I know he loves your hair."

Her mother's hand sank into the porous putrescent mass, into the heart of it. She looked at her daughter, her face a landscape of disgust and fear. She smiled her special loving smile and retched as it took her arm with its tentacles.

"Mother, I love you," Maureen cried. She felt too content to move. Her mother smiled at her again, overcome with love and revulsion. She was halfway into it: half mother, half blob. She became a distorted Greek legend squirming with love. Her face snapped in rictus, a mask of fright and love. Maureen could only watch. She loved her mother. "You are beautiful, Mother."

It belched and flattened itself on the rug. She could not smell it.

She finished the picture. Father came downstairs and tripped over a tentacle, waving bye-bye. She drew it quickly. It was easier that way. She could construct the memory later. She wanted the full bloom of love now.

Uncle Milton departed with a loving frown. She did not say good-bye. He had never really been.

The asterisk was perfect, fully grown, carefully tended by

its retinue of self. It spurted pus into the air. It was a cereal-box sun radiating cereal-box love.

The drum was upstairs. She ran into her room, found the drum on her toy chest, and carried it downstairs. Before she could reach the living room, it disappeared.

It was late. She had to get on with it. Now. For Mother. And Father. And maybe Uncle Milton.

Outstretching her palms, she walked toward the trembling star, measuring her steps with its palpitations. Sliding her hands under it, she lifted it into the air. It hung between her fingers.

She took it inside her; she ate it, she osmosed it; she transformed it. She felt it in her eyes, a heaviness, a largeness that could span anything, envision everything—with love.

Dream the dream, paint the picture. It's all in the cereal box ready to eat. Can't be changed now. The drum's disappeared again. You had the chance.

She opened the door carefully, squinting her oval eyes at the morning sun.

And everyone was there. Standing. Smiling. Laughing.

George W. Proctor is a Texan, an artist, a writer. He described the idea for the following story to me over the telephone during a conversation about something entirely different. I was intrigued and asked him to write it for this volume, and write it he did. The artist is here as well, a blending of two careers that provides a depth to the literal and psychological horrors and a realism to something that does not, of necessity, have to be supernatural.

THE GOOD IS OFT INTERRED

by George W. Proctor

Edging the velvet drapery farther aside, Gregory Broussard stared at the man partially hidden by a line of limousines parked in the circular driveway. Greater window area failed to enhance his perception.

Head bent atop rounded shoulders, arms dangling at his sides, the man outside the house stood quietly. He wore the clothing of a skid-row derelict: threadbare trousers, frayed sweater, and a tattered shirt. Sweat and dirt stained a hat that shadowed his face.

Disgust moved within Broussard. The man did nothing, just stood there. His mere presence violated the sanctity of the ground on which he stood.

An indefinable pressure squeezed across Broussard's chest. Animosity awoke, the inexplicable hatred that sparks between strangers when one senses a vulnerability existing within the other. It was the primordial instinct that draws a predator to its prey and leaves the weaker dead at the other's feet. Broussard relished the sensation, savored it.

"Are you certain he asked for me, Thomas?" Broussard turned from the window and faced his butler.

"He stated that you were acquainted during the war."

Nam? Everyone Broussard knew in the army had died in Vietnam, except Bill. Now William Favor was dead.

"He said to inform you that it was a matter of utmost urgency," Thomas concluded.

Nothing the man outside knew could possibly be of any consequence to Broussard. "I've never seen him before. Thomas, my guests will be leaving soon. I don't want him here when they do."

The butler stepped toward the door.

"Thomas, if he won't leave, call James." The image of the stranger cowering before the black chauffeur amused him.

The telephone rang. The butler redirected his steps down the mahogany-paneled hall. Broussard watched him with appreciation. Thomas was efficiency personified. Broussard would not tolerate less in himself or in others. Now that Bill could no longer interfere, Favor-Broussard, Inc., would be staffed as it should have been at its inception. Only those who could keep pace with Gregory Broussard would stay.

"Sir, a Miss Dunsmoor." Broussard glanced at the butler, uncertain that he had heard correctly. Thomas repeated, "A Miss Dunsmoor."

Broussard accepted the telephone and pressed it to his chest until the butler exited through the front door. Pushing the drapery aside, he watched Thomas walk down the steps to the waiting man.

The intruder turned to Thomas. The outside lights washed away the shadow of his hat brim for an instant. Broussard's pulse increased. There was something familiar yet totally alien about the face. He recognized it, but in the same moment he knew that he had never seen the man before.

His eyes clamped closed tightly, attempting to blot out the disturbing visage. Each detail of the face remained imprinted on his mind. Swollen and puffy, crevice-deep wrinkles creased the man's features. And the features themselves—they did not match. One eye stood wide and wild; the other was a mere slit. The mouth uplifted at one corner, while the other corner drooped to a knotty chin. A shudder of revulsion ran through Broussard.

"Greg? Hello? Greg, are you there?"

A woman's voice wedged into his thoughts. He lifted the receiver to his ear. "Yvonne?"

"Greg, is everything all right?" The concern in Yvonne's voice, like everything else about the young woman, was genuine.

"Just a minor problem." A calm spread through Broussard. "Hey, where are you calling from?"

"Home. The conference concluded a day early," she answered. "I missed you."

"A week is too long without you."

Since the young high school art teacher walked into his office six months ago, Broussard had learned the meaning of love. Before Yvonne it had only been a word that belonged in popular novels.

"I've nothing planned this weekend," she said. She did not ask to see him. She never made demands. "Time we should take advantage of."

"I was hoping you'd say that." He felt the warmth of her imagined smile.

"I love you, Greg. I . . . ."

"Gregory?" Grace's voice reverberated through the hall.

Broussard looked over his shoulder to find his wife by the living room door. He cupped a palm over the phone's mouthpiece. "It's a business call."

"We have guests." An impatient hand rested on Grace's hip.

"I'll be there when I can." He made no attempt to disguise his contempt. Turning his back on her, he listened to the crack of her heels on the tiled floor when she retreated. Despite three years of marriage, Grace remained a Rothyme. Like her father, Hadley Rothyme, she did not enjoy being defied. Broussard uncovered the mouthpiece. "I'm back."

"I shouldn't have called you at home," Yvonne said softly.

"Nonsense! Grace is entertaining a few friends. You've brightened what had all the appearances of being a dismal weekend." Outside, Thomas still talked with the intruder. What was taking him so long? "Can I interest you in a late dinner?"

"Tonight? What about Grace?"

"When the guests leave, she intends to drive to Springer Lake and visit her father for a couple of days," Broussard replied. "I believe I can find a use for every moment of your weekend."

"The whole weekend?" The distance separating them did not diminish Yvonne's surprise. "Greg, I can't imagine anything better."

Neither can I." Things had been hectic since Bill Favor's suicide. He needed time off. No one and no thing provided the renewed sense of life he drew from Yvonne. "I'll call you when she leaves."

"The minute you're free," she said emphatically.

The phone clicked. Broussard smiled, anticipating the moment when he once more would hold Yvonne close. The phone clicked again. "Hello? Is there anyone there?"

No answer came. Broussard placed the receiver onto the cradle and frowned. Grace? No. Grace would never suspect another woman. She was a Rothyme: What man needed more? Yet someone had been on the line. Who? He pushed the question away, realizing that a guest had picked up one of the extensions to find the phone in use.

He glanced back out the window. The stranger nodded at Thomas and then started toward the street. The man halted to look back. His gaze homed on Broussard, framed behind the window.

Something squirmed within Broussard. He tried to move, to break away from that gaze, but he couldn't.

A broad grin moved across the man's mismatched face. Broussard felt his hands and his body shake. He could not divert his eyes from that knowing grin, as though the man outside shared some secret buried deep in Broussard's subconscious.

No! Broussard railed against the soul-probing gaze. The man knew nothing. He had never seen him until tonight. How could he know anything? No one knew; no one suspected.

Broussard heard the door open. The man outside pulled his hat brim lower and walked onto the street. Every muscle in Broussard's body went flaccid. His arms shot out to the windowsill; he caught himself before his legs gave way.

"Mr. Broussard!" Thomas's arms locked about his employer's chest in support. "Are you all right?"

Broussard released the sill to stand on his own. He nodded to the butler. "That last drink was more potent than I realized."

Thomas stared questioningly but said nothing.

Broussard took a deep breath and then started down the hall to the guests. His body still trembled. Only once in his life had he experienced what he had sensed in the man's gaze. It had come in 1974 during a reconnaissance patrol along the Song Ba River, when a hand grenade fell from the jungle above him. Neither before nor since, until caught by the stranger's eyes, had he felt fear that dominated and controlled his whole being.

He stopped, remembering Yvonne's call. "Thomas, please inform the other servants that they may have the weekend off after Mrs. Broussard's departure this evening."

Thomas simply nodded.

"And Thomas, should that man ever return, call the police."

"Yes, sir," Thomas answered as Broussard entered the living room.

Without a glance to Grace, who stood chatting with a mincing little man, Broussard walked to the bar. He poured himself a double scotch and inhaled it in one swallow. He waited a moment, allowing the alcohol's warmth to quell the last of his tremblings.

Another double in hand, he surveyed the room. Since Vietnam, he had strived to be in the exact position in which he now stood, removing any obstacle that separated him from his goal. Now he found it difficult to stifle a yawn while he perused the guests. They were children, the pampered rich, cushioned from reality by "family" wealth. He had learned the rules to their games, the correct smiles, the meaningless words. Like Grace, like Bill Favor, they were a means to an end, to be discarded when they had served their purpose. The money, the doors it opened—those were his desires.

Bill had introduced him to the world of *real* money and power. Grace, through the Rothyme fortune, had provided the first taste of what wealth meant. When Bill died and the agency was completely under his control, he finally possessed the means to achieve his desires. All he needed was another year, perhaps two. Then there would be no further reason to endure these spoiled children.

For now, he maintained the required image.

He made his first stop at the sofa and a discourse on the merits of this and that playwright, director, and actor. After the necessary comments, thoughtful nods, and agreeing smiles, he maneuvered across the room to the fireplace, carefully avoiding the women congregated near a wall tapestry. The group remained off limits to men. The "tryst exchange" he dubbed it, where women shared and compared the attributes of their latest lovers. Once he had been tempted to sample its available pleasures. That was before Yvonne.

Suitably bemoaning the libertarian trends among American authors with the fireplace literary circle, Broussard moved to the "I just returned from" group that hovered near a table laid with trays of hors d'oeuvres. From there he slipped over to the "barracudas." Carefully, he listened to the gossip and character-assassinating innuendoes, never adding to the conversation. He could not risk being labeled the source of petty slander.

Returning to the bar, he glanced at his watch. Midnight, two hours since Yvonne's call. He reached for the decanter of scotch and then changed his mind. The last thing he wanted was to meet Yvonne with four sheets to the wind.

"Sorry to hear about Bill." A man's voice came from Broussard's side. He glanced around to find Paul Blackwater, one of Bill Favor's old friends, nursing a glass of wine. "He was a good man."

Broussard arranged his expression into a somber mask. The pain reflected in his eyes was no more difficult to achieve than the smiles he had used moments ago. "He was the best of friends. It's still hard to accept."

His last words quavered, the perfect touch to express the loss expected of him. But there was no loss, only gain. Bill Favor had offered him full partnership in the agency not out of friendship or sense of duty but to exploit his talents. In the end, the innocent patsy had turned the tables.

"Have they found anything more? For a man to place a pistol in his mouth and . . ." Blackwater said with a slow shake of his head.

"Only the note about pressures mounting beyond endurance. I never had any indication that anything was wrong. Even when Bill sold his share of the agency to me, I didn't realize he was troubled." Broussard had not foreseen the suicide, but there were no regrets. It made things easier. Bill could no longer interfere with his plans.

"Seems I recall Bill mentioning that you saved his life once in Vietnam." Blackwater sipped his wine.

Broussard's hand tightened around the empty highball glass. Once again, he stood in the dense jungle along the Song Ba. Overhead the foliage rustled.

"Sniper!" Kingston swung his rifle up to fire two bursts.

Broussard never saw the target. His gaze hung on a dark object that had dropped at his feet: a grenade. Fear solidly knotted his body. For an eternity, he stared mutely at death come to claim him.

He heard a scream, his own. His body responded. Arms wide, he flung himself on Kingston and Bill, hurtling them down the riverbank.

Then an exploding freight train plowed into his side, and there was oblivion.

When he awoke in a Tokyo hospital, the doctors told him he had died; at least his heart had stopped for three minutes during an operation to remove a piece of shrapnel lodged between the aorta and a pulmonary artery.

Bill came through the incident without a scratch. Kingston had not been as lucky. Shrapnel slammed into his temple, and he had died instantly.

For Broussard, except for the scars along the left side of his chest, the doctors declared him good as new. The army gave him a bronze star and a ticket home.

They had been wrong. Between the Song Ba and Tokyo, Gregory Broussard changed. He came away from the army better than new, stronger. He had been a sleeper; now he was awake, ready to take from life those things he had only dreamed of before. He saw the world as it was—those who used and those who were used. He had paid his dues in the latter category.

When Bill received his discharge, he found Broussard working in the lower echelons of a national advertising firm. With "family" money and Broussard's talent, Bill established Favor-Broussard.

"Greg? Greg?" Blackwater nudged his shoulder, jarring Broussard from his memories. "Is there anything wrong?"

Broussard smiled sheepishly. Tonight his mind had weaved back to the Song Ba twice. "Just recalling things Bill and I did in Nam, things I thought I had forgotten."

The image of the stranger standing by the driveway inched into Broussard's consciousness as he watched Blackwater join the "barracudas." The unexploded grenade superimposed over the mismatched face. Broussard's legs went rubbery. Sweat, cold and heavy, the sweat of fear, prickled over his body. The grenade, the man's face.

"Our guests are leaving. Will you see them off with me?" Grace pressed her side along his.

Releasing his breath, he looked at his wife. Her earlier icy edge had melted with a liberal dose of gin. He ignored her when she slipped an arm around him. He walked to the hall with her clinging to him and performed the needed rituals of departure.

When the last couple had exited, Grace called to Thomas, "Tell James I'll be ready to leave in an hour."

The butler nodded and left husband and wife alone in the hall. Grace hugged closer to Broussard. "I appreciate the way you entertained my friends this evening. Can I persuade you to entertain me for the weekend?"

"I've business appointments to attend this weekend." He enjoyed Hadley Rothyme's money, but he could not tolerate the man.

Broussard disentangled Grace's arm from his. Before he could step away, her arms circled his waist with a clinging desperation. Hurt flickered in her eyes.

"I have to go to my room and change for the drive." She nuzzled his shoulder, working toward his neck. "I don't have to leave until the morning. We have the rest of the night."

"At least you had the good taste not to say, 'The night is ours.'" Unlocking her hands, he stepped back, trying to visualize the attractive woman he had married three years before. The outside beauty remained, but beneath was Hadley Rothyme.

"Do you want me to beg?" Tears welled in her eyes. "I love you, Gregory. I want to share your bed again."

"Self-abuse is preferable to sharing a bed with you, my dear." Without another glance at his wife, Broussard pivoted sharply to climb the stairs to the privacy of his bedroom.

An hour later, he watched from a window as the chauffeur drove Grace away for a weekend with her father. Hadley Rothyme. The thought of a photograph-stuffed envelope locked in the safety of a desk drawer drifted through Broussard's mind. He smiled. Did Grace suspect her father's sexual preference?

He grinned. The envelope was an insurance measure. Eventually he would find a use for it, as he had with a similar envelope he had presented to Bill Favor. His grin widened. While "family" wealth offered opportunities, "family" demands and expectations served as a counterbalance. The Favors could never tolerate a son who was less than a man. The photographs of Bill and his pretty-boy lovers were all it took to persuade him to sell his share of the agency.

Brushing aside Bill Favor and Hadley Rothyme, Broussard crossed the room and lifted the phone from a bedside table. Yvonne answered sleepily from the nap he had disturbed, but she was fully awake when he said that he would be at her apartment in a half hour.

Spirits rising in anticipation of the weekend with Yvonne, Broussard moved back downstairs. He found Thomas supervising the servants while they cleaned away the last traces of

Grace's guests. He ordered the butler to bring his car to the front of the house, and in a few minutes he slid behind the wheel of the Jaguar.

"Sir," Thomas said when Broussard gripped the gearshift, "the staff would like to inquire whether you have any objections to their leaving after the house has been straightened. Many of us have families outside the city."

"By all means, tell them to take off tonight."

Broussard shifted into first and eased his foot from the clutch. The car edged forward along the circular driveway. Despite the late hour, Broussard stopped at the gate, checking for traffic. A movement to the left caught his attention. His head turned slightly and froze.

Walking beneath the harsh glow of a streetlight was the stranger, the man Thomas had ordered from the house hours ago.

"Gregory Broussard." The man's voice flowed soft and soothing, yet it grated on Broussard's ears. As with the mismatched features of his face, the man's enunciation held an incongruity. One syllable did not blend with the next. "Gregory, we need to speak."

The man extended a hand. Conflicting urges coursed through Broussard. His hands trembled, as if they wanted to grasp of their own volition.

"No!" Broussard moaned. His fingers locked around the steering wheel. To touch that hand, irrational fear flooded him, to feel that knotty flesh, would. . . . His skin crawled. There was no definition for the fear. Yet he knew. He *knew*!

"Gregory, there's time to correct the error," the man's twisted voice continued. "The Song Ba, Tokyo . . . something happened that. . . ."

The hand grenade, the explosion. Broussard's head jerked away from the stranger. He saw the relationship, understood the man's purpose, his own revulsion. Death! The man was death. To feel his touch. . . .

Broussard's foot slammed the accelerator to the floor. Tires screamed, rubber biting concrete. Broussard risked only one glance into the rear-view mirror as he fled. The man, spotlighted by the street lamp, stood behind him, empty hand reaching out.

"I feel wonderful." Yvonne hugged Broussard when they exited from the restaurant's parking lot.

He bathed in the radiance of her presence. She filled a void in him that he had been unaware of until she was there, overflowing with life.

"Can you believe that six months have passed since the day I walked into your office?" Her green eyes flashed with child-like exuberance.

He squeezed her hand. "I barely noticed you. I was more impressed by your portfolio. The artwork was fantastic!"

It had been. After two months of part-time summer employment, he had offered her a job at three times her teacher's salary. She had turned him down.

"Teaching is what I like," she had said with a shrug of her shoulders. "It's definitely a financial disaster, but it's what I want. It gives me something I've never found elsewhere. I don't know. It's hard to explain."

Had anyone else said that, Broussard would have laughed in his face. But from Yvonne. . . . He could not find the correct words. She gave, and in giving, she received.

Perhaps that was the void she touched within him. Yvonne taught him to give again. When she was beside him, the money, the agency, the things he scrambled after were empty and hollow. Giving, caring, sharing, loving—all the emotions he had discarded on the Song Ba's bank gained new meaning with Yvonne.

The Song Ba. It brought the man outside the house to mind. Nervous relief tickled through Broussard. He felt ashamed. He had reacted to the man like a frightened child. Death personified? The image belonged to overly imaginative, melodramatic literature. The man was a man, nothing more. Death did not walk on two legs, seeking victims.

What could the man want? What did he know about the Song Ba or Tokyo?

"Hey?" Yvonne's voice cut into his thoughts. "This isn't the way to my apartment."

"No." He grinned and shook his head. "Grace is gone, and I've dismissed the servants for the weekend. We'll have the house to ourselves."

Yvonne answered with a hug and then nestled beside him.

A few lights dimly lit the house's interior when they entered. Broussard reached for the light switch, but Yvonne stopped his hand. She waved off a tour of the house and asked directions to his bedroom. The abundance of wealth seemed to have no effect on her. That pleased him. Taking her hand, he led her upstairs.

Ten minutes later, Yvonne lay atop his bed. Crossing the dark room, Broussard drew open the draperies. Moonlight invaded the bedroom, bathing Yvonne's sleek nakedness in gleaming silver. She opened her arms to him.

He came to her slowly, savoring the love and need that glowed within him. Their lips met tenderly.

"It's so right to have you here," he whispered when their mouths parted. "You belong beside me. One day, you'll be here . . . forever."

"Shhhhh." She pressed a finger to his lips. "What we have now is enough."

Urging arms and hands encircled him. He followed her gentle guidance, immersing himself in her soothing warmth.

Lights flared overhead.

A startled cry quavered from Yvonne's throat. More lights exploded, blinding him. A photographic strobe?

"Get out." He heard Grace. "I'll contact you later."

Broussard blinked. Beyond the hovering red glow that dominated his vision, he saw a man dart from the bedroom. Grace glared at him, her face indignant and victorious.

"And you," she said, her gaze shifting between the lovers. "You've got five minutes to get this slut out of my house."

As she stormed from the room, Broussard rose and jerked a robe from the closet. Yvonne looked at him with a dazed uncertainty. She slipped from the bed and reached for her clothes.

"Wait here!" Anger harshened his words. "Grace will leave tonight, not you!"

"But Greg?" Yvonne stared at him blankly.

"Trust me." His tone softened to an assuring caress. "We have nothing to worry about. Please wait."

She hesitated and then nodded. "I'll wait."

Acknowledging her answer with a light kiss, he ran after Grace. He caught his wife at the bottom of the stairs. Grabbing her arm, he yanked her after him.

"What in hell do you think you've accomplished by this?" He pulled her into the study and slammed the door behind them.

"Evidence," she said defiantly when he stepped behind the desk and unlocked the lower drawer. "I've got all I need for a divorce."

He reached into the drawer, found a manila envelope, and tossed it at her feet. "I wouldn't be so certain. I don't believe your father would enjoy it if these fell into the wrong hands."

"My father?" Her haughty confidence sagged for an instant. Hesitantly, she stooped to lift the envelope from the floor.

His pulse quieting, Broussard watched his wife open the sealed flap and extract the first of twenty photographs. Defiance and victory melted from her face. Grace sank into a chair in front of the desk. One by one, she pulled each explicit color print from the envelope.

"They're no more than children," she muttered.

"Hadley Rothyme, community leader, philanthropist." Broussard prolonged the sarcasm of each word. "Who would ever suspect that 'Daddy dear' had a taste for little girls . . . mere children?"

Grace's head rose to him. Defeat and resignation were reflected in her eyes.

"Keep those." Broussard savored the power he held over her. "I've other sets . . . and the negatives, in case you or your father decide to remove me before I'm ready to leave."

"What do you want?" Her voice was trembly, drained of strength.

"Just you, my lovely wife." He walked across the room and softly brushed a fingertip over her cheek. She shuddered. "Eventually, you'll get the divorce. But not until I'm ready. For the moment, I need you and Daddy's money."

She stuffed the photos back into the envelope. Unquestioning, she nodded acceptance of his terms.

"Now, I suggest that you proceed with your weekend visit." He watched her rise and walk to the door. "And Grace, make certain your photographer has all the prints and negatives from tonight on my desk Monday morning. Understand?"

Again she nodded subserviently, and then she left. Broussard grinned. Perhaps it was for the best. Grace understood her position now. All she had to do was play the part of the loving wife for a year or two more.

He moved to a brandy decanter on a bookcase behind the desk. Pouring two swallows into a snifter, he sipped with satisfaction. It would be easier. Yvonne and he would no longer have to steal time together.

A soft smile moved across Broussard's face, erasing the harsh traces of the victory over Grace. Downing the last of the brandy in a single gulp, he walked to the door and flicked off the lights.

A woman's scream rent the house's stillness.

Yvonne! Grace!

He ran while his mind patched together the imagined scenario. He had pushed Grace too far. She had broken. Seeking revenge, she had struck directly at his only vulnerability, Yvonne.

He took the stairs two at a time. The house sat silent now, with no sounds of struggle, no cries, no running feet. The quiet was worse than the screams. Was it over? Had Grace achieved her purpose?

Broussard ran through the open bedroom door and stopped. The room was empty! There was no sign of a struggle, no Grace, no Yvonne.

A muffled groan came from the far side of the bed.

Covering the distance around the bed in less than a heartbeat, Broussard halted. An uninhibited moan of horror pushed from his throat. Yvonne lay on the floor. An angry red gash ran across half her forehead. She moaned again.

She was alive.

Lifting her half-nude body from the floor, Broussard placed her on the bed and then ran from the room. He returned from the bathroom a few moments later with a moist washcloth and a towel. Carefully, he bathed the wound. Relief quieted his initial fears. The flow of blood had made the injury appear worse than it was.

"Greg?" Yvonne's eyes flickered open.

"How did Grace manage this?" His hands trembled as he finished cleaning the cut. He pressed the towel atop it to staunch the flow of blood.

"Grace?" Yvonne looked up at him, puzzled. "It was a man. He frightened me. I slipped and fell. I hit my head on the bed table."

Grace's photographer had come back for a few shots of his own, Broussard figured. Yvonne's screams and fall had spoiled his blackmail attempt. Frightened, the photographer had fled. But the man was not out of the woods yet. He would pay for what he had done to Yvonne.

"I don't believe that the cut is serious, but I'd like a doctor to look at it."

"Give me a few more minutes rest," Yvonne replied with a weak smile.

The shattering of glass came from below, followed by the sound of someone stumbling into furniture.

"Your visitor is still in the house." Broussard opened a drawer to the bed table. He pulled out a chrome-plated revolver.

"Greg?" Yvonne sat up, her eyes wide.

He kissed her cheek lightly. "I'll be back in a moment."

Gun leveled before him, he cautiously made his way downstairs. He paused at the foot of the stairway, listening. The sound of shuffling feet came from the study.

Flattening himself against the wall, Broussard slid toward the door. Inside, he saw the silhouette of a man move in front of an open drapery. Reaching inside the doorway, Broussard's hand crept along the wall to locate the light switch.

He tightened his grip on the pistol. His fingers flicked the switch. "Right there. Freeze!"

Light flooded the room. The man within halted and then turned. Broussard's blood ran cold; it was the man from outside! A pleased grin spread across that mismatched face.

The man stepped toward Broussard. "Gregory, I've followed you since Tokyo, but until you met Yvonne no way existed for us to speak."

Fear, muscle, and brain-paralyzing fear transfixed Broussard. He willed his finger to squeeze the trigger, but it would not respond. The Song Ba, the grenade, Tokyo—they crowded his mind, melting into a single vision of death. The man was death. As impossible as it seemed, the man was *Death!*

"I've tried to talk with you." The man's voice contained a disturbing melancholy. "You had no need of me, couldn't hear or see me. Yvonne changed that. She touched the emptiness within you, the emptiness only I can remove."

The man came forward in slow, shuffling steps. Motionless, unable to break the muscle freezing terror, Broussard stood helpless before his steady advance.

"Did I detect a glimmer of recognition?" the man asked. "You know me now, don't you, Gregory?"

"Death." The ice gripping Broussard's vocal chords shattered in splintering fragments. "DEATH!"

He felt his finger move. Once, twice, six times it pumped the trigger. Sadness, the very heart of sadness, weaved in the stranger's expression. Yet, he continued toward Broussard. Six bullets had entered his chest, but he bore no wounds.

"Not death, Gregory, but the very essence of life itself." The man's hand reached out. "Once we walked together. The grenade, the closeness to death opened the chasm. Then in Tokyo, those three heartless minutes on the operating table tore me loose. You noticed my absence, but the hunger for power never needs what I offer."

There was a flicker of realization in Broussard's mind. He rejected it. It could not be. It could not.

"Through Yvonne, you found love," the man said. "Love cannot exist without me."

"No." Broussard's writhing lips formed the single word as the man's hand touched his heaving chest.

Warmth, soothing and caressing, suffused through every cell of Broussard's body. The stranger, no longer a stranger, melted into the corporeal flesh that was Gregory Broussard.

"My soul." It came as a piteous cry of naked recognition.

Broussard stood alone. An inner warmth filled the hollowness within him, a sense of completeness, oneness with himself. Hotter it glowed, to burn in actinic flarings. Six years of personal depravities found a conscience. A wailing scream tore from his lips as his legs wilted beneath him. He crumpled to the floor, his body locking itself in a defenseless ball.

Through the screams, he heard Yvonne enter the study, heard her terrified cries mingle in a chorus with his. Within the consuming fires, he isolated one untouched point of serenity. Yvonne's screams would be transitory. She, though never comprehending, would eventually accept what had happened this night.

For him, the screams would never end.

William F. Nolan continues his welcome return to the fantasy field with an original story that, like all his best work, reflects a spare style that invites the reader to fill in the details and multiply the horror. Those who accept the invitation seldom have any regrets.

THE POOL

by William F. Nolan

As they turned from Sunset Boulevard and drove past the high iron gates, swan-white and edged in ornamented gold, Lizbeth muttered under her breath.

"What's the matter with you?" Jaimie asked. "You just said 'shit,' didn't you?"

"Yes, I said it."

"Why?"

She turned toward him in the MG's narrow bucket seat, frowning. "I said it because I'm angry. When I'm angry, I say shit."

"Which is my cue to ask why you're angry."

"I don't like jokes when it comes to something this important."

"So who's joking?"

"You are, by driving us here. You *said* we were going to look at our new house."

"We are. We're on the way."

"This is *Bel Air*, Jaimie!"

"Right. Says so, right on the gate."

"Obviously, the house isn't in Bel Air."

"Why obviously?"

"Because you made just $20,000 last year on commercials, and you haven't done a new one in three months. Part-time actors who earn $20,000 a year don't buy houses in Bel Air."

"Who says I bought it?"

She stared at him. "You told me you *owned* it, that it was yours!"

He grinned. "It is, sweetcake. All mine."

"I hate being called 'sweetcake.' It's a sexist term."

"Bullshit! It's a term of endearment."

"You've changed the subject."

"No, *you* did," he said, wheeling the small sports roadster smoothly over the looping stretch of black asphalt.

Lizbeth gestured toward the mansions flowing past along the narrow, climbing road, castles in sugar-cake pinks and milk-chocolate browns and pastel blues. "So we're going to live in one of these?" Her voice was edged in sarcasm.

Jaimie nodded, smiling at her. "Just wait. You'll see!"

Under a cut-velvet driving cap, his tight-curled blond hair framed a deeply tanned, sensual actor's face. Looking at him, at that open, flashing smile, Lizbeth told herself once again that it was all too good to be true. Here she was, an ordinary small-town girl from Illinois, in her first year of theater arts at UCLA, about to hook up with a handsome young television actor who looked like Robert Redford and who now wanted her to live with him in Bel Air!

Lizbeth had been in California for just over a month, had known Jaimie for only half that time, and was already into a major relationship. It was dreamlike. Everything had happened so fast: meeting Jaimie at the disco, his divorce coming through, getting to know his two kids, falling in love after just three dates.

Life in California was like being caught inside one of those silent Chaplin films, where everything is speeded up and people whip dizzily back and forth across the screen. Did she *really* love Jaimie? Did he *really* love her? Did it matter?

Just let it happen, kid, she told herself. Just flow with the action.

"Here we are," said Jaimie, swinging the high-fendered little MG into a circular driveway of crushed white gravel. He braked the car, nodding toward the house. "Our humble abode!"

Lizbeth drew in a breath. Lovely! Perfect!

Not a mansion, which would have been too large and too intimidating, but a just-right two-story Spanish house topping a green-pine bluff, flanked by gardens and neatly trimmed box hedges.

"Well, do you like it?"

She giggled. "Silly question!"

"It's no castle."

"It's perfect! I hate big drafty places." She slid from the MG and stood looking at the house, hands on hips. "Wow. Oh, wow!"

"You're right about twenty-thou-a-year actors," he admitted, moving around the car to stand beside her. "This place is way beyond me."

"Then how did you . . . ?"

"I won it at poker last Thursday. High-stakes game. Went into it on borrowed cash. Got lucky, cleaned out the whole table, except for this tall, skinny guy who asks me if he can put up a house against what was in the pot. Said he had the deed on him and would sign it over to me if he lost the final hand."

"And you said yes."

"Damn right I did."

"And he lost?"

"Damn right he did."

She looked at the house and then back at him. "And it's legal?"

"The deed checks out. I own it all, Liz—house, gardens, pool."

"There's a *pool*?" Her eyes were shining.

He nodded. "And it's a beaut. Custom design. I may rent it out for commercials, pick up a little extra bread."

She hugged him. "Oh, Jaimie! I've always wanted to live in a house with a pool!"

"This one's unique."

"I want to see it!"

He grinned and then squeezed her waist. "First the house, *then* the pool. Okay?"

She gave him a mock bow. "Lead on, master!"

Lizbeth found it difficult to keep her mind on the house as Jaimie led her happily from room to room. Not that the place wasn't charming and comfortable, with its solid Spanish furniture, bright rugs, and beamed ceilings. But the prospect of finally having a pool of her own was so delicious that she couldn't stop thinking about it.

"I had a cleaning service come up here and get everything ready for us," Jaimie told her. He stood in the center of the living room, looking around proudly, reminding her of a captain on the deck of his first ship. "Place needed work. Nobody's lived here in ten years."

"How do you know that?"

"The skinny guy told me. Said he'd closed it down ten years ago, after his wife left him." He shrugged. "Can't say I blame her."

"What do you know about her?"

"Nothing. But the guy's a creep, a skinny creep." He flashed his white smile. "Women prefer *attractive* guys."

She wrinkled her nose at him. "Like *you*, right?"

"Right!"

He reached for her, but she dipped away from him, pulling off his cap and draping it over her dark hair.

"You look cute that way," he said.

"Come on, show me the pool. You promised to show me."

"Ah, yes, madame . . . the pool."

They had to descend a steep flight of weathered wooden steps to reach it. The pool was set in its own shelf of woodland terrain, notched into the hillside and screened from the house by a thick stand of trees.

"You never have to change the water," Jaimie said as they walked toward it. "Feeds itself from a stream inside the hill. It's self-renewing. Old water out, new water in. All the cleaning guys had to do was skim the leaves and stuff off the surface." He hesitated as the pool spread itself before them. "Bet you've never seen one like it!"

Lizbeth never had, not even in books or magazine photos.

It was *huge*, at least ten times larger than she'd expected, edged on all sides by gray, angular rocks. It was designed in an odd, irregular shape that actually made her . . . made her . . . suddenly made her . . .

Dizzy. I'm dizzy.

"What's wrong?"

"I don't know." She pressed a hand against her eyes. "I . . . I feel a little . . . sick."

"Are you having your . . . ?"

"No, it's not that. I felt fine until. . . ." She turned away toward the house. "I just don't like it."

"What don't you like?"

"The pool," she said, breathing deeply. "I don't like the pool. There's something wrong about it."

He looked confused. "I thought you'd love it!" His tone held irritation. "Didn't you just tell me you always wanted. . . ."

"Not one like this," she interrupted, overriding his words. "Not *this* one." She touched his shoulder. "Can we go back to the house now? It's cold here. I'm freezing."

He frowned. "But it's *warm*, Liz! Must be eighty at least. How can you be cold?"

She was shivering and hugging herself for warmth. "But I am! Can't you feel the chill?"

"All right," he sighed. "Let's go back."

She didn't speak during the climb up to the house.

Below them, wide and black and deep, the pool rippled its dark skin, a stirring, sluggish, patient movement in the windless afternoon.

Upstairs, naked in the Spanish four-poster bed, Lizbeth could not imagine what had come over her at the pool. Perhaps the trip up to the house along the sharply winding road had made her carsick. Whatever the reason, by the time they were back in the house, the dizziness had vanished, and she'd enjoyed the curried chicken dinner Jaimie had cooked for them. They'd sipped white wine by a comforting hearth fire and then made love there tenderly late into the night, with the pulsing flame tinting their bodies in shades of pale gold.

"Jan and David are coming by in the morning," he had told her. "Hope you don't mind."

"Why should I? I think your kids are great."

"I thought we'd have this first Sunday together, just the two of us; but school starts for them next week, and I promised they could spend the day here."

"I don't mind. Really I don't."

He kissed the top of her nose. "That's my girl."

"The skinny man. . . ."

"What about him?"

"I don't understand why he didn't try to sell this house in the ten years when he wasn't living here."

"I don't know. Maybe he didn't need the money."

"Then why bet it on a poker game? Surely the pot wasn't anywhere near equal to the worth of this place."

"It was just a way for him to stay in the game. He had a straight flush and thought he'd win."

"Was he upset at losing the place?"

Jaimie frowned at that question. "Now that you mention it, he didn't seem to be. He took it very calmly."

"You said that he left after his wife split. Did he talk about her at all?"

"He told me her name."

"Which was?"

"Gail. Her name was Gail."

Now, lying in the upstairs bed, Lizbeth wondered what had happened to Gail. It was odd somehow to think that she and the skinny man had made love in this same bed. In a way, she'd taken Gail's place.

Lizbeth still felt guilty about saying no to Jaimie when he'd suggested a postmidnight swim. "Not tonight, darling. I've a slight headache. Too much wine, maybe. You go' on without me."

And so he'd gone on down to the pool alone, telling her that such a mild, late-summer night was just too good to waste, that he'd take a few laps around the pool and be back before she finished her cigarette.

Irritated with herself, Lizbeth stubbed out the glowing Pall Mall in the bedside ashtray. Smoking was a filthy habit—ruins your lungs, stains your teeth. And smoking in bed was doubly stupid. You fall asleep . . . the cigarette catches the bed on fire. She *must* stop smoking. All it took was some real will power, and if . . .

Lizbeth sat up abruptly, easing her breath to listen. Nothing. No sound.

That was wrong. The open bedroom window overlooked the pool, and she'd been listening, behind her thoughts, to Jaimie splashing about below in the water.

Now she suddenly realized that the pool sounds had ceased, totally.

She smiled at her own nervous reaction. The silence simply meant that Jaimie had finished his swim and was out of the pool and headed back to the house. He'd be there any second.

But he didn't arrive.

Lizbeth moved to the window. Moonlight spilled across her breasts as she leaned forward to peer out into the night. The pale mirror glimmer of the pool flickered in the darkness below, but the bulk of trees screened it from her vision.

"Jaimie!" Her voice pierced the silence. "Jaimie, are you still down there?"

No reply. Nothing from the pool. She called his name again, without response.

Had something happened while he was swimming? Maybe a sudden stomach cramp or a muscle spasm from the cold water? No, he would have called out for help. She would have heard him.

Then . . . what? Surely this was no practical joke, an attempt to scare her? No, impossible. That would be cruel, and Jaimie's humor was never cruel. But he might think of it as fun, a kind of hide and seek in a new house. *Damn him!*

Angry now, she put on a nightrobe and stepped into her slippers. She hurried downstairs, out the back door, across the damp lawn, to the pool steps.

"Jaimie! If this is a game, I don't like it! Damn it, I *mean* that!" She peered downward; the moonlit steps were empty. "*Answer* me!"

Then, muttering "Shit!" under her breath, she started down the clammy wooden steps, holding to the cold iron pipe rail. The descent seemed even more precipitous in the dark, and she forced herself to move slowly.

Reaching level ground, Lizbeth could see the pool. She moved closer for a full view. It was silent and deserted. Where was Jaimie? She suddenly was gripped by the familiar sense of dizzy nausea as she stared at the odd, weirdly angled rock shapes forming the pool's perimeter. She tried to look away. And *couldn't*.

It wants me!

That terrible thought seized her mind. But what wanted her? The pool? No . . . something *in* the pool.

She kicked off the bedroom slippers and found herself walking toward the pool across moon-sparkled grass, spiky and cold against the soles of her bare feet.

Stay back! Stay away from it!

But she couldn't. Something was drawing her toward the black pool, something she could not resist.

At the rocks, facing the water, she unfastened her nightrobe, allowing it to slip free of her body.

She was alabaster under the moon, a subtle curving of leg, of thigh, of neck and breast. Despite the jarring fear hammer of her heart, Lizbeth knew that she had to step forward into the water.

It wants me!

The pool was black glass, and she looked down into it, at the reflection of her body, like white fire on the still surface.

Now . . . a ripple, a stirring, a deep-night movement from below.

Something was coming—a shape, a dark mass, gliding upward toward the surface.

Lizbeth watched, hypnotized, unable to look away, unable to obey the screaming, pleading voice inside her: *Run! Run!*

And then she saw Jaimie's hand. It broke the surface of the pool, reaching out to her.

His face bubbled free of the clinging black water, and acid bile leaped into her throat. She gagged, gasped for air, her eyes wide in sick shock.

It was *part* Jaimie, part something else!

It smiled at her with Jaimie's wide, white-toothed open mouth, but, oh God! only *one* of its eyes belonged to Jaimie. It had three others, all horribly different. It had *part* of Jaimie's face, *part* of his body.

Run! Don't go to it! Get away!

But Lizbeth did not run. Gently, she folded her warm, pink-fleshed hand into the icy wet horror of that hand in the pool and allowed herself to be drawn slowly forward. Downward. As the cold, receiving waters shocked her skin, numbing her, as the black liquid rushed into her open mouth, into her lungs and stomach and body, filling her as a cup is filled, her final image, the last thing she saw before closing her eyes, was Jaimie's wide-lipped, shining smile—an expanding patch of brightness fading down . . . deep . . . very deep . . . into the pool's black depths.

Jan and David arrived early that Sunday morning, all giggles and shouts, breathing hard from the ride on their bikes.

A whole Sunday with Dad. A fine, warm-sky summer day with school safely off somewhere ahead and not bothering them. A big house to roam in, and yards to run in, and caramel-ripple ice cream waiting (Dad had promised to buy some!), and games to play, and . . .

"Hey! Look what I found!"

Jan was yelling at David. They had gone around to the back of the house when no one answered the bell, looking for their father. Now eight-year-old Jan was at the bottom of a flight of high wooden steps, yelling up at her brother. David was almost ten and tall for his age.

"What you find?"

"Come and see!"

He scrambled down the steps to join her.

"Jeez!" he said. "A pool! I never saw one this big before!"

"Me neither."

David looked over his shoulder, up at the silent house.

"Dad's probably out somewhere with his new girlfriend."

"Probably," Jan agreed.

"Let's try the pool while we're waiting. What do you say?"

"Yeah, let's!"

They began pulling off shirts and slacks.

Motionless in the depths of the pool, at the far end, where rock and tree shadows darkened the surface, it waited, hearing the tinkling, high child voices filtering down to it in the sound-muted waters. It was excited because it had never absorbed a child; a child was new and fresh—new pleasures, new strengths.

It had formed itself within the moist deep soil of the hill, and the pool had nurtured and fed it, helping it grow, first with small, squirming water bugs and other yard insects. It had absorbed them, using their eyes and their hard, metallic bodies to shape itself. Then the pool had provided a dead bird, and now it had feathers along part of its back, and the bird's sharp beak formed part of its face. Then a plump gray rat had been drawn into the water, and the rat's glassy eye became part of the thing's body. A cat had drowned here, and its claws and matted fur added new elements to the thing's expanding mass.

Finally, when it was still young, a golden-haired woman, Gail, had come here alone to swim that long-ago night, and the pool had taken her, given her as a fine new gift to the thing in its depths. And Gail's long silk-gold hair streamed out of the thing's mouth (one of its mouths, for it had several), and it had continued to grow, to shape itself.

Then, last night, this man, Jaimie, had come to it. And his right eye now burned like blue phosphor from the thing's face. Lizbeth had followed, and her slim-fingered hands, with their long, lacquered nails, now pulsed in wormlike convulsive motion along the lower body of the pool-thing.

Now it was excited again, trembling, ready for new bulk, new lifestuffs to shape and use. It rippled in dark anticipation, gathering itself, feeling the pleasure and the hunger.

Faintly, above it, the boy's cry: "Last one in's a fuzzy green monkey!"

It rippled to the vibrational splash of two young bodies striking the water.

It glided forward swiftly toward the children.

Stephen King is the world's best-selling author of dark fantasy. One reason for this is his uncanny ability to take what is right and normal and give it a nudge so that it becomes anything but right, definitely not normal. As with, for instance, a child's toy . . .

THE MONKEY

by Stephen King

When Hal Shelburn saw it, when his son Dennis pulled it out of a mouldering Ralston-Purina carton that had been pushed far back under one attic eave, such a feeling of horror and dismay rose in him that for a moment he thought he surely must scream. He put one fist to his mouth as if to cram it back . . . and then merely coughed into his fist. Neither Terry nor Dennis noticed, but Petey looked around, momentarily curious.

"Hey, neat," Dennis said respectfully. It was a tone Hal rarely got from the boy any more himself. Dennis was twelve.

"What is it?" Petey asked. He glanced at his father again before his eyes were dragged back to the thing his big brother had found. "What is it, Daddy?"

"It's a monkey, fartbrains," Dennis said. "Haven't you ever seen a monkey before?"

"Don't call your brother fartbrains," Terry said automatically, and she began to examine a box of curtains. The curtains were slimy with mildew, and she dropped them quickly. "Uck."

"Can I have it, Daddy?" Petey asked. He was nine.

"What do you mean?" Dennis cried. "*I* found it!"

"Boys, please," Terry said. "I'm getting a headache."

Hal barely heard them—any of them. The monkey glimmered up at him from his older son's hands, grinning its old familiar grin. The same grin had haunted his nightmares as a child, haunted them until he had . . .

Outside a cold gust of wind rose, and for a moment lips with no flesh blew a long note through the old, rusty gutter outside. Petey stepped closer to his father, eyes moving uneasily to the rough attic roof through which nailheads poked.

"What was that, Daddy?" he asked as the whistle died to a guttural buzz.

"Just the wind," Hal said, still looking at the monkey. Its cymbals, crescents of brass rather than full circles in the weak light of the one naked bulb, were moveless, perhaps a foot apart, and he added automatically, "Wind can whistle, but it can't carry a tune." Then he realized that that was a saying of his Uncle Will's, and a goose ran over his grave.

The long note came again, the wind coming off Crystal Lake in a long, droning swoop and then wavering in the gutter. Half a dozen small drafts puffed cold October air into Hal's face—God, this place was so much like the back closet of the house in Hartford that they might all have been transported twenty-five years back in time.

I won't think about that.

But the thought wouldn't be denied.

In the back closet where I found that goddamned monkey in that same box.

Terry had moved away to examine a wooden crate filled with knickknacks, duck walking because the pitch of the eave was so sharp.

"I don't like it," Petey said; he felt for Hal's hand. "Dennis can have it if he wants. Can we go, Daddy?"

"Worried about ghosts, chickenguts?" Dennis enquired.

"Dennis, you stop it," Terry said absently. She picked up a wafer-thin cup with a Chinese pattern. "This is nice. This . . ."

Hal saw that Dennis had found the wind-up key in the monkey's back. Terror flew through him on dark wings.

"Don't do that!"

It came out more sharply than he had intended, and he had snatched the monkey out of Dennis's hands before he was really aware that he had done it. Dennis looked around at him, startled. Terry had also glanced back over her shoulder, and Petey looked up. For a moment they were all silent, and the wind whistled again, very low this time, like an unpleasant invitation.

"I mean, it's probably broken," Hal said.

It used to be broken . . . except when it wanted to be fixed.

"Well, you didn't have to *grab*," Dennis said.

"Dennis, shut up."

Dennis blinked at him and for a moment looked almost uneasy. Hal hadn't spoken to him so sharply in a long time, not since he had lost his job with National Aerodyne in California two years earlier and they had moved to Texas. Dennis decided not to push it . . . for now. He turned back to the Ralston-Purina carton and began to root through it again, but the other stuff was nothing but shit: broken toys, bleeding springs, and stuffings.

The wind was louder now, hooting instead of whistling. The attic began to creak softly, making a noise like footsteps.

"Please, Daddy?" Petey asked, loud enough for only his father to hear.

"Yeah," he said. "Terry, let's go."

"I'm not through with this. . . ."

"I said let's *go*."

It was her turn to look startled.

They had taken two adjoining rooms in a motel. By ten that night the boys were asleep in their room and Terry was asleep in the adults' room. She had taken two valium on the ride back from the home place in Casco, to keep her nerves from giving her a migraine. Lately she took a lot of valium. It had started around the time National Aerodyne had laid Hal off. For the last two years he had been working for Texas Instruments—it was $4,000 less a year, but it was work. He had told Terry that they were lucky. She agreed. There were plenty of software architects drawing unemployment, he said. She agreed. The company housing in Arnette was every bit as good as the place in Fresno, he said. She agreed, but he thought her agreement was a lie.

And he had been losing Dennis. He could feel the kid going, achieving a premature escape velocity: so long, Dennis, bye-bye, stranger, it was nice sharing this train with you. Terry said that she thought the boy was smoking reefer. She smelled it sometimes. You have to talk to him, Hal. And *he* agreed, but so far he had not.

The boys were asleep. Terry was asleep. Hal went into the bathroom and locked the door and sat down on the closed lid of the john and looked at the monkey.

He hated the way it felt, that soft brown nappy fur, worn bald in spots. He hated its grin. "That monkey grins just like a nigger," Uncle Will had said once, but it didn't grin like a nigger, or like anything human. Its grin was all teeth, and if you wound up the key the lips would move, the teeth would seem to get bigger, to become vampire teeth, the lips would writhe and the cymbals would bang, stupid monkey, stupid clockwork monkey, stupid, stupid—

He dropped it. His hands were shaking, and he dropped it.

The key clicked on the bathroom tile as it struck the floor. The sound seemed very loud in the stillness. It grinned at him with its murky amber eyes, doll's eyes, filled with idiot glee, its brass cymbals poised as if to strike up a march for some black band from hell, and on the bottom the words "MADE IN HONG KONG" were stamped.

"You can't be here," he whispered. "I threw you down the well when I was nine."

The monkey grinned up at him.

Hal Shelburn shuddered.

Outside in the night, a black capful of wind shook the motel.

Hal's brother Bill and Bill's wife, Collette, met them at Uncle Will's and Aunt Ida's the next day. Terry and Collette went into the house, and Hal walked with his brother toward the overgrown patch of ground that had been their uncle's garden for so many years. Hal could still see the stakes the beans had grown on, now heaved every way by the early frost, like canted gravestones.

"Did it ever cross your mind that a death in the family is a really lousy way to renew the family connection?" Bill asked him with a bit of a grin. He had been named for Uncle Will. Will and Bill, champions of the rodayo, Uncle Will used to say, and ruffle Bill's hair. It was one of his sayings . . . like "The wind can whistle, but it can't carry a tune." Uncle Will had died six years ago, and Aunt Ida had lived on here alone until a stroke had taken her just the previous week. Very sudden, Bill had said when he called long distance to give Hal the news. As if he could know; as if anyone could know. She had died alone.

"Yeah," Hal said. "The thought had crossed my mind."

They looked at the place together, the home place where

they had finished growing up. Their father, a merchant mariner, had simply disappeared as if from the very face of the earth when they were young; Bill claimed to remember him vaguely, but Hal had no memories of him at all. Their mother had died when Bill was ten and Hal eight. They had come to Uncle Will's and Aunt Ida's from Hartford, and they had been raised here, had gone to college here. Bill had stayed and now had a healthy law practice in Portland.

Hal saw that Petey had wandered off toward the blackberry tangles that lay on the eastern side of the house in a mad jumble. "Stay away from there, Petey," he called.

Petey looked back, questioning. Hal felt simple love for the boy rush him . . . and he suddenly thought of the monkey again.

"Why, Dad?"

"The old well's in there someplace," Bill said. "But I'll be damned if I remember just where. Your dad's right, Petey—those blackberry tangles are a good place to stay away from. Thorns'll do a job on you. Right, Hal?"

"Right," Hal said automatically. Pete moved away, not looking back, and then started down the embankment toward the small shingle of beach where Dennis was skipping stones over the water. Hal felt something in his chest loosen a little.

"Let's go inside," Bill said. "They'll have coffee on."

"The kids—"

"—will be fine," Bill finished, just as if he and Collette had some. He clapped Hal affectionately on the back. "Same old worrywart. You still have trouble getting to sleep, little brother?"

"No," Hal said. He had gotten one very troubled hour last night, just before dawn. "No trouble."

"Good. There's hope for you yet. Listen, there's something I want to talk to you about."

Bill might have forgotten where the old well had been, but late that afternoon Hal went to it unerringly, shouldering his way through the brambles that tore at his old flannel jacket and hunted for his eyes. He reached it and stood there, breathing hard, looking at the rotted, warped boards that covered it. After a moment's debate he knelt (his knees fired twin pistol shots) and moved two of the boards aside.

From the bottom of that wet, rock-lined throat a face stared up at him—wide eyes, grimacing mouth—and a moan escaped him. It was not loud, except in his heart. There it had been very loud.

It was his own face, reflected up from dark water, *not* the monkey's. For a moment he had thought it was the monkey's.

He sat back and closed his eyes. White light, dull and overcast, added ten years to his thirty-five. The wind clattered in the skeletal blackberry tangles, and somewhere a crow uttered a harsh cry. It liked the sound so well that it did it again.

He was shaking, shaking all over.

I threw it down the well. I threw it down the well, please God, don't let me be crazy, I threw it down the well.

He opened his eyes. He dug a clod of earth out of the ground and threw it into the hole and listened to the splash. Oh, yes, there was water again, quite a lot by the sound. Thirty feet deep, Uncle Will had told him once. Hand-dug, hand-faced with good Maine rock. Work was a bitch in those days, Hal. Artesian wells was for rich folks.

The well had gone dry the summer Johnny McCabe died, the year after Bill and Hal came to stay at the home place with Uncle Will and Aunt Ida. Uncle Will had borrowed money from the bank to have an artesian well sunk, and the blackberry tangles had grown up around the old dug well, the dry well.

Except the water had come back. Like the monkey.

This time the memory would not be denied. Hal sat there helplessly, letting it come, trying to go with it, to ride it like a surfer riding a monster wave that will crush him if he falls off the board, just trying to get through it so that it would be gone again.

He had crept out here with the monkey late that summer, and the blackberries had been out, the smell of them thick and cloying. No one came in here to pick, although Aunt Ida would sometimes stand at the edge of the tangles and pick a cupful of berries into her apron. In here the blackberries had gone past ripe to overripe; some of them were rotting, sweating a thick white fluid like pus, and the crickets sang maddeningly in the high grass underfoot, their endless cry: *Reeeeeeee*—

The thorns tore at him, brought dots of blood onto his bare arms. He made no effort to avoid their sting. He had been blind with terror, so blind that he had come within inches of stumbling onto the boards that covered the well, perhaps within inches of crashing thirty feet to the well's muddy bottom. He had pinwheeled his arms for balance, and more thorns had branded his forearms. It was that memory that had caused him to call Petey back sharply.

That was the day Johnny McCabe had died—his best friend. Johnny had been climbing the rungs up to his treehouse in his backyard. The two of them had spent many hours up there that summer playing pirate, seeing make-believe galleons out on the lake, unlimbering the cannons, preparing to board. Johnny had been climbing up to the treehouse as he had done a thousand times before, and the rung just below the trap door in the bottom of the treehouse had snapped off in his hands, and Johnny had fallen thirty feet to the ground and had broken his neck, and it was the monkey's fault, the monkey, the goddamn hateful monkey. When the phone rang, when Aunt Ida's mouth dropped open and then formed an O of horror as her friend Milly from down the road told her the news, when Aunt Ida said, "Come out on the porch, Hal, I have to tell you some bad news," he had thought with sick horror, *The monkey! What's the monkey done now?*

There had been no reflection of his face trapped at the bottom of the well that day, only the stone cobbles going down into the darkness and the smell of wet mud. He had looked at the monkey lying there on the wiry grass that grew between the blackberry tangles, its cymbals poised, its grinning teeth huge between its splayed lips, its fur, rubbed away in balding, mangy patches here and there, its glazed eyes.

"I hate you," he had hissed at it. He wrapped his hand around its loathsome body, feeling the nappy fur crinkle. It grinned at him as he held it up in front of his face. "Go on!" He dared it, beginning to cry for the first time that day. He shook it. The poised cymbals trembled minutely. It spoiled everything good, everything. "Go on, clap them! Clap them!"

The monkey only grinned.

"Go on and clap them!" His voice rose hysterically. "Fraidy-cat, fraidy-cat, go on and clap them! I dare you!"

Its brownish-yellow eyes. Its huge and gleeful teeth.

He threw it down the well then, mad with grief and terror. He saw it turn over once on its way down, a simian acrobat doing a trick, and the sun glinted one last time on those cymbals. It struck the bottom with a thud, and that must have jogged its clockwork, for suddenly the cymbals *did* begin to beat. Their steady, deliberate, and tinny banging rose to his ears, echoing and fey in the stone throat of the dead well: *Jang-jang-jang-jang—*

Hal clapped his hands over his mouth, and for a moment he could see it down there, perhaps only in the eye of imagination . . . lying there in the mud, eyes glaring up at the small circle of his boy's face peering over the lip of the well (as if marking its shape forever), lips expanding and contracting around those grinning teeth, cymbals clapping, funny wind-up monkey.

Jang-jang-jang-jang, who's dead? *Jang-jang-jang-jang,* is it Johnny McCabe, falling with his eyes wide, doing his own acrobatic somersault as he falls through the bright summer vacation air with the splintered rung still held in his hands to strike the ground with a single bitter snapping sound? Is it Johnny, Hal? Or is it you?

Moaning, Hal had shoved the boards across the hole, getting splinters in his hands, not caring, not even aware of them until later. And still he could hear it, even through the boards, muffled now and somehow all the worse for that. It was down there in stone-faced dark, clapping its cymbals and jerking its repulsive body, the sounding coming up like the sound of a prematurely buried man scrabbling for a way out.

Jang-jang-jang-jang, who's dead this time?

He fought and battered his way back through the blackberry creepers. Thorns stitched fresh lines of welling blood briskly across his face, and burdocks caught in the cuffs of his jeans, and he fell full-length once, his ears still jangling, as if it had followed him. Uncle Will found him later, sitting on an old tire in the garage and sobbing, and he thought Hal had been crying for his dead friend. So he had; but he had also cried in the aftermath of terror.

He had gone to Johnny's funeral with his aunt and uncle, had stood by the open grave, really aware of nothing save how uncomfortable he was in his suit, which he had had for a year and a half and which was now getting too tight at the crotch and under his arms.

He had thrown the monkey down the well in the afternoon. That evening, as twilight crept in through a shimmering mantle of ground fog, a car moving too fast for the reduced visibility had run down Aunt Ida's Manx cat in the road and had gone right on. There had been guts everywhere. Bill had thrown up, but Hal had only turned his face away, his pale, still face, hearing Aunt Ida's sobbing (this on top of the news about the McCabe boy had caused a fit of weeping that was almost hysterics, and it was almost two hours before Uncle Will could calm her completely) as if from miles away. In his heart there was a cold and exultant joy. It hadn't been his turn. It had been Aunt Ida's Manx, not him, not his brother Bill or his Uncle Will (just two champions of the rodayo). And now the monkey was gone, it was down the well, and one scruffy Manx cat with ear mites was not too great a price to pay. If the monkey wanted to clap its hellish cymbals now, let it. It could clap and clash them for the crawling bugs and beetles, the dark things that made their home in the well's stone gullet. It would rot down there in the darkness, and its loathsome cogs and wheels and springs would rust in darkness. It would die down there, in the mud and the darkness. Spiders would spin it a shroud.

But . . . it had come back.

Slowly, Hal covered the well again as he had on that day, and in his ears he heard the phantom echo of the monkey's cymbals: *Jang-jang-jang-jang, who's dead, Hal? Is it Terry? Dennis? Is it Petey, Hal? He's your favorite, isn't he? Is it him? Jang-jang-jang—*

Hal closed his eyes and put a trembling hand to his mouth. And the blackberry bushes clattered together in the October wind under a white October sky, making a sound like the nodding, bony laughter of skeletons who are sharing a good joke.

"Put that *down!*

Petey flinched and dropped the monkey, and for one nightmare moment Hal thought that that would do it, that the jolt would jog its machinery and the cymbals would begin to beat and clash.

"Daddy, you scared me."

"I'm sorry. I just . . . I don't want you to play with that."

The others had gone to see a movie, and he had thought he would beat them back to the motel. But he had stayed at the home place longer than he would have guessed; the old, hateful memories seemed to move in their own eternal time zone.

Terry was sitting near Dennis, watching *The Beverly Hillbillies.* She watched the old, grainy print with a steady, bemused concentration that spoke of a recent valium pop. Dennis was reading a rock magazine with the group Styx on the cover. Petey had been sitting cross-legged on the carpet, goofing with the monkey.

"It doesn't work anyway," Petey said. *Which explains why Dennis let him have it,* Hal thought, and then felt ashamed and angry at himself. He seemed to have no control over the hostility he felt toward Dennis more and more often, but in the aftermath he felt demeaned and tacky . . . helpless.

"No," he said. "It's old. I'm going to throw it away. Give it to me."

He held out his hand, and Petey, looking troubled, handed it over.

Dennis said to his mother, "Pop's turning into a friggin' schizophrenic."

Hal was across the room even before he knew he was going, the monkey in one hand, grinning as if in approbation. He hauled Dennis out of his chair by the shirt. There was a purring sound as a seam came adrift somewhere. Dennis looked almost comically shocked. His copy of *Tiger Beat* fell to the floor.

"Hey!"

"You come with me," Hal said grimly, pulling his son toward the door to the connecting room.

"Hal!" Terry nearly screamed. Petey just goggled.

Hal pulled Dennis through. He slammed the door and then slammed Dennis against it. Dennis was starting to look scared. "You're getting a mouth problem," Hal said.

"Let *go* of me! You tore my shirt, you. . . ."

Hal slammed the boy against the door again. "Yes," he said. "A real mouth problem. Did you learn that in school? Or back in the smoking area?"

Dennis flushed, his face momentarily ugly with guilt. "I wouldn't be in that shitty school if you didn't get canned!" he burst out.

Hal slammed Dennis against the door again. "I didn't get canned, I got laid off, you know it, and I don't need any of your shit about it. You have problems? Welcome to the world, Dennis. Just don't you lay off all your problems on me. You're eating. Your ass is covered. At eleven, I don't . . . need any . . . shit from you." He punctuated each phrase by pulling the boy forward until their noses were almost touching and then slamming him back into the door. It was not hard enough to hurt, but Dennis was scared—his father had not laid a hand on him since they had moved to Texas—and now he began to cry with a young boy's loud, braying, healthy sobs.

"Go ahead, beat me up!" he yelled at Hal, his face twisted and blotchy. "Beat me up if you want. I know how much you fucking hate me!"

"I don't hate you. I love you a lot, Dennis. But I'm your dad and you're going to show me respect or I'm going to bust you for it."

Dennis tried to pull away. Hal pulled the boy to him and hugged him. Dennis fought for a moment and then put his face against Hal's chest and wept as if exhausted. It was the sort of cry Hal hadn't heard from either of his children in years. He closed his eyes, realizing that he felt exhausted himself.

Terry began to hammer on the other side of the door. "Stop it, Hal! Whatever you're doing to him, stop it!"

"I'm not killing him," Hal said. "Go away, Terry."

"Don't you. . . ."

"It's all right, Mom," Dennis said, muffled against Hal's chest.

He could feel her perplexed silence for a moment, and then she went. Hal looked at his son again.

"I'm sorry I badmouthed you, Dad," Dennis said reluctantly.

"When we get home next week, I'm going to wait two or three days and then I'm going to go through all your drawers, Dennis. If there's something in them you don't want me to see, you better get rid of it."

That flash of guilt again. Dennis lowered his eyes and wiped away snot with the back of his hand.

"Can I go now?" He sounded sullen once more.

"Sure," Hal said, and he let him go. *Got to take him camping in the spring, just the two of us. Do some fishing, like Uncle Will used to do with Bill and me. Got to get close to him. Got to try.*

He sat down on the bed in the empty room and looked at the monkey. *You'll never be close to him again, Hal,* its grin seemed to say. *Never again. Never again.*

Just looking at the monkey made him feel tired. He laid it aside and put a hand over his eyes.

That night Hal stood in the bathroom, brushing his teeth, and thought: *It was in the same box. How could it be in the same box?*

The toothbrush jabbed upward, hurting his gums. He winced.

He had been four and Bill six the first time he saw the monkey. Their missing father had bought a house in Hartford, and it had been theirs, free and clear, before he died or disappeared or whatever it had been. Their mother worked as a secretary in an insurance company, and a series of sitters came in to stay with the boys, except by then it was just Hal that the sitters had to mind through the day—Bill was in first grade, big school. None of the baby-sitters stayed for long. They got pregnant and married their boyfriends or got work at Holmes Aircraft, the helicopter plant out in Westville, or Mrs. Shelburn would discover that they had been at the cooking sherry or her bottle of brandy that was kept in the sideboard for special occasions. Most of them were stupid girls who seemed only to want to eat or sleep. None of them wanted to read to Hal as his mother would do.

The sitter that long winter was a huge, sleek black girl named Beulah. She fawned over Hal when Hal's mother was around and sometimes pinched him when she wasn't. Still, Hal had some liking for Beulah, who once in a while would read him a lurid tale from one of her confession or true-detective magazines ("Death Came for the Voluptuous Red-head," Beulah would intone ominously in the dozy daytime silence of the living room, and pop another Reese's Peanut Butter Cup into her mouth while Hal solemnly studied the grainy tabloid pictures and drank milk from his Wish-Cup). And the liking made what happened worse.

He found the monkey on a cold, cloudy day in March. Sleet ticked sporadically off the windows, and Beulah was asleep on the couch, a copy of *My Story* tented open on her admirable bosom.

So Hal went into the back closet to look at his father's things.

The back closet was a storage space that ran the length of the second floor on the left side, extra space that had never been finished off. One got into the back closet by using a small door—a down-the-rabbithole sort of door—on Bill's side of the boys' bedroom. They both liked to go in there, even though it was chilly in winter and hot enough in summer to wring a bucketful of sweat out of your pores. Long and narrow and somehow snug, the back closet was full of fascinating junk. No matter how much stuff you looked at, you never seemed to be able to look at it all. He and Bill had spent whole Saturday afternoons up there, barely speaking to each other, taking things out of boxes, examining them, turning them over and over so that their hands could absorb each unique reality, putting them back. Now Hal wondered whether he and Bill hadn't been trying as best they could to somehow make contact with their vanished father.

He had been a merchant mariner with a navigator's certificate, and there were stacks of charts back there, some marked with neat circles (and the dimple of the compass's swing point in the center of each). There were twenty volumes of something called *Barron's Guide to Navigation.* A set of cockeyed binoculars that made your eyes feel hot and funny if you looked through them too long. There were touristy things from a dozen ports of call—rubber hula-hula dolls, a black cardboard bowler with a torn band that said "YOU PICK A GIRL AND I'LL PICCADILLY," a glass globe with a tiny Eiffel Tower inside—and there were also envelopes with foreign stamps tucked carefully away inside, and foreign coins; there were rock samples from the Hawaiian island of Maui, a glassy black, heavy and somehow ominous, and funny records in foreign languages.

That day with the sleet ticking hypnotically off the roof just above his head, Hal worked his way all the way down to the far end of the back closet. This was where Bill had found the funny postcards that showed women who were wearing high-heeled shoes and stockings and nothing else so that you could see their bosoms and the hair between their legs. Down here the light was dim and yellow, making him feel faintly uneasy. It was cobwebby down here and a little spooky.

Hal moved a box aside and saw another box behind it, a Ralston-Purina box. Looking over the top was a pair of glassy hazel eyes. They gave him a start, and he skittered back for a moment, heart thumping, as if he had discovered a deadly pygmy. Then he saw its silence, the glaze in those eyes, and realized that it was some sort of toy. He moved forward again and lifted it carefully from the box.

It grinned its ageless, toothy grin in the yellow light, its cymbals held apart.

Delighted, Hal had turned it this way and that, feeling the crinkle of its nappy fur. Its funny grin pleased him. Yet hadn't there been something else, an almost instinctive feeling of disgust that had come and gone almost before he was aware of it? Perhaps it was so, but with an old, old memory like this one, you had to be careful not to believe too much. Old memories could lie. But . . . hadn't he seen that same expression on Petey's face, in the attic of the home place?

He had seen the key set into the small of its back, and had

turned it. It had turned far too easily; there were no winding-up clicks. Broken, then. Broken, but still neat.

He took it out to play with it.

"What you got, Hal?" Beulah asked, waking from her nap.

"Nothing," Hal said. "I found it."

He put it up on the shelf on his side of the bedroom. It stood atop his Lassie coloring books, grinning, staring into space, cymbals poised. It was broken, but it grinned nonetheless. That night Hal awakened from some uneasy dream, bladder full, and got up to use the bathroom in the hall. Bill was a breathing lump of covers across the room.

Hal came back, almost asleep again . . . and suddenly the monkey began to beat its cymbals together in the darkness.

Jang-jang-jang-jang—

He came fully awake, as if snapped in the face with a cold, wet towel. His heart gave a staggering leap of surprise, and a tiny, mouselike squeak escaped his throat. He stared at the monkey, eyes wide, lips trembling.

Jang-jang-jang-jang—

Its body rocked and humped on the shelf. Its lips spread and closed, spread and closed, hideously gleeful, revealing huge carnivorous teeth.

"Stop," Hal whispered.

His brother turned over and uttered a loud single snore. All else was silent . . . except for the monkey. The cymbals clapped and clashed, and surely it would wake his brother, his mother, the world. It would wake the dead.

Jang-jang-jang-jang—

Hal moved toward it, meaning to stop it somehow, perhaps put his hand between its cymbals until it ran down (*but it was broken, wasn't it?*), and then it stopped on its own. The cymbals came together one last time—*Jang!*—and then spread slowly apart to their original position. The brass glimmered in the shadows. The monkey's dirty yellowish teeth grinned their improbable grin.

The house was silent again. His mother turned over in her bed and echoed Bill's single snore. Hal got back into his bed and pulled the covers up, his heart still beating fast, and he thought: *I'll put it back in the closet again tomorrow. I don't want it.*

But the next morning he forgot all about putting the monkey back because his mother didn't go to work. Beulah was dead. Their mother wouldn't tell them exactly what happened.

"It was an accident, just a terrible accident" was all she would say. But that afternoon Bill bought a newspaper on his way home from school and smuggled page 4 up to their room under his shirt ("TWO KILLED IN APARTMENT SHOOT-OUT," the headline read) and read the article haltingly to Hal, following along with his finger, while their mother cooked supper in the kitchen. Beulah McCaffery, nineteen, and Sally Tremont, twenty, had been shot by Miss McCaffery's boyfriend, Leonard White, twenty-five, following an argument over who was to go out and pick up an order of Chinese food. Miss Tremont had expired at Hartford Receiving; Beulah McCaffery had been pronounced dead at the scene.

It was as if Beulah had just disappeared into one of her own detective magazines, Hal Shelburn thought, and he felt a cold chill race up his spine and then circle his heart. And then he realized that the shootings had occurred at about the same time the monkey . . .

"Hal?" It was Terry's voice, sleepy. "Coming to bed?"

He spat toothpaste into the sink and rinsed his mouth. "Yes," he said.

He had put the monkey in his suitcase earlier and locked it up. They were flying back to Texas in two or three days. But before they went, he would get rid of the damned thing for good.

Somehow.

"Have you thought about what Bill said?" Terry asked in the dark.

"Yeah," Hal said.

"Are you going to say okay?"

"Yes, I think so."

Bill had told him that a development corporation had made an offer on Uncle Will's and Aunt Ida's fourteen acres, which included their half a mile of Crystal Lake shorefront, of course. The home place would have to be razed, and that hurt, but there would be $20,000 apiece, enough to cinch Dennis's college if it was invested properly; and if the condominiums actually went up, he and Bill might make a hundred thousand apiece coming out the other side.

"Good," Terry said, sounding relieved. She paused. "This has been a hard trip for you, hasn't it?"

"Yes," he said. "I loved Ida, and I loved that place."

"Hal. . . ."

He looked over at her in the darkness.

"You were pretty rough on Dennis this afternoon."

"Dennis has needed somebody to start being rough on him for quite a while now, I think. He's been drifting. I just don't want him to start falling."

"Psychologically, beating the boy isn't a very productive—"

"I didn't *beat* him, Terry, for Christ's sake!"

"—way to assert parental authority."

"Oh, don't give me that encounter-group shit," Hal said angrily.

"I can see you don't want to discuss this." Her voice was cold.

"I told him to get the dope out of the house, too."

"You did?" Now she sounded apprehensive. "How did he take it? What did he say?"

"Come on, Terry! What *could* he say? 'You're fired'?"

"Hal, what's the matter with you? You're not like this. What's *wrong?*"

"Nothing," he said, thinking of the monkey locked away in his Samsonite. Would he hear it if it began to clap its cymbals? Yes, he surely would. Muffled, but audible. Clapping doom for someone, as it had for Beulah, Johnny McCabe, Uncle Will's dog Daisy. *Jang-jang-jang*, is it you, Hal? "I've just been under strain."

"I *hope* that's all it is. Because I don't like you this way."

"No?" And the words escaped before he could stop them; he didn't even want to stop them. "So pop a few valium, and everything will look okay again, right?"

He heard her draw breath in and let it out shakily. She began to cry then. He could have comforted her (maybe), but there seemed to be no comfort in him. There was too much terror. It would be better when the monkey was gone again, gone for good. Please, God, gone for good.

After a while her tears stopped and a while after that, when she thought he was asleep (oh yes, he could almost read her thoughts), she got up and went into the bathroom. White light seeped under the crack at the bottom of the door. He listened to the toilet flush. Water ran as she washed her hands. There was a pause. Then, faintly, the minute click of the medicine bottle being opened. She filled a glass. The light under the door went out, and she came back to bed. Five minutes later she was breathing deeply. He remembered reading somewhere that the drugged do not dream, and he thought about getting up and taking two of her valium himself, but he didn't move.

He lay wakeful until very late, until morning began to gray the air outside. But he thought he knew what to do.

Bill had found the monkey the second time.

That was about a year and a half after Beulah McCaffery had been pronounced dead at the scene. It was summer. Hal had just finished kindergarten.

He came in from playing with Stevie Arlingen, and his mother called, "Wash your hands, Hal, you're feelthy like a peeg." She was on the porch, drinking an iced tea and reading a book. It was her vacation; she had two weeks.

Hal gave his hands a token pass under cold water and printed dirt on the hand towel. "Where's Bill?"

"Upstairs. You tell him to clean his side of the room. It's a mess."

Hal, who enjoyed being the messenger of unpleasant news in such matters, rushed up. Bill was sitting on the floor. The small down-the-rabbithole door leading to the back closet was ajar. He had the monkey in his hands.

"That don't work," Hal said immediately. "It's busted."

He was apprehensive, although he barely remembered coming back from the bathroom that night, and the monkey suddenly beginning to clap its cymbals. A week or so after that, he had had a bad dream about the monkey and Beulah—he couldn't remember exactly what—and had awakened screaming, thinking for a moment that the soft weight on his chest was the monkey, that he would open his eyes and see it grinning down at him. But of course the soft weight had only been his pillow, clutched with panicky tightness. His mother came in to soothe him with a drink of water and two chalky-orange baby aspirins, those valium for childhood's troubled times. She thought it was the fact of Beulah's death that had caused the nightmare. So it was, but not in the way she thought.

He barely remembered any of this now, but the monkey still scared him, particularly its cymbals. And its teeth.

"I know that," Bill said, and he tossed the monkey aside. "It's stupid." It landed on Bill's bed, staring up at the ceiling, cymbals poised. Hal did not like to see it there. "You want to go down to Teddy's and get Popsicles?"

"I spent my allowance already," Hal answered. "Besides, Mom says you got to clean up your side of the room."

"I can do that later. And I'll loan you a nickel, if you want." Bill was not above giving Hall an Indian rope burn sometimes, grinning fiendishly and twisting until the tears started from Hal's eyes ("Smell an onion, kid?" Bill would enquire unkindly as he twisted the flesh of Hal's wrist clock and counterclock at the same time, until the skin was bright red and Hal began to scream "I say uncle! I say uncle!"), and Bill would occasionally trip him up or punch him for no particular reason, but mostly he was okay.

"Sure," Hal said gratefully. "I'll just put that busted monkey back in the closet first, okay?"

"Nah," Bill said, getting up. "Let's go-go-go."

Hal went. Bill's moods were changeable, and if he paused to put the monkey away, he might lose his Popsicle. They went down to Teddy's and got them, then down to the Rec, where some kids were getting up a baseball game. Hal was too small to play, but he sat far out in foul territory, sucking his root beer Popsicle and chasing what the big kids called "Chinese home runs." They didn't get home until almost dark, and their mother whacked Hal for getting the hand towel dirty and whacked Bill for not cleaning up his side of the room, and after supper there was TV, and by the time all of that had happened, Hal had forgotten all about the monkey. It somehow found its way up onto *Bill's* shelf, where it stood right next to Bill's autographed picture of Bill Boyd. And there it stayed for nearly two years.

By the time Hal was seven, the string of baby-sitters had played out. There was a recession on, and money was tight. There was an atmosphere of worry in the house. Three secretaries had already been laid off at Holmes Aircraft. Ruth Shelburn had been saved because of her seniority, but only so far. Baby-sitters had become an extravagance, and Mrs. Shelburn's last word to the two of them each morning was, "Bill, look after your brother."

That day, however, Bill had to stay after school for a Safety Patrol Boy meeting and Hal came home alone, stopping at each corner until he could see absolutely no traffic coming in either direction and then skittering across, shoulders hunched, like a doughboy crossing no man's land. He let himself into the house with the key under the mat and went immediately to the refrigerator for a glass of milk. He got the bottle . . . and then it slipped through his fingers and crashed to smithereens on the floor, pieces of glass flying everywhere, as the monkey suddenly began to beat its cymbals together upstairs.

Jang-jang-jang-jang, on and on.

He stood there immobile, looking down at the broken glass and the puddle of milk, full of a terror he could not name or understand. It was simply there, seeming to ooze from his pores.

He turned and rushed upstairs to their room. The monkey stood on Bill's shelf, seeming to stare at him. He had knocked the autographed picture of Bill Boyd face down onto Bill's bed. The monkey rocked and grinned and beat its cymbals together. Hal approached it slowly, not wanting to, not able to stay away. Its cymbals jerked apart and crashed together and jerked apart again. As he got closer, he could hear the clockwork running in the monkey's guts.

Abruptly, uttering a cry of revulsion and terror, he swatted it from the shelf as one might swat a large, loathsome bug. It struck Bill's pillow and then fell on the floor, cymbals still beating together, *jang-jang-jang,* lips flexing and closing as it lay there on its back in a patch of late-April sunshine.

Then, suddenly, he remembered Beulah. The monkey had clapped its cymbals that night, too.

Hal kicked it with one Buster Brown shoe, kicked it as hard as he could, and this time the cry that escaped him was one of fury. The clockwork monkey skittered across the floor, bounced off the wall, and lay still. Hal stood staring at it, fists bunched, heart pounding. It grinned saucily back at him, the sun a burning pinpoint in one glass eye. *Kick me all you want,* it seemed to tell him. *I'm nothing but cogs and clockwork and a worm-gear or two, kick me all you feel like, I'm not real, just a funny clockwork monkey is all I am, and who's dead? There's been an explosion at the helicopter plant! What's that rising up into the sky like a big bloody bowling ball with eyes where the finger holes should be? Is it your mother's head, Hal? Down at Brook Street Corner! The car was going too fast! The driver was drunk! There's one Patrol Boy less! Could you hear the crunching sound when the wheels ran over Bill's skull and his brains squirted out of his ears? Yes? No? Maybe? Don't ask me, I don't know, I can't know, all I know how to do is beat these cymbals together jang-jang-jang, and who's dead, Hal? Your mother? Your brother? Or is it you, Hal? Is it you?*

He rushed at it again, meaning to stomp on it, smash its loathsome body, jump on it until cogs and gears flew and its horrible glass eyes rolled across the floor. But just as he reached it, its cymbals came together once more, very softly

(*jang*)

as a spring somewhere inside expanded one final minute notch . . . and a sliver of ice seemed to whisper its way through the walls of his heart, impaling it, stilling its fury, and leaving him sick with terror again. The monkey almost seemed to know—how gleeful its grin seemed!

He picked it up, tweezing one of its arms between the thumb and first finger of his right hand, mouth drawn down in a bow of loathing, as if it were a corpse he held. Its mangy fake fur seemed hot and fevered against his skin. He fumbled open the tiny door that led to the back closet and turned on the bulb. The monkey grinned at him as he crawled down the length of the storage area between boxes piled on top of boxes, past the set of navigation books and the photograph albums with their fumes of old chemicals and the souvenirs and the old clothes, and Hal thought: *If it begins to clap its cymbals together now and move in my hand I'll scream, and if I scream it'll do more than grin, it'll start to laugh, to laugh at me, and then I'll go crazy and they'll find me in here, drooling and laughing, crazy, I'll be crazy, oh please, dear God, please, dear Jesus, don't let me go crazy—*

He reached the far end and clawed two boxes aside, spilling one of them, and jammed the monkey back into the Ralston-Purina box in the farthest corner. It leaned in there, comfortably, as if home at last, cymbals poised, grinning its simian grin, as if the joke were still on Hal. Hal crawled backward, sweating, hot and cold, all fire and ice, waiting for the cymbals to begin, and when they began, the monkey would leap from its box and scurry beetlelike toward him, clockwork whirring, cymbals clashing madly, and—

—and none of that happened. He turned off the light, slammed the small down-the-rabbithole door, and leaned against it, panting. At last he began to feel a little better. He went downstairs on rubbery legs, got an empty bag, and began carefully to pick up the jagged shards and splinters of the broken milk bottle, wondering whether he was going to cut himself and bleed to death, whether that was what the clapping cymbals had meant. But that didn't happen either. He got a towel and wiped up the milk and then sat down to see whether his mother and brother would come home.

His mother came first, asking, "Where's Bill?"

In a low, colorless voice, now sure that Bill must be dead,

Hal started to explain about the Patrol Boy meeting, knowing that, even given a very long meeting, Bill should have been home half an hour ago.

His mother looked at him curiously and started to ask what was wrong, and then the door opened and Bill came in—only it was not Bill at all, not really. This was a ghost-Bill, pale and silent.

"What's wrong?" Mrs. Shelburn exclaimed. "Bill, what's wrong?"

Bill began to cry, and they got the story through his tears. There had been a car, he said. He and his friend Charlie Silverman were walking home together after the meeting, and the car came around Brook Street Corner too fast, and Charlie had frozen. Bill had tugged Charlie's hand once but had lost his grip, and the car—

Bill began to bray out loud, hysterical sobs, and his mother hugged him to her, rocking him, and Hal looked out on the porch and saw two policemen standing there. The squad car in which they had conveyed Bill home was at the curb. Then he began to cry himself . . . but his tears were tears of relief.

It was Bill's turn to have nightmares now—dreams in which Charlie Silverman died over and over again, knocked out of his Red Ryder cowboy boots and flipped onto the hood of the old Hudson Hornet the drunk had been driving. Charlie Silverman's head and the Hudson's windshield had met with an explosive noise, and both had shattered. The drunken driver, who owned a candy store in Milford, suffered a heart attack shortly after being taken into custody (perhaps it was the sight of Charlie Silverman's brains drying on his pants), and his lawyer was quite successful at the trial with his "this man has been punished enough" theme. The drunk was given sixty days (suspended) and lost his privilege to operate a motor vehicle in the state of Connecticut for five years . . . which was about as long as Bill Shelburn's nightmares lasted. The monkey was hidden away again in the back closet. Bill never noticed that it was gone from his shelf . . . or if he did, he never said.

Hal felt safe for the next four years. He even began to forget about the monkey again, or to believe it had only been a bad dream. But when he came home from school on the afternoon his mother died, it was back on his shelf, cymbals poised, grinning down at him.

He approached it slowly, as if from outside himself—as if his own body had been turned into a wind-up toy at the sight of the monkey. He saw his hand reach out and take it down. He felt the nappy fur crinkle under his hand, but the feeling was muffled, mere pressure, as if someone had shot him full of novocaine. He could hear his breathing, quick and dry, like the rattle of wind through straw.

He turned it over and grasped the key, and years later he would think that his drugged fascination was like that of a man who puts a six-shooter with one loaded chamber against a closed and jittering eyelid and pulls the trigger.

No don't let it alone throw it away don't touch it—

He turned the key, and in the silence he heard a perfect tiny series of winding-up clicks. When he let the key go, the monkey began to clap its cymbals together, and he could feel its body jerking, bend-and-*jerk*, bend-and-*jerk*, as if it were alive, it *was* alive, writhing in his hand like some loathsome pygmy, and the vibration he felt through its balding brown fur was not that of turning cogs but the beating of its black and cindered heart.

With a groan, Hal dropped the monkey and backed away, fingernails digging into the flesh under his eyes, palms pressed to his mouth. He stumbled over something and nearly lost his balance (then he would have been right down on the floor with it, his bulging blue eyes looking into its glassy hazel ones). He scrambled toward the door, backed through it, slammed it, and leaned against it. Suddenly he bolted for the bathroom and vomited.

It was Mrs. Stukey from the helicopter plant who brought the news and stayed with them those first two endless nights, until Aunt Ida got down from Maine. Their mother had died of a brain embolism in the middle of the afternoon. She had been standing at the water cooler with a cup of water in one hand and had crumpled as if shot, still holding the paper cup in one hand. With the other she had clawed at the water cooler and had pulled the great glass bottle of Poland water down with her. It had shattered . . . but the plant doctor, who came on the run, said later that he believed Mrs. Shelburn was dead before the water had soaked through her dress and her underclothes to wet her skin. The boys were never told any of this, but Hal knew anyway. He dreamed it again and again on the long nights that followed his mother's death. "You still have trouble gettin' to sleep, little brother?" Bill had asked him, and Hal supposed Bill thought all the thrashing and bad dreams had to do with their mother dying so suddenly, and that was right . . . but only partly right. There was the guilt, the certain, deadly knowledge that he had killed his mother by winding the monkey up on that sunny after-school afternoon.

When Hal finally fell asleep, his sleep must have been deep. When he awoke, it was nearly noon. Petey was sitting cross-legged in a chair across the room, methodically eating an orange section by section and watching a game show on TV.

Hal swung his legs out of bed, feeling as if someone had punched him down into sleep . . . and then punched him back out of it. His head throbbed. "Where's your mom, Petey?"

Petey glanced around. "She and Dennis went shopping. I said I'd stay here with you. Do you always talk in your sleep, Dad?"

Hal looked at his son cautiously. "No, I don't think so. What did I say?"

"It was all muttering, I couldn't make it out. It scared me, a little."

"Well, here I am in my right mind again," Hal said, and he managed a small grin. Petey grinned back, and Hal felt simple love for the boy again, an emotion that was bright and strong and uncomplicated. He wondered why he had always been able to feel so good about Petey, to feel that he understood Petey and could help him, and why Dennis seemed a window too dark to look through, a mystery in his ways and habits, the sort of boy he could not understand because he had never been that sort of boy. It was too easy to say that the move from California had changed Dennis, or that—

His thoughts froze. The monkey. The monkey was sitting on the windowsill, cymbals poised. Hal felt his heart stop dead in his chest and then suddenly begin to gallop. His vision wavered, and his throbbing head began to ache ferociously.

It had escaped from the suitcase and now stood on the windowsill, grinning at him. *Thought you got rid of me, didn't you? But you've thought that before, haven't you?*

Yes, he thought sickly. Yes, I have.

"Pete, did you take that monkey out of my suitcase?" he asked, knowing the answer already. He had locked the suitcase and had put the key in his overcoat pocket.

Petey glanced at the monkey, and something—Hal thought it was unease—passed over his face. "No," he said. "Mom put it there."

"Mom did?"

"Yeah. She took it from you. She laughed."

"Took it from me? What are you talking about?"

"You had it in bed with you. I was brushing my teeth, but Dennis saw. He laughed, too. He said you looked like a baby with a teddybear."

Hal looked at the monkey. His mouth was too dry to swallow. He'd had it in *bed* with him? In *bed*? That loathsome fur against his cheek, maybe against his *mouth*, those glass eyes staring into his sleeping face, those grinning teeth near his neck? Dear *God*.

He turned abruptly and went to the closet. The Samsonite was there, still locked. The key was still in his overcoat pocket.

Behind him, the TV snapped off. He came out of the closet slowly. Petey was looking at him soberly. "Daddy, I don't like that monkey," he said, his voice almost too low to hear.

"Nor do I," Hal said.

Petey looked at him closely to see whether he was joking and found that he was not. He came to his father and hugged him tight. Hal could feel him trembling.

Petey spoke into his ear, then, very rapidly, as if afraid he might not have courage enough to say it again . . . or that the monkey might overhear.

"It's like it looks at you. Like it looks at you no matter where you are in the room. And if you go into the other room, it's like it's looking through the wall at you. I kept feeling like it . . . like it wanted me for something."

Petey shuddered. Hal held him tight.

"Like it wanted you to wind it up," Hal said.

Pete nodded violently. "It isn't really broken, is it, Dad?"

"Sometimes it is," Hal said, looking over his son's shoulder at the monkey. "But sometimes it still works."

"I kept wanting to go over there and wind it up. It was so quiet, and I thought, I can't, it'll wake up Daddy, but I still wanted to, and I went over and I . . . I *touched* it, and I hate the way it feels . . . but I liked it, too . . . and it was like it was saying, 'Wind me up, Petey, we'll play, your father isn't going to wake up, he's never going to wake up at all, wind me up, wind me up.' "

The boy suddenly burst into tears. "It's bad, I know it is. There's something wrong with it. Can't we throw it out, Daddy? Please?"

The monkey grinned its endless grin at Hal. He could feel Petey's tears between them. Late-morning sun glinted off the monkey's brass cymbals—the light reflected upward and put sunstreaks on the motel's plain white stucco ceiling.

"What time did your mother think she and Dennis would be back, Petey?"

"Around one." He swiped at his red eyes with his shirt-sleeve, looking embarrassed at his tears. But he wouldn't look at the monkey. "I turned on the TV," he whispered. "And I turned it up loud."

"That was all right, Petey."

"I had a crazy idea," Petey said. "I had this idea that if I wound that monkey up, you . . . you would have just died there in bed. In your sleep. Wasn't that a crazy idea, Daddy?" His voice had dropped again, and it trembled helplessly.

How would it have happened? Hal wondered. *Heart attack? An embolism, like my mother? What? It doesn't really matter, does it?*

And on the heels of that, another, colder thought: *Get rid of it, he says. Throw it out. But can it be gotten rid of? Ever?*

The monkey grinned mockingly at him, its cymbals held a foot apart. Did it suddenly come to life on the night Aunt Ida died? he wondered suddenly. Was that the last sound she heard, the muffled *jang-jang-jang* of the monkey beating its cymbals together up in the black attic while the wind whistled along the drainpipe?

"Maybe not so crazy," Hal said slowly to his son. "Go get your flight bag, Petey."

Petey looked at him uncertainly. "What are we gong to do?"

Maybe it can be got rid of. Maybe permanently, maybe just for a while . . . a long while or a short while. Maybe it's just going to come back and come back and that's what all this is about . . . but maybe I—we—can say good-bye to it for a long time. It took twenty years to come back this time. It took twenty years to get out of the well. . . .

"We're going to go for a ride," Hal said. He felt fairly calm but somehow too heavy inside his skin. Even his eyeballs seemed to have gained weight. "But first I want you to take your flight bag out there by the edge of the parking lot and find three or four good-sized rocks. Put them inside the bag and bring it back to me. Got it?"

Understanding flickered in Petey's eyes. "All right, Daddy."

Hal glanced at his watch. It was nearly 12:15. "Hurry. I want to be gone before your mother gets back."

"Where are we going?"

"To Uncle Will's and Aunt Ida's," Hal said. "To the home place."

Hal went into the bathroom, looked behind the toilet, and got the brush bowl leaning there. He took it back to the window and stood there with it in his hand like a cut-rate magic wand. He looked out at Petey in his melton shirt jacket, crossing the parking lot with his flight bag, "DELTA" showing clearly in white letters against a blue field. A fly bumbled in an upper corner of the window, slow and stupid with the end of the warm season. Hal knew how it felt.

He watched Petey hunt up three good-sized rocks and then start back across the parking lot. A car came around the corner of the motel, a car that was moving too fast, much too fast, and without thinking, reaching with the kind of reflex a good shortstop shows going to his right, his hand flashed down, as if in a karate chop . . . and stopped.

The cymbals closed soundlessly on his intervening hand, and he felt something in the air. Something like rage.

The car's brakes screamed. Petey flinched back. The driver motioned to him impatiently, as if what had almost happened was Petey's fault, and Petey ran across the parking lot with his collar flapping and into the motel's rear entrance.

Sweat was running down Hal's chest; he felt it on his forehead like a drizzle of oily rain. The cymbals pressed coldly against his hand, numbing it.

Go on, he thought grimly. *Go on, I can wait all day. Until hell freezes over, if that's what it takes.*

The cymbals drew apart and came to rest. Hal heard one faint *click!* from inside the monkey. He withdrew his hand and looked at it. On both the back and the palm there were grayish semicircles printed into the skin, as if he had been frostbitten.

The fly bumbled and buzzed, trying to find the cold October sunshine that seemed so close.

Pete came bursting in, breathing quickly, cheeks rosy. "I got three good ones, Dad, I. . . ." He broke off. "Are you all right, Daddy?"

"Fine," Hal said. "Bring the bag over."

Hal hooked the table by the sofa over to the window with his foot so that it stood below the sill and put the flight bag on it. He spread its mouth open like lips. He could see the stones Petey had collected glimmering inside. He used the toilet bowl brush to hook the monkey forward. It teetered for a moment and then fell into the bag. There was a faint *jing!* as one of its cymbals struck one of the rocks.

"Dad? Daddy?" Petey sounded frightened. Hal looked around at him. Something was different; something had changed. What was it?

Then he saw the direction of Petey's gaze, and he knew. The buzzing of the fly had stopped. It lay dead on the windowsill.

"Did the monkey do that?" Petey whispered.

"Come on," Hal said, zipping the bag shut. "I'll tell you while we ride out to the home place."

"How can we go? Mom and Dennis took the car."

"I'll get us there," Hal said, and he ruffled Petey's hair.

He showed the desk clerk his driver's license and a twenty-dollar bill. After taking Hal's Texas Instruments digital watch as further collateral, the clerk handed Hal the keys to his own car, a battered AMC Gremlin. As they drove east on Route 302 toward Casco, Hal began to talk, haltingly at first and then a little faster. He began by telling Petey that his father had probably brought the monkey home with him from overseas as a gift for his sons. It wasn't a particularly unique toy; there was nothing strange or valuable about it. There must have been hundreds of thousands of wind-up monkeys in the world, some made in Hong Kong, some in Taiwan, some in Korea. But somewhere along the line—perhaps even in the dark back closet of the house in Connecticut where the two boys had begun their growing up—something had happened to the monkey. Something bad, evil. It might be, Hal told Petey as he tried to coax the clerk's Gremlin up past forty (he was very aware of the zipped-up flight bag on the back seat, and Petey kept glancing around at it), that some evil—maybe even most evil—isn't even sentient and aware of what it is. It might be that most evil is very much like a monkey full of clockwork that you wind up; the clockwork turns, the cymbals begin to beat, the teeth grin, the stupid glass eyes laugh . . . or appear to laugh . . .

He told Petey about finding the monkey, but he found himself skipping over large chunks of the story, not wanting to terrify the scared boy any more than he was already. The story thus became disjointed, not really clear, but Petey asked no questions; perhaps he was filling in the blanks for himself,

Hal thought, in much the same way that he had dreamed his mother's death over and over, although he had not been there.

Uncle Will and Aunt Ida had both been there for the funeral. Afterward, Uncle Will had gone back to Maine—it was harvest time—and Aunt Ida had stayed on for two weeks with the boys to neaten up her sister's affairs. But more than that, she spent the time making herself known to the boys, who were so stunned by their mother's sudden death that they were nearly sleepwalking. When they couldn't sleep, she was there with warm milk; when Hal woke at three in the morning with nightmares (nightmares in which his mother approached the water cooler without seeing the monkey that floated and bobbed in its cool sapphire depths, grinning and clapping its cymbals, each converging pair of sweeps leaving trails of bubbles behind); she was there when Bill came down with first a fever and then a rash of painful mouth sores and then hives three days after the funeral; she was there. She made herself known to the boys, and before they rode the New England Flyer from Hartford to Portland with her, both Bill and Hal had come to her separately and wept on her lap while she held them and rocked them, and the bonding began.

The day before they left Connecticut for good to go "down Maine" (as it was called in those days), the rag man came in his great old rattly truck and picked up the huge pile of useless stuff that Bill and Hal had carried out to the sidewak from the back closet. When all the junk had been set out by the curb for pickup, Aunt Ida had asked them to go through the back closet again and pick out any souvenirs or remembrances they wanted. "We just don't have room for it all, boys," she told them, and Hal supposed that Bill had taken her at her word and had gone through all those fascinating boxes their father had left behind, one final time. Hal did not join his older brother. Hal had lost his taste for the back closet. A terrible idea had come to him during those first two weeks of mourning: Perhaps his father hadn't just disappeared, or run away because he had an itchy foot and had discovered marriage wasn't for him.

Maybe the monkey had gotten him.

When he heard the rag man's truck roaring and farting and backfiring its way down the block, Hal nerved himself, snatched the scruffy wind-up monkey from his shelf where it had been since the day his mother died (he had not dared to touch it until then, not even to throw it back into the closet), and ran downstairs with it. Neither Bill nor Aunt Ida saw him. Sitting on top of a barrel filled with broken souvenirs and mouldy books was the Ralston-Purina carton, filled with similar junk. Hal had slammed the monkey back into the box it had originally come out of, hysterically daring it to begin clapping its cymbals (*go on, go on, I dare you, dare you, DARE YOU*), but the monkey only waited there, leaning back nonchalantly as if expecting a bus and grinning its awful, knowing grin.

Hal stood by, a small boy in old corduroy pants and scuffed Buster Browns, as the rag man, an Italian who wore a crucifix and whistled through the space in his teeth, began loading boxes and barrels into his ancient truck with the high wooden sides. Hal watched as he lifted both the barrel and the Ralston-Purina box balanced atop it; he watched the monkey disappear into the maw of the truck; he watched as the rag man climbed back into the cab, blew his nose mightily into the palm of his hand, wiped his hand with a huge red handkerchief, and started the truck's engine with a mighty roar and a stinking blast of oily blue smoke; he watched the truck draw away. And a great weight had dropped away from his heart—he actually felt it go. He had jumped up and down twice, as high as he could jump, his arms spread, palms held out, and if any of the neighbors had seen him, they would have thought it odd almost to the point of blasphemy, perhaps: *Why is that boy jumping for joy* (for that was surely what it was; a jump for joy can hardly be disguised) *with his mother not even a month in her grave?*

He was jumping for joy because the monkey was gone, gone forever. Gone forever, but not three months later Aunt Ida had sent him up into the attic to get the boxes of Christmas decorations, and as he crawled around looking for them, getting the knees of his pants dusty, he had suddenly come face to face with it again, and his wonder and terror had been so great that he had had to bite sharply into the side of his hand to keep from screaming . . . or fainting dead away. There it was, grinning its toothy grin, cymbals poised a foot apart and ready to clap, leaning nonchalantly back against one corner of a Ralston-Purina carton as if waiting for a bus, seeming to say: *Thought you got rid of me, didn't you? But I'm not that easy to get rid of, Hal. I like you, Hal. We were made for each other, just a boy and his pet monkey, a couple of good old buddies. And somewhere south of here there's a stupid old Italian rag man lying in a claw-foot tub with his eyeballs bulging and his dentures half popped out of his mouth, his screaming mouth, a rag man who smells like a burned-out Exide battery. He was saving me for his grandson, Hal, he put me on the shelf with his soap and his razor and his Burma-Shave and the Philco radio he listened to the Brooklyn Dodgers on, and I started to clap and one of my cymbals hit that old radio and into the tub it went and then I came to you, Hal, I worked my way along country roads at night and the moonlight shone off my teeth at three in the morning and I left death in my wake, Hal, I came to you, I'm your Christmas present, Hal, wind me up, who's dead? Is it Bill? Is it Uncle Will? Is it you, Hal? Is it you?*

Hal had backed away, grimacing madly, eyes rolling, and nearly fell going downstairs. He told Aunt Ida that he hadn't been able to find the Christmas decorations—it was the first lie he had ever told her, and she had seen the lie on his face but had not asked him why he had told it, thank God—and later when Bill came in, she asked him to look and he brought the Christmas decorations down. Later, when they were alone, Bill hissed at him that he was a dummy who couldn't find his own ass with both hands and a flashlight. Hal said nothing. Hal was pale and silent, only picking at his supper. And that night he dreamed of the monkey again, one of its cymbals striking the Philco radio as it babbled out Dean Martin singing "Whenna da moon hitta you eye like a big pizza pie *ats-a moray*," the radio tumbling into the bathtub as the monkey grinned and beat its cymbals together with a *JANG* and a *JANG* and a *JANG*; only it wasn't the Italian rag man who was in the tub when the water turned electric.

It was him.

Hal and his son scrambled down the embankment behind the home place to the boathouse that jutted out over the water on its old pilings. Hal had the flight bag in his right hand. His throat was dry; his ears were attuned to an unnaturally keen pitch. The bag seemed very heavy.

"What's down here, Daddy?" Petey asked.

Hal didn't answer. He set down the flight bag. "Don't touch that," he said, and Petey backed away from it. Hal felt in his pocket for the ring of keys Bill had given him and found one neatly labeled "B'HOUSE" on a scrap of adhesive tape.

The day was clear and cold, windy, the sky a brilliant blue. The leaves of the trees that crowded up to the verge of the lake had gone every bright fall shade from blood red to sneering yellow. They rattled and talked in the wind. Leaves swirled around Petey's sneakers as he stood anxiously by, and Hal could smell November on the wind, with winter crowding close behind it.

The key turned in the padlock, and he pulled the swing doors open. Memory was strong; he didn't even have to look to kick down the wooden block that held the door open. The smell in there was all summer: canvas and bright wood, a lingering, musty warmth.

Uncle Will's little rowboat was still here, the oars neatly shipped as if he had last loaded it with his fishing tackle and two six packs of Black Label on ice yesterday afternoon. Bill and Hal had both gone out fishing with Uncle Will many times, but never together; Uncle Will maintained that the boat was too small for three. The red trim that Uncle Will had touched up each spring was now faded and peeling, though, and spiders had spun their silk in the boat's bow.

Hal laid hold of it and pulled it down the ramp to the little shingle of beach. The fishing trips had been one of the best parts of his childhood with Uncle Will and Aunt Ida. He had a feeling that Bill felt much the same. Uncle Will was ordinarily the most taciturn of men, but once he had the boat positioned to his liking, some sixty or seventy yards offshore, lines set and bobbers floating on the water, he would crack a beer for himself and one for Hal (who rarely drank more than half of the one can Uncle Will would allow, always with the ritual admonition from Uncle Will that Aunt Ida must never be told because "she'd shoot me for a stranger if she knew I was givin' you boys beer, don't you know"), and wax expansive. He would tell stories, answer questions, rebait Hal's hook when it needed rebaiting; and the boat would drift where the wind and the mild current wanted it to be.

"How come you never go right out to the middle, Uncle Will?" Hal had asked once.

"Look over the side there, Hal," Uncle Will had answered.

Hal did. He saw blue water and his fish line going down into black.

"You're looking into the deepest part of Crystal Lake," Uncle Will said, crunching his empty beer can in one hand and selecting a fresh one with the other. "A hundred feet if she's an inch. Amos Culligan's old Studebaker is down there somewhere. Damn fool took it out on the lake one early December, before the ice was made. Lucky to get out of it alive, he was. They'll never get that Studebaker out, nor see it until Judgment Trump blows. Lake's one deep son of a whore right here, it is. Big ones are right here, Hal. No need to go out no further. Let's see how your worm looks. Reel that son of a whore right in."

Hal did, and while Uncle Will put a fresh crawler from the old Crisco tin that served as his bait box on his hook, he stared into the water, fascinated, trying to see Amos Culligan's old Studebaker, all rust and waterweed drifting out of the open driver's side window through which Amos had escaped at the absolute last moment, waterweed festooning the steering wheel like a rotting necklace, waterweed dangling from the rear-view mirror and drifting back and forth in the currents like some strange rosary. But he could see only blue shading to black, and there was the shape of Uncle Will's nightcrawler, the hook hidden inside its knots, hung up there in the middle of things, its own sunshafted version of reality. Hal had a brief, dizzying vision of being suspended over a mighty gulf, and he had closed his eyes for a moment until the vertigo passed. That day, he seemed to recollect, he had drunk his entire can of beer.

... *the deepest part of Crystal Lake ... a hundred feet if she's an inch.*

He paused a moment, panting, and looked up at Petey, still watching anxiously. "You want some help, Daddy?"

"In a minute."

He had his breath again, and now he pulled the rowboat across the narrow strip of sand to the water, leaving a groove. The paint had peeled, but the boat had been kept under cover, and it looked sound.

When he and Uncle Will went out, Uncle Will would pull the boat down the ramp, and when the bow was afloat he would clamber in, grab an oar to push with, and say: "Push me off, Hal ... this is where you earn your truss!"

"Hand that bag in, Petey, and then give me a push," he said. And, smiling a little, he added: "This is where you earn your truss."

Petey didn't smile back. "Am I coming, Daddy?"

"Not this time. Another time I'll take you out fishing, but ... not this time."

Petey hesitated. The wind tumbled his brown hair, and a few yellow leaves, crisp and dry, wheeled past his shoulders and landed at the edge of the water, bobbing like boats themselves.

"You should have muffled them," he said, low.

"What?" But he thought he understood what Petey had meant.

"Put cotton over the cymbals. Taped it on. So it couldn't . . . make that noise."

Hal suddenly remembered Daisy coming toward him—not walking but lurching—and how, quite suddenly, blood had burst from both of Daisy's eyes in a flood that soaked her ruff and pattered down on the floor of the barn, how she had collapsed on her forepaws . . . and on the still, rainy spring air of that day he had heard the sound, not muffled but curiously clear, coming from the attic of the house fifty feet away: *Jang-jang-jang-jang* . . .

He began to scream hysterically, dropping the armload of wood he had been getting for the fire. He ran for the kitchen to get Uncle Will, who was eating scrambled eggs and toast, his suspenders not even up over his shoulders yet.

"She was an old dog, Hal," Uncle Will had said, his face haggard and unhappy—he looked old himself. "She was twelve, and that's old for a dog. You mustn't take on, now—old Daisy wouldn't like that."

"Old," the vet had echoed, but he had looked troubled all the same, because dogs don't die of explosive brain hemorrhages even at twelve ("like as if someone had stuck a firecracker in his head," Hal overheard the vet saying to Uncle Will as Uncle Will dug a hole in back of the barn not far from the place where he had buried Daisy's mother in 1950: "I never seen the beat of it, Will.").

And later, terrified almost out of his mind but unable to help himself, Hal had crept up to the attic.

Hello, Hal, how you doing? the monkey grinned from its shadowy corner. Its cymbals were poised, a foot or so apart. The sofa cushion Hal had stood on end between them was now all the way across the attic. Something—some force— had thrown it hard enough to split its cover, and stuffing foamed out of it. *Don't worry about Daisy,* the monkey whispered inside his head, its glassy hazel eyes fixed on Hal Shelburn's wide blue ones. *Don't worry about Daisy, she was old, old, Hal, even the vet said so, and by the way, did you see the blood coming out of her eyes, Hal? Wind me up, Hal. Wind me up, let's play, and who's dead, Hal? Is it you?*

And when he came back to himself, he had been crawling toward the monkey as if hypnotized. One hand had been outstretched to grasp the key. He scrambled backward then, and almost fell down the attic stairs in his haste—probably would have if the stairwell had not been so narrow. A little whining noise had been coming from his throat.

Now he sat in the boat, looking at Petey. "Muffling the cymbals doesn't work," he said. "I tried it once."

Petey cast a nervous glance at the flight bag. "What happened?"

"Nothing I want to talk about now," Hal said, "and nothing you want to hear about. Come on and give me a push."

Petey bent to it, and the stern of the boat grated along the sand. Hal dug in with an oar, and suddenly that feeling of being tied to the earth was gone and the boat was moving lightly, its own thing again after years in the dark boathouse, rocking on the light waves. Hal unshipped the oars one at a time and clicked the oarlocks shut.

"Be careful, Daddy," Petey said. His face was pale.

"This won't take long," Hal promised, but he looked at the flight bag and wondered.

He began to row, bending to the work. The old, familiar ache in the small of his back and between his shoulderblades began. The shore receded. Petey was magically eight again, six, a four-year-old standing at the edge of the water. He shaded his eyes with one infant hand.

Hal glanced casually at the shore but would not allow himself to actually study it. It had been nearly fifteen years, and if he studied the shoreline carefully he would see the changes rather than the similarities and become lost. The sun beat on his neck, and he began to sweat. He looked at the flight bag, and for a moment he lost the bend-and-pull rhythm. The flight bag seemed . . . seemed to be bulging. He began to row faster.

The wind gusted, drying the sweat and cooling his skin. The boat rose, and the bow slapped water to either side when it came down. Hadn't the wind freshened, just in the last minute or so? And was Petey calling something? Yes. Hal couldn't make out what it was over the wind. It didn't matter. Getting rid of the monkey for another twenty years—or maybe forever (please, God, forever)—that was what mattered.

The boat reared and came down. He glanced left and saw baby whitecaps. He looked shoreward again and saw Hunter's Point and a collapsed wreck that must have been the Burdons' boathouse when he and Bill were kids. Almost there, then. Almost over the spot where Amos Culligan's Studebaker had plunged through the ice one long-ago December. Almost over the deepest part of the lake.

Petey was screaming something, screaming and pointing. Hal still couldn't hear. The rowboat rocked and bucked, flatting off clouds of thin spray to either side of its peeling bow. A tiny rainbow glowed in one, was pulled apart. Sunlight and shadow raced across the lake in shutters, and the waves were not mild now; the whitecaps had grown up. His sweat had dried to gooseflesh, and spray had soaked the back of his jacket. He rowed grimly, eyes alternating between the shoreline and the flight bag. The boat rose again, this time so high that for a moment the left oar pawed at air instead of water.

Petey was pointing at the sky, his screams now only a faint, bright runner of sound.

Hal looked over his shoulder.

The lake was a frenzy of waves. It had gone a deadly dark shade of blue sewn with white seams. A shadow raced across the water toward the boat, and something in its shape was familiar, so terribly familiar, that Hal looked up, and then the scream was there, struggling in his tight throat.

The sun was behind the cloud, turning it into a hunched, working shape with two gold-edged crescents held apart. Two holes were torn in one end of the cloud, and sunshine poured through in two shafts.

As the cloud crossed over the boat, the monkey's cymbals, barely muffled by the flight bag, began to beat. *Jang-jang-jang-jang, it's you, Hal, it's finally you, you're over the deepest part of the lake now and it's your turn, your turn, your turn—*

All the necessary shoreline elements had clicked into their places. The rotting bones of Amos Culligan's Studebaker lay somewhere below, this was where the big ones were, this was the place.

Hal shipped the oars to the locks in one quick jerk, leaned forward, unmindful of the wildly rocking boat, and snatched the flight bag. The cymbals made their wild, pagan music; the bag's sides bellowsed as if with tenebrous respiration.

"*Right here, you son of a bitch!*" Hal screamed. "*RIGHT HERE!*"

He threw the bag over the side.

It sank fast. For a moment he could see it going down, sides moving, and for that endless moment *he could still hear the cymbals beating*. And for a moment the black waters seemed to clear, and he could see down into that terrible gulf of waters to where the big ones lay; there was Amos Culligan's Studebaker, and his mother was behind its slimy wheel, a grinning skeleton with a lake bass staring coldly from the skull's nasal cavity. Uncle Will and Aunt Ida lolled beside her, and Aunt Ida's gray hair trailed upward as the bag fell, turning over and over, a few silver bubbles trailing up: *jang-jang-jang-jang* . . .

Hal slammed the oars back into the water, scraping blood from his knuckles (*and, ah God, the back of Amos Culligan's Studebaker had been full of dead children! Charlie Silverman . . . Johnny McCabe . . .*), and began to bring the boat about.

There was a dry pistol-shot crack between his feet, and suddenly clear water was welling up between two boards. The boat was old; the wood had shrunk a bit, no doubt; it was just a small leak. But it hadn't been there when he rowed out. He would have sworn to it.

The shore and lake changed places in his view. Petey was at his back now. Overhead, that awful, simian cloud was breaking up. Hal began to row. Twenty seconds was enough to convince him that he was rowing for his life. He was only a so-so swimmer, and even a great one would have been put to the test in this suddenly angry water.

Two more boards suddenly shrank apart with that pistol-shot sound. More water poured into the boat, dousing his shoes. There were tiny metallic snapping sounds that he realized were nails breaking. One of the oarlocks snapped and flew off into the water. Would the swivel itself go next?

The wind now came from his back, as if trying to slow him down or even to drive him into the middle of the lake. He was terrified, but he felt a crazy kind of exhilaration through the terror. The monkey was gone for good this time. He knew it somehow. Whatever happened to him, the monkey would not be back to draw a shadow over Dennis's life, or Petey's. The monkey was gone, perhaps resting on the roof or the hood of Amos Culligan's Studebaker at the bottom of Crystal Lake. Gone for good.

He rowed, bending forward and rocking back. That cracking, crimping sound came again, and now the rusty old bait can that had been lying in the bow of the boat was floating in three inches of water. Spray blew in Hal's face. There was a louder snapping sound, and the bow seat fell into two pieces and floated next to the bait box. A board tore off the left side of the boat, and then another, this one at the waterline, tore off at the right. Hal rowed. Breath rasped in his mouth, hot and dry, and his throat swelled with the coppery taste of exhaustion. His sweaty hair flew.

Now a crack ran directly up the bottom of the rowboat, zigzagged between his feet, and ran up to the bow. Water gushed in; he was in water up to his ankles, then to the swell of calf. He rowed, but the boat's shoreward movement was sludgy now. He didn't dare look behind him to see how close he was getting.

Another board tore loose. The crack running up the center of the boat grew branches, like a tree. Water flooded in.

Hal began to make the oars sprint, breathing in great failing gasps. He pulled once . . . twice . . . and on the third pull both oar swivels snapped off. He lost one oar and held onto the other. He rose to his feet and began to flail at the water with it. The boat rocked, almost capsized, and spilled him back onto his seat with a thump.

Moments later more boards tore loose, the seat collapsed, and he was lying in the water that filled the bottom of the boat, astounded at its coldness. He tried to get on his knees, desperately thinking: *Petey must not see this, must not see his father drown right in front of his eyes, you're going to swim, dogpaddle if you have to, but do, do something—*

There was another splintering crack—almost a crash—and he was in the water, swimming for the shore as he never had swum in his life . . . and the shore was amazingly close. A minute later he was standing waist deep in water, not five yards from the beach.

Petey splashed toward him, arms out, screaming and crying and laughing. Hal started toward him and floundered. Petey, chest deep, foundered.

They caught each other.

Hal, breathing in great, winded gasps, nevertheless hoisted the boy into his arms and carried him up to the beach, where both of them sprawled, panting.

"Daddy? Is it really gone? That monkey?"

"Yes. I think it's really gone."

"The boat fell apart. It just . . . fell apart all around you."

Disintegrated, Hal thought, and he looked at the boards floating loose on the water forty feet out. They bore no resemblance to the tight, hand-made rowboat he had pulled out of the boathouse.

"It's all right now," Hal said, leaning back on his elbows. He shut his eyes and let the sun warm his face.

"Did you see the cloud?" Petey whispered.

"Yes. But I don't see it now . . . do you?"

They looked at the sky. There were scattered white puffs here and there, but no large dark cloud. It was gone, as he had said.

Hal pulled Petey to his feet. "There'll be towels up at the house. Come on." But he paused, looking at his son. "You were crazy, running out there like that."

Petey looked at him solemnly. "You were brave, Daddy."

"Was I?" The thought of bravery had never crossed his mind. Only his fear. The fear had been too big to see anything else. If anything else had indeed been there. "Come on, Pete."

"What are we going to tell Mom?"

Hal smiled. "I don't know, big guy. We'll think of something."

He paused a moment longer, looking at the boards floating on the water. The lake was calm again, sparkling with small wavelets. Suddenly Hal thought of summer people he didn't even know—a man and his son, perhaps, fishing for the big one. "I've got something, Dad!" the boy screams. "Well, reel it up and let's see," the father says, and coming up from the depths, weed draggling from its cymbals, grinning its terrible, welcoming grin . . . the monkey.

He shuddered, but those were only things that might be.

"Come on," he said to Petey again, and they walked up the path through the flaming October woods toward the home place.

From the Bridgton News, October 24th, 1980:

MYSTERY OF THE DEAD FISH
By Betsy Moriarty

Hundreds of dead fish were found floating belly-up on Crystal Lake in the neighboring township of Casco late last week. The largest numbers appeared to have died in the vicinity of Hunter's Point, although the lake's currents make this a bit difficult to determine. The dead fish included all types commonly found in these waters —bluegills, pickerel, sunnies, carp, brown, and rainbow trout, even one landlocked salmon. Fish and Game authorities say they are mystified, and caution fishermen and women not to eat any sort of fish from Crystal Lake until tests have determined . . .

MASTERWORKS OF MODERN HORROR